M000232939

HIGH MOOR

Graeme Reynolds

First published in 2011 by
Horrific Tales Publishing
http://www.horrifictales.co.uk
http://www.facebook.com/HighMoorNovel
Copyright © 2011 Graeme Reynolds
http://www.graemereynolds.com
The moral right of Graeme Reynolds to be
identified as the author of this work has been
asserted in accordance with the Copyright,
Designs and Patents Act, 1988.

A CIP catalogue record for this book is available from the
British Library
ISBN: 0957010311
ISBN-13: 978-0957010338

For Donna.

ACKNOWLEDGMENTS

I owe a great deal of thanks to the following people. Without their help and guidance, this book would probably never have seen the light of day.

My editors, Rick Taubold and Lisa Jenkins for all your advice and help.

Stu Smith from Graviton Creations for putting up with my constant tinkering and producing a wonderful cover.

My beta readers, Neil John Buchanan, John Arthur Miller, Tony Smith, Paula Ray and Jodi Macarthur for helping me work out the kinks in the plot.

And thanks to everyone in my critique group on Zoetrope, especially Scott Gamboe, Karl Rademacher, Shari Wice, Sandra Ramos O'Briant, Shell Willby, Shane McKenzie, RLB Hartman and everyone else who helped me whip this story into shape.

Prologue

28th October 2008. Llanllugan, Mid Wales. 17.40.

The metallic shriek of the alarm clock cut through the silence, jarring John back to consciousness. He thrust an arm out to hit the snooze button, but found only empty air. A second alarm sounded from another room, its sound muffled through the heavy walls, then a third alarm joined the chorus, followed by the insistent beep of his wristwatch and the alarm on his mobile phone.

John's eyes snapped open. He sat upright in the leather chair, alert and fearful. He checked the time and looked at the sky outside. The clouds burned against the purple blanket of the approaching night.

Oh no.

He pushed himself up from the chair and started down the hall to the kitchen, his heart racing in time to the pulsating alarms.

Please, God. Let there be enough time.

Still groggy, John jerked open the refrigerator door and removed three large raw steaks, then applied the deadbolt to the back door before hurrying to the cellar. The steaks dripped blood on the wooden floor in his wake.

It's all right. I'm going to make it.

A bang resounded through the house, rattling the windows. Fireworks outside, much louder than they should have been. He'd left a window open.

Fear clenched John's stomach, fear and perhaps something else.

No. It can't start now. Not yet.

John sprinted from room to room as his heart raced, and sweat beaded on his forehead. The rising tide of panic numbed his legs. He knocked over a small wooden table as he hurled himself down the hallway. He found the open window in the study and wrenched it closed. It was almost dark outside.

He pushed aside the wooden cellar door, stumbling as he took the stairs two at a time. He reached the bottom, yanked open the heavy steel door, then doubled over as a sharp pain tore through his stomach.

John threw the steaks into the corner of the windowless, concrete room and shouldered the reinforced door closed. Its base scraping across the floor set his teeth on edge. Another burst of pain dropped him to his knees. Fire spread from his stomach to his limbs. Sweat dripped into his eyes, stinging them and blurring his vision. Panting now, he managed to reach across to turn the heavy key in the lock with unsteady hands. The key fell from his grasp and jangled as it bounced across the concrete floor.

Ignoring it, he kicked his shoes off and undid the belt of his jeans, when another spasm hit. The pain lanced through him in wave after agonising wave. Nothing else mattered but the acid-fire setting his nerve endings alight.

The change began in earnest. John could think no more. He opened his mouth and screamed as fangs burst through his gums in a spray of bloodstained foam.

***

High Moor

28th October 2008. High Moor. 22:50.

Malcolm Harrison thrust his hands deeper into his pockets and hunched his neck down in a vain attempt to warm up.

The dog stopped again and sniffed a wooden fence post, taking its own sweet time, oblivious to the rain and the cold wind that were making its owner's life such a misery.

"Have a fucking shit so we can go home, you bastard." Malcolm growled at the animal.

The dog, a large good-natured Rottweiler called Samson, ignored him and trotted off to investigate the trees.

The dog had not been Malcolm's idea. He had known who would end up taking the thing for walks at all hours, in all weathers, scooping up the shit with a carrier bag. The wife and the kids had kept on about it for months, about how it would be good for home security as well as a pet for the children. There had been promises to walk it and take care of it, and yet here he was, following it round the park in the middle of the bloody night, with a pocket full of plastic bags, waiting for it to take a shit.

"Fuck it!"

The dog appeared from the darkness near the trees, running back to Malcolm. The great beast cowered behind his legs and whimpered, pushing in so close that he almost lost his balance.

"What the fuck's the matter with you, Samson? Are you done yet?"

A branch snapped, back along the tree line.

A bolt of fear shot from his stomach, up his spine. Malcolm held his breath, the silent chill air reminding him just how isolated he was. The nearest house was a good four hundred yards away, and at this late hour there was not even a reassuring background hum of traffic. The faint twinkle of street lights on the far side of the trees could be seen, while to his left the park stretched out for almost half a mile until it reached the town centre.

"Probably just kids messing about," he whispered to the dog without much conviction. His pace quickened as he made his way out of the park to the safety of his home.

For once he felt comforted by the presence of Samson, despite almost tripping over the animal as it strived to stay close to him.

Yeah, probably kids, or some druggie out there, but there was that thing when I was a kid and...

He forced the thought from his head, instead focusing on the rush of warmth he would feel as he came into the house.

I'll dry Samson off, get a beer, sit in my chair then...

A growl came from the darkness. Thick. Guttural. The harsh amber glow of the sodium street lights bathed the first row of trees in an orange haze, but showed only pitch darkness beyond.

Malcolm pulled down the hood of his heavy coat and looked into the shadows, the rain forgotten now. Beside him, Samson snarled.

Was that movement?

Another growl came from the trees, longer and deeper than the first.

"I'll set the fucking dog on you, if you don't piss off."

The growl went up an octave.

"You asked for it. Get 'em, Samson."

Samson whined and looked at his owner.

"What are you waiting for, you soft shite? Go on, get in there."

Samson snarled, barked a challenge, then ran into the darkness. Silence followed.

Malcolm stood rooted to the spot for what seemed like forever. The wind picked up again, driving the rain into his face, its steady hiss the only sound that reached his strained ears.

A rustle of leaves beyond the tree line. The hint of movement in the inky shadows.

"Samson?"

A bark shattered the silence. A deep growl followed, then a long high-pitched whine of agony.

The dog's screaming! What the fuck could make a Rottweiler scream?

The sound broke Malcolm's paralysis, and he sprinted down the path, leaving that awful sound behind. He crashed through the rusted iron gate, out into the street, then ran across the road into a dark lane between the houses. He slipped on something soft that squelched under his shoe, and almost lost his footing. Spurred by terror, he somehow regained his balance and burst from the lane, onto the street where he lived.

He cast nervous glances over his shoulder while he fumbled for his keys, then struggled to keep his shaking hands steady enough to get the key into the lock. The door swung open and he fell inside. After scrambling to his feet, he slammed the door and slid the deadbolt and chain into place. His heart pounded in his chest. He thought that he might be about to have a heart attack.

Karen, his wife, looked at him from the kitchen, with a can of lager in her hand. "Did you remember my fags, Malcolm? And where's the fucking dog?"

***

29th October 2008. Llanllugan. Mid Wales. 06.49.

John awoke from dreams of rage. The cold concrete floor pressed against his naked body, and the bitter taste of blood lingered on his tongue. He opened his eyes, wincing at the harsh fluorescent light, and tried to stand up.

Nausea bubbled up from his stomach. He fell to his knees and retched. Dark brown liquid and chunks of meat splashed across the floor and his legs. He wiped his mouth in disgust and forced himself to stand.

The basement door remained closed and was still intact, with the exception of a few new dents in its steel surface. He'd made it. He stumbled across the room and reached up for the key, in its hiding place atop the door frame, but found nothing.

"Oh shit. Please, God. Don't tell me I ate the fucking key. Again."

High Moor

He checked the door frame once more, then turned his attention to the shredded pile of rags that had been his clothes. He kicked at the pile and felt a surge of relief as the key skittered across the concrete floor, then dismay as it came to rest in the pool of vomit.

Holding his breath, he retrieved the key from the stinking puddle, unlocked the door, pulled it open, and ascended the wooden stairs to his house.

***

John emerged from the shower half an hour later, feeling much better. The rank animal musk on his skin had been scrubbed away, but despite washing his hair several times, it still smelled like wet dog. He cleaned his teeth until he saw flecks of blood on his toothbrush, then he got dressed and went downstairs to make breakfast.

Soon, the smell of frying bacon filled the house. John poured himself a cup of strong, black coffee and turned the portable television in the corner of the room on to the BBC news channel. He returned his attention to the bacon, flipping the rashers over while trying to ignore the rumbling of his stomach.

The news droned on in the background. A story about the impending financial crisis and the U.S. elections finished and another story began. John wasn't really paying attention, until he heard the reporter say two words. "High Moor."

He picked up the remote control and turned up the volume. A female reporter stood in a park, attempting to look sympathetic and sensitive, when it was clear that she would rather be anywhere else than there. Someone off camera held an umbrella above her head, in an unsuccessful attempt to protect her hair from the heavy rain. Behind her, men in white forensics suits worked in a taped off area. One of them picked up what looked like a dog's hind-leg and put it in a white plastic bag.

"Over twenty years have passed since there have been any sightings of the legendary High Moor Beast, but today it is feared that it again stalks the countryside, after a local man and his dog were attacked in Coronation Park.

"It was here, by this children's play area late last night, that the police discovered the remains of Samson, after they were alerted by his owner, Mr Malcolm Harrison.

"It is thought that the beast may be a puma or leopard, released in the late 1960s when the Dangerous Animals act was passed. In 1986 a local farmer shot, and killed, a large puma that was thought to be responsible for a number of deaths in the area.

"It would seem that without Samson's brave sacrifice, his owner might have become the first human casualty of the High Moor Beast in over twenty years. Police are warning people to only leave the house after dark if necessary, not to travel alone, and to avoid wooded and rural areas.

This is Kate Monty, BBC News."

High Moor

John's mouth hung open as he stared at the television, unable to process what he'd just seen. A shrill alarm rang out, shocking him out of his stupor. His bacon was on fire.

He removed the flaming pan from the gas, doused a tea towel in cold water and threw it over the conflagration that had been his breakfast. Smoke filled the room. He opened the window, then pushed the button on the smoke alarm. When the alarm refused to stop, he reached up, removed the cover, and disconnected the battery. Then, he sat on a barstool and rubbed his face with both hands.

"Puma? Puma my big fat arse. Shit."

He walked into the hallway, removed a business card from the table, and dialled the number.

The phone rang six times before a man answered. "John? It's seven-fifteen in the morning. Can't this wait until I'm in the office?"

"No, Frank, it can't. I'm not going to be able to do the Morgan job. You'll have to get Luke or Dan to do it instead."

"You can't pull this shit on me, John. We've got the specifications meeting this morning, and I need you there. No one else will be able to get up to speed in time."

"I'm sorry, Frank, but something's come up and I can't do it. Don't send me anything else for the next month, either. I won't be around."

"What the fuck could be so important that you'd risk losing your contract with us?"

"It's personal. Family business. I have to go back home."

Part 1

Chapter 1

24th February 1986. High Moor. 14:35.

David climbed the wooden fence and turned to his two friends. "Keep up you two. This'll take all day at this rate."

Behind him, Michael and John struggled with the wooden boards and rope. David, being the oldest at eleven years old, and the leader of their little group, carried the tools stolen from his father's workshop in a blue plastic sports bag.

John stumbled and almost dropped his end of the board. "I still don't see why we had to go all the way out here. It's bloody miles away." Michael grunted his agreement.

David sat on the fence and waited for the younger boys to catch up. "John, what happened to the tree house?"

John reached David's side and put down the boards and rope. "Malcolm Harrison and his dickhead mates trashed it and stole all our stuff."

"Right and, Michael, what happened to the camp we built on the waste ground by the pub?"

Michael wiped the sweat from his forehead. "Malcolm fucking Harrison and his mates trashed it and stole all our stuff."

David reached across and ruffled Michael's hair. "Well done. So now you know why we're heading off into the woods. We need to build this year's camp somewhere that prick won't find it. You two are thick as pig shit, I swear. Mike, sometimes I think you were adopted or something."

Michael grinned at his older brother. "Fuck you, tosspot. At least I'm not half monkey".

John climbed onto the fence and sat beside David. "Malcolm Harrison is half arse monkey."

David took out a pack of cigarettes and handed one each to John and Michael. "What's the other half?"

Michael thought about this for a moment. "Arse ferret?"

John lit his cigarette and passed the lighter to Michael. "So he's half monkey, half ferret and all big fat arse?"

David and Michael snorted with laughter. The mental image the description conjured up fit Malcolm perfectly.

Michael stopped laughing and frowned. "Wait, I have a serious question."

David rolled his eyes. "What?"

"Which one's his Mam?"

John chuckled. "Have you seen her? She's definitely the arse."

David laughed and got down from the fence. "Come on, you two. Finish your fags and let's get moving. We need to get the camp finished and get back before dinner tonight."

John and Michael took a long drag from their cigarettes, flicked the ends onto the track and ground them into the dirt with their feet. Then they picked up the building materials and followed David across the fields.

High Moor

The sun beat down with uncharacteristic warmth. It was the first really nice day of the year. The winter snow had only melted a week before, and traces were still visible on the hills. Apart from the chill in the wind, the day could have been mistaken for a summer afternoon, instead of a day in late February.

With the two-week Easter Holiday just over a month away, the long days away from school and the adventures that awaited them were at the front of their minds. The first job of the year was to set up their new base of operations, away from the prying eyes of adults and the attentions of Malcolm and his gang.

They arrived at the small brook that bordered the woodlands. The site of their camp lay in the deeper parts of the forest, beyond where the broad-leaved trees gave way to towering pines.

John looked at the flowing water, and then turned to David. "How are we going to get these across?"

David slapped himself across the forehead. "Duh! How do you think, dipshit? We make a bridge with the planks, get across and then pull them over. Do I have to think of everything?"

The boys laid the planks across the stream and rested them on the opposite bank, and then David and John made their way across.

Michael looked at the wobbling boards and shook his head. "I don't want to."

John walked back to the water's edge. "Come on, Mike, you big girl. It's easy."

David joined John and looked at his brother with a mocking smile on his face. "Our Marie could do it. Maybe we should leave you at home next time and bring her if you are going to be a baby."

Michael looked at the planks and his face creased in concentration. He put one foot on the wood and tested his weight, then made his way across.

The plank bowed as he reached the half way point. He overcompensated for the sudden movement and slipped from the board, backwards into the stream.

David and John's laughter stopped short when Michael, up to his waist in the cold water, began to cry. David jumped from the riverbank to help his younger brother up.

"I'm soaked. I'm gonna get KILLED!"

"Let's get this stuff to the camp and I'll make a fire to dry you off. Mam will be alright."

Michael wiped his nose on his sleeve. "It's not me mam I'm worried about." He and David exchanged looks, and for a moment an uneasy silence settled over the boys. Then David grinned.

"I'll tell Mam we had a water fight with the hose and that it's all my fault."

Michael thought about this and came to the conclusion that it was an acceptable lie, which did wonders for his mood. The boys picked up their burdens and continued on their way.

David turned his head to look at his brother. "You realise that you were just sitting in all the piss and shit from the new housing estate? It all empties into the beck about a mile upstream. Still, you always smell like you just pissed your pants, so I don't think anyone will notice."

Michael smiled at his brother. "Fuck you, monkey boy. They only smell like that 'cos they're your hand-me-downs."

Once under the canopy of the trees, the day lost its warmth and Michael complained about the cold while they trudged through the woods. Water oozed from his trainers, making a squelching sound and leaving a trail of wet footprints on the forest floor.

They walked for ten minutes before they came to their marker, a small piece of yellow plastic nailed to the sap laden trunk of a pine tree. The boys left the path and walked for a few minutes more until they came to another yellow marker, at which point they turned to their right and made their way through the bracken until they arrived at the site of their new camp.

While David and John had been working on the camp for the past few weekends, it was the first time that Michael had seen their new base. He'd been grounded by his parents for an incident involving fireworks, dog excrement, and the local vicar that had not ended well.

He looked up at the tree house and his mouth dropped open in awe. "Wow."

Tree house was too small a word to describe what stood before them. On one of the tall pine trees stood two platforms, one at fifteen feet from the forest floor and the other at thirty five feet. A makeshift ladder of wooden boards nailed to the tree trunk was the only way up.

The actual tree house was on an adjacent oak tree. The top of the trunk had been destroyed by a lightning strike years before, leaving a flat area. The branches then grew up around the flattened area like a cage. It was here the boys built a solid wooden floor, doorway and walls, using the natural growth as a framework. Only the roof remained incomplete.

Michael walked around the base of the tree, looking for a ladder. When he found no obvious means of getting into the tree house, he turned to the other two boys and frowned in confusion.

"How do you get in?"

David looked at John and then grinned at his little brother.

"That's the best part."

David and John each picked up a coil of rope and headed to the trees. John climbed the wooden ladder, while David wrapped the rope around himself, from his shoulders to his waist, and shimmied up the side of the oak. Michael stood on the ground and watched his best friend and brother ascend into the canopy, his wet clothes forgotten.

As John reached the highest platform, David scrambled onto the base of the tree house through a large gap in the wall.

David nodded to John. "OK. Do it."

John threw the coil of rope across the gap between the trees. David stretched his arm out, but the rope caught on a branch and dangled just out of David's reach.

John grabbed the rope and reeled it back. "Bollocks. Sorry, Dave. You ready?"

David nodded and John threw the rope again. This time, David caught it, and both boys tied the ends off on their respective trees.

John finished his knot and tested it, then yelled across to David. "Knew there was a reason I joined the Boy Scouts."

David checked his knot. "Well, it sure as hell wasn't to do Bob-a-Job. If Mitchell thinks I am going round, scrounging for his pocket this Easter, he can fuck right off."

John climbed down to the lower platform, while David gathered up the second rope.

He tied his end off, next to the first and hurled the remainder across the gap to John. "Catch."

John reached for the unravelling coils and almost slipped from the platform, but managed to grab the rope with one hand and use the other to steady himself. He tied the rope around the trunk of the tree at head height, and double checked his knot. Ropes now extended out from the tree house to the two platforms to form a triangle.

Michael shivered in his wet clothes. "I still don't get it? What are you doing?"

David gave his brother a knowing smile. "Watch and learn."

21

He reached into the bag and produced a strange piece of metal. The metal was bent into the shape of an omega symbol, to form two hand holds, with a large loop in between. The hand grips and the centre of the loop were wrapped with over an inch of heavy silver tape.

Michael realised what David and John were planning, and his mouth hung open in amazement. "No way. You're not fucking serious?"

David hooked the metal over the rope, leaned back and allowed his weight to be supported, then lifted his feet up.

The boy rocketed down the taut line, screaming as he went. "GET IN!" He traversed the distance between the two trees in seconds and came to rest on the lower platform, next to John.

"You get in the same way. You climb to the top platform and slide down into the tree house. We have a grip each, so even if those dickheads find the place, they won't be able to get in."

Michael was, for a change, silent. He looked up at his older brother in awe.

John grabbed the makeshift metal slide from David. "My go." He ran to the tree and climbed up to the higher level with the metal handle tucked into the back of his jeans.

Michael found his voice again. "This summer is going to be great."

His brother winked at him. "I told you it was worth the walk. This year is going to be the best year ever."

Neither of the other boys disagreed.

***

22

High Moor

The sun sat low in the sky, its light casting an orange glow on the forest floor, when David hammered in the last nail.

He stood back and admired his work, then turned to John and Michael, who were carving their names into the walls with their knives. "Finished."

The camp was, at this stage, nothing more than a wooden box with the two ropes suspended from the wide entrance, but that didn't matter. It was finished, and it was theirs.

John looked at his watch and groaned. "We better get going. It's going to be dark soon, and me mam and dad will have a fit if I miss dinner."

Michael and David exchanged worried glances.

"What time is dinner?" said Michael.

David frowned. "Six on the dot. What time is it now, John?"

"Quarter to."

Michael grabbed his metal hoop and hooked it over the rope. "We are so dead. We're gonna have to leg it all the way back." Michael launched himself into space and shot along the zip line, with John and David close behind.

They ran through the darkening woodlands, towards the path.

John came alongside David and gasped. "How are we gonna get across the river? We don't have a bridge anymore."

"We're going to have to take the long way around. We'll nick some more wood from the building site tomorrow and make a permanent bridge."

Michael looked worried. "That's if we can still walk tomorrow. You know what Dad's like about meal times."

David frowned, but nodded his assent and picked up the pace as the sun dipped below the horizon and darkness spread across the forest like a cloak.

The boys burst from the woodlands, onto the open expanse of fields that lay between them and their homes. The fields were bathed in a cool monochrome from the full moon, a welcome respite from the looming shadows of the forest.

"What time is it John?" asked David, in between gasping lungfuls of cold air.

A long, shrieking howl broke the silence, drifting across the open countryside and echoing around the boys.

John stopped dead in his tracks. "What the hell was that?"

David and Michael looked at him, the fear on their faces visible in the moonlight.

"No idea, mate. Someone's dog?" said David. An edge crept into his voice.

Another howl rang out and reverberated through the trees behind them. The boys exchanged glances and sprinted across the fields to the safety of their homes.

They arrived, panting and sweaty from their run, at ten past six.

David scowled. "Better go and face the music. See you tomorrow, John?"

John nodded his understanding. "Sure. See you later. You too, Mike, and good luck with your dad. Maybe you will be OK, we're only ten minutes late, and you two don't have watches."

David looked at Michael, then back to John. "Yeah, maybe. See you tomorrow."

Chapter 2

25th February 1986. High Moor. 10.15.

Sergeant Steven Wilkinson fished in his pockets for cigarettes. "So, tell me what I'm looking at here, Constable Phillips?"

"It's a sheep, boss."

Steven sighed. Constable Phillips had an incredible talent for stating the fucking obvious, which was probably why he had been assigned to the Durham Constabulary Wildlife Liaison Office. If a bigger career dead-end existed, Steven was not aware of it.

He took a cigarette from the pack and stood with his back to the wind, swearing under his breath as a rogue gust extinguished his lighter. He cupped his hands around it and tried again. The flame sprang to life and the cigarette finally lit.

"I know that it's a bloody sheep, Constable Phillips, the white wool like substance is a dead giveaway. What I want to know is what do you think happened to it?"

Both men cast their eyes down at the mangled carcass. The animal's insides had been laid open, its innards spread around the immediate vicinity. One of its legs was missing, and the sheep's head had been severed, lying five feet away from the rest of the corpse.

Around the field, another twenty-nine carcasses existed in similar conditions. Steven had worked in the Wildlife Liaison Office for ten years and had never seen anything like it.

Constable Phillips shrugged. "Someone's dog got off the lead?"

"Maybe, but it would have to be a big bloody dog. And to do this? To this many animals? It would have to be a pack of them, and they'd have to be in here for quite a while."

An unmarked, white Ford Escort pulled up at the entrance to the field. Two men got out and walked to the rear of the vehicle, opened the boot, and took out two pairs of white coveralls.

"Forensics is here, then?" said Constable Phillips.

Steven suppressed the sarcastic comment on the tip of his tongue. He hated call outs on Sunday mornings. His hangover reverberated inside his skull, his stomach lurched when he looked at the slaughtered animals, and he was losing patience with his colleague. Sundays were his day off, but whenever an incident occurred that involved animals, as Wildlife Liaison Officer the call was sent to him.

He massaged his temples. "So, let's step back from this and look at the evidence. We have thirty sheep torn apart by an unknown animal or animals. The gate to the field was closed so either they jumped the fence, or someone let them in."

"You think someone did this deliberately?"

"It's possible. We either have a pack of wild dogs roaming the area, we have a bloody lion on the loose, or someone that has access to a number of large dogs brought them here and let them loose in the field."

"Gypos?"

A grin broke out on Steven's face, despite his best efforts. "We don't refer to them as Gypos, Constable. The official term is members of the travelling community. Still, I think it might be an idea to drop by and pay them a visit."

This was the last thing he needed on a Sunday morning. His wife was snoring in bed, while he had to go to the local traveller's camp and ask questions to a bunch of hostile gypsies. "Come on, let's have another chat with the farmer to see if he's had any problems with travellers, then we can pop by the camp outside of High Moor for a friendly visit."

He smoked the cigarette down to the butt, flicked it into the grass, and the two men headed back across the field to their squad car.

***

The roads were quiet as they headed into the town. The early morning rush of churchgoers had ended, the congregations settled in their pews awaiting the Sunday morning service. They passed occasional vehicles occupied by families on their way to visit relatives.

The only people on the streets were old men on their way to the working men's club, and a smattering of young men and women still dressed in their clothes from the night before.

Steven hated this town. In its history it had been home to a small steel works and a coal mine, but these had long since closed. Now, only a few factories on the outskirts provided any sort of large scale employment for its residents.

High Moor

The town was dying. Over half the shops in the high street were boarded up, casualties of the new supermarket on the outskirts of town. Those that remained provided cheap, low-quality clothes to those on benefits, or were charity shops filled with the detritus of the town folks' lives.

The police car left the dual carriageway and headed into the town centre, past the towering grey concrete flats and prefabricated box-shaped houses of the council estates and into the older part of High Moor. The red bricks of the small, terraced houses were blackened with age and a century's worth of soot and filth.

The car drove up the high street, over pavements strewn with litter and sporadic pools of vomit, past the old cinema, now boarded up, and a pub called The Railway on the site of the old train station. No trains had come to this town for over twenty years, the lines long since torn up to make way for new roads and housing estates.

Abandoned cardboard boxes tumbled across the empty town square as gusts of wind caught them. The market was the bustling hub of the town on Saturdays, but on Sunday mornings it was nothing more than a flat expanse of tarmac containing steel skeletons of the stalls and the rubbish from the previous day. he refuse would spread across the town until the bin men arrived on Monday morning to load the wet cardboard and rotting vegetables into the backs of their large white trucks.

Steven thought the town was like a monstrous parasite, sucking the life, hope, and ambition from everyone unfortunate enough to live here. High Moor had the largest number of violent crimes and incidents of drug abuse, teenage pregnancy and petty theft in a twenty mile radius. Only the more deprived suburbs of Newcastle and Middlesbrough were worse.

"What a shit hole." said Constable Phillips.

"Could be worse. You could live here instead of just having to drive through it every once in a while."

"I thought you lived in Neville's Cross, Sarge?"

"I do now, but I was born and raised here. Back then it didn't seem so bad. It wasn't until the pit closed that things went downhill."

The police car left the centre of the town, past rows of takeaways with graffiti-covered steel shutters masking their entrances, into rows of terraced houses. They headed south, out of the town, towards the moor that gave the town its name and the Traveller's camp that resided upon it.

Steven turned left, off the tarmac road, onto a rough gravel track that tested both the suspension of the police car and the stomach of its driver. They passed the closed mine surrounded by high chain fencing, its gates secured by a rusty padlock. Then the camp came into view.

The site was made up of a number of vehicles: expensive motor homes, heavily modified transit vans, and even some ornate, horse-drawn caravans, crowded together in a circular formation.

High Moor

Steven pulled over and parked the car. The gravel crunched under the tires as he applied the brakes. The two police officers got out of the car and walked towards a gap in the trailers that formed the entrance.

The remains of a fire smouldered in the centre of the circle. Three people sitting around it got up and entered their vehicles, the door locks clicking behind them.

An old woman sat on the steps of a wooden horse-drawn caravan, its once extravagant paint work faded and cracked with age. The woman's white hair was mostly hidden by a red-head scarf, and her shoulders were wrapped with a thick woollen shawl. She glared at the two men, and as they passed her she spat a wad of chewing tobacco onto the ground by Steven's foot.

Several dogs barked at the men's approach. A couple of Staffordshire Bull Terriers and an aging Alsatian, none capable of committing the sort of damage they had witnessed earlier.

The door of one of the expensive motor-homes opened and a man emerged. His moustache twitched as he suppressed a grin. "Can I help you, officers? Are you lost?"

Steven's headache worsened. *Here we go.*

***

25th February 1986. Aykley Head's Police HQ. 15.25.

"..and there were no dogs in evidence at the site that, in your opinion, could have caused the damage to the livestock?"

Steven looked at his boss. Inspector Franks was responsible for most of the smaller departments that made up Durham Constabulary and made no secret of his intention to rise as far and as fast in the Force as he could. That translated into bad news for the people working under him.

"No sir, at the time we visited the site, there did not appear to be any animals capable of destroying that many livestock."

Inspector Franks regarded Steven for a few seconds, his face impassive. "Do you have any other thoughts as to what might have been responsible, Sergeant?"

"No sir, not at this time."

The Inspector took a deep breath and paused for a second. "What I am about to tell you does not leave this room. The press will have a field day if they get hold of it."

The Inspector pushed a large manila envelope across the desk.

"This was taken this morning by a rambler, scarcely five miles from the scene of the incident. When he reported the matter to us, we had the film processed here."

Steven opened the envelope and took out an enlarged photograph. It took a few moments for him to realise exactly what he was looking at.

High Moor

The photograph was grainy, a result of the enlargement, and had been taken from long range. A large, tawny-coloured animal was walking across a field with a river bank visible in the background. The animal held a rabbit it its mouth, giving the picture a sense of scale. It was the size of a large dog, sleek and muscular, with a long tail and small pointed ears.

"Do you know what that is, Sergeant Wilkinson?"

"It's a big cat, sir. If I had to make a guess I would say probably a Puma or a Cougar. You say this was taken this morning?"

The Inspector frowned. "Yes, sergeant, this morning by the River Wear. Here is what's responsible for attacking those sheep, and I want you to resolve the situation before the press find out about it, or before it does any more damage."

Steven sighed. The day was just getting better and better.

Chapter 3

25th March 1986. High Moor. 13:05.

John hurled the ball at the side of his house, putting more force behind the throw than he'd intended. The ball soared overhead, and he backpedalled to grab it before it hit the window of David and Michael's house next door.

He bounced the ball off the floor again. "Come on. Get a bloody move on."

David and Michael had been to church with their mother and little sister that morning before having their Sunday lunch. John had been waiting for what seemed like an eternity for his friends to appear. The woods beckoned, and he wanted to get back to the camp. David was making some modifications that required supplies from a building site. If they left things too late, there was always the risk of running into nosey adults out for an afternoon walk. That was a complication they could do without.

The ball struck the wall again. The sound of its impact echoed through the narrow space between the two houses. As John caught the ball, the door of his friend's house opened and David appeared, followed by Michael and Marie, their eight year old sister.

John put the ball in his pocket and walked over to his friends. "About bloody time you showed up. I've been waiting for you all morning. Can we get going now?"

"We gotta go to the shop for some milk and stuff," replied David. "And we gotta take the squirt with us."

High Moor

Marie stuck her tongue out at her older brother, and then gave John a shy smile. John pretended not to notice.

"Aw, man, that's miles away! Can't we just go on our bikes? We'll be back in half an hour."

"Can't, mate. Mam and Dad want some time by themselves so we are stuck babysitting for the afternoon. Anyway, Marie isn't allowed to take hers on the main road yet, so we're walking."

Marie put her hands on her hips in indignation. "I'm not a baby, David. I'm eight. That's only a year younger than Michael, and I can do anything you can. If you run off and leave me like you did last time, I'm going to tell."

The boys looked at one another and shrugged.

"We can pick up some World Cup stickers at the shop," said John. "I've got almost all of England. Just need Gary Linker and Bryan Robson now."

They walked out of the alley, towards the shop. Michael came alongside John. "You got any swaps?"

"Yeah, loads. What ones do you need?"

"I need Peter Beardsley."

"Na, not got any spares of him. I have about five Graeme Souness though."

"Graeme Souness? He is in every pack! I wouldn't mind, but he's shit an' all."

"You're only jealous 'cos his hair's better than yours."

Michael considered this for a second then punched John in the arm. "At least I haven't got a girl perm like Chris Waddle and you."

Marie folded her arms in a huff, disgusted at the topic of conversation. "Boys. You never talk about anything interesting."

David grinned at his sister. "What would you rather talk about squirt? Dolls and Ponies?"

"No, just not football. It's boring."

"You're boring." said Michael.

"At least I'm not ugly! No girl will ever fancy you. Not even a dog like Lizzie Fletcher. You've got ears like the bloody world cup."

Michael's face went red, and he looked to be on the verge of losing his temper.

"Pack it in you two," said David, an edge in his voice. "It's bad enough that we have to change our plans for today without you two arguing like a pair of babies. Give it a rest, or you can both go and play on the swings like little kids while me and John go and do something else."

At this, the siblings quietened down, and they followed behind the two older boys, exchanging murderous glances.

The shop was situated in the middle of a small council estate, mostly made up of two-storey flat-roofed houses. It stood at the junction of two residential streets. A solitary building had once been two homes, but now contained the small convenience store and a fish and chip shop. Overgrown patches of grass that had once been gardens flanked the building. The grassy area was enclosed with a wooden fence with peeling green paint and a low brick wall that was covered in graffiti.

High Moor

In honesty, none of the children minded the errand. The shop was a special place, almost magical in its lure. A small refrigerator at the rear of the shop held pints of milk and cold cans of lager. The three aisles were packed with tins of food, racks of vegetables, and a stand with assorted pieces of sewing materials. Behind the counter, a wall-mounted shelf held the tea, coffee, and a rack of cigarettes. What caught the children's eye, however, was the array of glass jars standing on the shelves behind the shop assistant.

There were hardly any shops like this in High Moor anymore. A dazzling array of different confectionary delights filled the jars. Cola bottles, pear drops, penny chews, liquorice laces, peanut brittle, gobstoppers, and hard candy peered out at the children from behind their glass prisons, calling to them.

David put two bottles of milk on the counter along with two loaves of white bread, while John rooted through his pockets for change, and the two younger children stared open-mouthed at the sweets.

"Can we have four twenty-five pence mix ups and five packs of World Cup stickers please?" said John to the elderly woman behind the counter.

David looked surprised. "You sure, John?"

"Yeah, I got my pocket money yesterday, and I got a bit extra for helping Dad with the lawn, so I'm fine. If I just got them for myself, then you lot'd just sit there, looking at me while I ate them, so this way I can eat mine in peace." He winked at Michael and Marie. Marie blushed, and a grin spread across Michael's face.

They sat on the low brick wall outside the shop, eating the sweets and watching John as he opened his new stickers. A sudden squeal of bicycle tires cut through the silence.

John looked up and saw Malcolm Harrison getting off his BMX, along with the rest of his gang: Billy Phillips, Simon Dobbs, and Lawrence Mitchell. "Aw shit."

David, John, and Michael got off the wall, their fists balled, ready for trouble.

David stood face to face with Malcolm. "What the fuck do you want, Harrison?"

Malcolm put his hands out, an innocent expression on his face. "Just wanted to say hello and to see what you are doing. Let me see those stickers, John."

"I'm not letting you see anything, Malcolm. Why don't you piss off and bother someone else."

"That's not very friendly. Maybe I'll just take them off you, make you look bad in front of your little skank girlfriend over there."

Marie reddened.

David moved between Malcolm and John. "Oi! Don't call my sister a skank, you tosser."

The rest of Malcolm's gang spread out and formed a loose semicircle around them, darting in and making half-hearted snatches at the foil packets in John's hands.

Billy Phillips produced the carrier bag of shopping from behind the wall. "Oh, look what I found. Finders keepers and all that."

Michael lunged at the bag. "That's me mam's shopping. Put it down, you prick."

Billy grinned. "Anything you say, Mikey boy," and hurled the plastic bag high into the air.

David and Michael watched the bag as it somersaulted through space. The milk bottles fell from it as it reached the top of its arc and shattered on the concrete paving stones below.

"Me dad will go mental!" screamed Michael and hurled himself at Billy, who shoved the smaller boy back against the wall. David squared up to Malcolm, who planted both hands on his shoulders and pushed him back.

"You want some, Dave? You wanna go? Right here, right now?"

Marie strode forward, her face flushed with rage.

"Malcolm Harrison, you are a fucking twat!" she screamed and brought her right foot up, striking the boy between his legs. Malcolm's face went purple and he almost folded in half. As his head came down, David brought his knee up into Malcolm's face. The boy's nose exploded in a shower of blood, and he fell to the floor, trying to catch his breath through agonised sobs.

John turned and punched Lawrence Mitchell square in the face as he stood gawping at his fallen friend. The boy fell back and put his hands over his face. John pummelled him, launching punch after punch at the cowering boy.

David and Michael turned to the other two boys, their faces twisted with fury. They knew what would happen to them if they returned without the shopping and were prepared to pass along the pain.

David balled his fists and stepped forward with murder in his eyes. "You owe me 50p Billy. Now."

Billy looked at Malcolm, who was still on the floor crying, and to Lawrence, now curled into a foetal position while John rained punches on his head.

Billy held out a shiny gold coin with trembling hands. "I've only got a quid."

David grabbed the coin from Billy's hand. "That'll do. Now piss off and take your cry babies with you before you get some of the same." He turned to John. "Leave him, mate, he's not worth the bother."

Lawrence got to his feet and grabbed his bike, then pedalled off in floods of tears. Billy and Simon followed close behind him. Malcolm struggled to his feet and tried to mount his bike, shrieking with pain as his bruised genitals landed on the saddle. With tears and snot running across his face, he wobbled off after his friends.

"Bother us once more, arse wipe, and I'll set my little sister on you again!" yelled David. Michael and John laughed at this. Marie was still glaring at the retreating boys, her lips pursed and her face flushed with anger.

John patted Marie on the shoulder. "Marie. You were awesome."

"Yeah," said Michael, "I can't believe you kicked Malcolm Harrison in the balls."

David walked up to his little sister and gave her a hug. "You're alright, Marie, but we can't call you squirt anymore after you kicked his arse. Gonna have to call you Scrapper instead, I reckon."

Marie flushed with pride and grinned at the three boys. "So I can play with you guys now? The girls around ours are so boring. All they ever talk about is dolls and ponies."

The boys looked at each other. Michael and John shrugged.

"Sure thing, Scrapper, you can hang with us from now on."

Chapter 4

25th March 1986. High Moor. 17:13.

The day flew by. The children dropped off the shopping at home, then took their bicycles and made a makeshift ramp from some bricks and a couple of old pieces of wood. Marie fell off hers while attempting a jump one-handed and skinned her knees. Mindful of John's presence, however, the tears soon stopped. The secret camp in the woods was not mentioned by any of the boys. While Marie was a provisional member of their gang, she was not to be trusted with their greatest secret. Not yet anyway.

The sun was low in the sky when they made their way home.

"I can't believe it's school tomorrow," said Michael.

John pulled a face. "I know. I've got a stack of history homework to do tonight after tea, and I really can't be arsed."

David rolled his eyes. "You wait until you get to secondary school. I swear I get more to do at home than I do in class."

Now it was Michael's turn to pull a face. "More homework? It's so unfair. It's bad enough that we have to sit there, bored all day without them ruining our nights and weekends."

"I think they should ban homework," said Marie. "Or we should get everyone to do what they did on the telly. Go on stroke or something?"

David laughed. "I think you mean go on strike, squirt."

"Whatever. And you said you weren't gonna call me squirt anymore."

David put his hands up in mock terror. "Alright, alright, Scrapper. I don't want you to kick me in the balls as well. Come on you two, we'd better get in for dinner, before we get in trouble. See you tomorrow, John?"

"Yeah, as long as that cow in history doesn't give me even more bloody homework to do. See you tomorrow at break, Michael, Marie. See you later, Dave," said John. Then he opened the rear door to his house and disappeared inside.

David opened their own back door and walked into the kitchen with Michael and Marie on his heels. A waft of warm damp air, laden with the smells of cooking hit them, and the children smiled. It had been a busy day, and they were all starving.

David hung his jacket up on the pegs behind the door. "Evening, Mam. What's for dinner?"

His mother looked up at him, and a shadow fell over her face. She opened her mouth to speak, when her husband's voice came from the front room.

"Joan? Is that them back?"

"Yes, Norman. They just came in now," she replied, a tremble in her voice.

They heard sounds of a newspaper being folded and heavy footsteps in the hallway. The children looked at their mother. She turned away and gave the evening meal her full attention.

43

Norman Williams appeared in the kitchen doorway. He was a large, barrel-chested man with heavily muscled arms and thinning dark brown hair combed across his scalp in a vain attempt to hide his encroaching baldness. His eyes were bloodshot, and the stink of alcohol and sweat billowed from him like a cloud. He curled his lip into a snarl.

"Where are they?"

David shrugged. "Where's what?"

Norman slapped David across the face with the back of his hand. The boy staggered and fell against the kitchen worktop.

"Don't you talk back to me, you little bastard. You know what I mean. Where are my good fucking tools?

David's stomach somersaulted. He had forgotten about the tools, left in their camp the previous day. His father tightened his fists and turned to Michael.

"It was you, wasn't it? You've been messing about with my tools again, you little fucking cunt. I've told you I don't know how many times, but you just don't listen."

Norman raised his fist to strike Michael. David moved between them.

"It was me, Dad. I've been building a tree house in the woods. I used them."

"You took our Marie in the woods? With all the perverts and glue sniffers?"

The fist lashed out and caught David in the ribs.

David crumpled to the floor and gasped for breath. Tears ran across his cheeks. "No. It was yesterday, I used them yesterday."

Norman bent over, grabbed the boy and pulled him to his feet.

"Then where the fucking hell are they today?"

"Still there, I forgot them last night."

Norman's face turned red and he balled his fists so tight that his knuckles turned white. The fist lashed out again and connected with the boy's stomach. David collapsed to the floor, gagging. His father kicked out and lifted him into the air. He crashed to the floor against the kitchen units.

"You did WHAT? With my best tools? If some pikey hasn't stolen them, they'll have rust all over them. You little–fucking–bastard," he screamed, punctuating the final three words with savage kicks to David's prone body.

He reached over, grabbed a fistful of David's hair and pulled him to his feet again. "You get out there, and you bring them back before I fucking cripple you. GET OUT. NOW."

He opened the back door and pushed David out into the night. David leaned against the wall and gasped for breath, tears of pain and rage flowing across his cheeks.

"Bastard," he said to the night. The word unblocked a dam, deep inside. All the pain and humiliation that he had suffered in the course of his short life flowed up and out of him.

"You miserable, fucking bastard," he screamed at the house. "I hope you die of cancer." He kicked out at the passenger door of his father's car and put a fresh dent in the beaten bodywork.

The porch light came on, and he heard the lock click open on the back door. Without a backward glance, David ran off into the night as the moon rose over the roof of the houses.

***

David reached the end of the street and stopped running. The moon shone from a cloudless sky, and the temperature had plummeted after the sun had gone down. David's denim jacket did little to keep him warm, and he wrapped his arms around himself. The movement made him wince as he brushed his bruised ribs.

I should run away. Just keep going and never go back. Not until I'm eighteen anyway. Then I'll go back with a baseball bat and put that fucker in a wheelchair. Shove his good tools right up his big fat arse.

He smiled at the thought and played it over and over in his head. His hate kept him warm, even if he knew deep down that it was all a fantasy. If he wasn't there to take the brunt of his father's rage, then it would be taken out on Michael and Marie.

The full moon lit his path across the fields, towards the dark line of the woods on the horizon. Off in the darkness, a dog barked, and from the hedgerow that separated the fields an owl hooted as it searched the night for its prey.

David made it to the tree line. The path snaked off into the darkness, branching left towards the town centre, straight across to the new housing estate where the faintest glimmer of orange light could be seen through the trees, and right into the deep woods where it continued for two or three miles before reaching the river.

Visions of strange men with bags of glue welded to their faces and their trousers around their ankles flashed through his mind. All his life he'd been taught that the woods were full of perverts, especially after dark. For a moment he considered turning back and telling his father that the tools were gone. Then he thought about the beating he would get if he returned empty-handed.

"Fuck it," he said and headed off down the right-hand path, into the deep woods.

David found it difficult to judge time in the darkness as he stumbled along the path. It seemed like he'd been in the woods for hours, but he was sure no more than ten minutes had passed. Grasping brambles reached out from the undergrowth and snagged his trousers. Once or twice he fell, wincing in pain as he skinned his hands. The woods were silent. No sounds of shambling glue sniffers crashing through the undergrowth towards him. He started to relax.

He missed the first marker and had to backtrack when he reached the stepping stones over the stream. He made his way back along the track and checked each tree until he spotted the yellow plastic tag nailed to the dark shape of the pine.

He pushed his way through the undergrowth. Building their camp all the way out here seemed less and less like a good idea with every passing second. He reached the second marker, spotting it more by luck than judgement.

Not far to go. A few more minutes and I'll be at the tree house. I'll get the bastard's tools, take the short cut back across the beck, and pray that the fat fuck passed out after dinner.

47

A howl echoed through the woods. The sound came from everywhere at once, resounding through the trees until it faded into silence. David felt warmth run down his leg and realised that he'd wet himself.

He stood in silence, breathing in short, sharp gasps, and listened to the sounds of the woods. He heard crashing in the undergrowth behind him. Something was heading in his direction. Fast. David sprinted towards the camp, pushing any thought of what might be behind him out of his mind.

The camp loomed up at him, its outline visible in silhouette against the full moon. The sounds of pursuit were closer now. He grasped the first plank of the makeshift ladder and climbed as if his life depended on it.

He reached the first platform and sighed with relief. His limbs trembled, and he grasped the thick trunk of the tree, holding onto it as if it were his mother. The crashing in the undergrowth stopped. David held his breath and peered over the edge of the platform.

Something made its way through the bracken towards the tree. Whatever it was, it was huge. At least the size of a full grown man, perhaps even bigger, although at this angle it was impossible to tell. David got a sense of mass and power from the shape beneath him. It wore no clothes, but seemed to be covered in something white. Fur?

The creature sniffed the air and turned its head upwards towards the terrified boy. It howled, and then David knew exactly what it was. Werewolf.

It circled the base of the tree, growling in frustration and then moved beyond David's line of sight, under the platform. He heard ripping sounds, and despite his terror, he craned his head over the side, to look.

The monster was climbing the trunk of the tree. Claws like knives dug into the bark as it hauled itself up towards him. Its progress was slow, but it was relentless, unerring. David choked back a sob, and with shaking arms, began the climb to the second platform, only too aware that he was only gaining a temporary respite.

David reached the second platform, almost forty feet from the forest floor, just as the beast reached the first. It raised its head and howled once more at the boy.

"Fuck off!" he screamed, his voice cracking. "Fuck off and bother someone else."

The creature snarled and continued climbing the tree towards the sobbing boy nestled high in its branches.

David broke down in tears. He didn't want to die. He didn't want to be torn apart and eaten by this thing that was climbing towards him. He had nowhere left to go. Nowhere left to run.

Unless...

The beast was almost half way up the tree now. Its progress slowed as the trunk thinned. Its every move sent shudders up to David in his hiding place and made the tree sway. It would be on him in moments.

An idea formed through the black wall of terror in his mind. David removed his denim jacket, wrapped the arms around his hands and threw the coat over the rope zip-line. Without a second's thought, he launched himself into the air. He swore he felt the wind from claws slash at empty air behind him. He hit the platform and rolled across it, feeling splinters from the wooden planks embed themselves in his knees. He looked back. The werewolf was still on the tree, just beneath the highest platform. It howled in fury.

"Let's see you get over here, you flea-bitten, mangy twat."

The monster snarled at him and stayed where it was for a moment. David felt a wave of relief crash over him. It would have to climb down, and then climb back up this tree to get him, at which point he could escape to the lower platform and then do it all again. He could keep this up all night, or until the monster got bored and went off in search of easier prey.

The werewolf bunched its muscles and launched itself into space. It covered the distance between the trees with ease and crashed down into the tree house, through the flimsy timber roof.

David whimpered and pushed himself back into the corner. He felt something stick into his back. His father's tool bag. His hands shook as he reached inside and produced a long, sharp chisel, which he held out before him like a sword.

The werewolf got to its feet, snarled at the terrified boy, then pounced.

Chapter 5

26th March 1986. Durham Wildlife Liaison Office. 09:15

Steven Wilkinson leaned forward in his chair and regarded the man sitting on the other side of the desk. "So? What do you think?"

"About what?"

Steven pushed the photographs across the table.

"What do you think? About these. The big cat and the attack on those sheep."

The other man grinned, which accentuated the furrows in his face, and lit a cigarette.

"Well, which do you want to know about first?"

"What? Aren't we talking about the same thing here?"

"Nope. One has now't to do with 'tother."

Steven felt his patience evaporate. Matt Wilshire was a local hunter who carried out consultancy for the Police on occasions such as this. The old bugger was playing with him, and Steven was not in the mood.

"Come on, Matt. I've been chasing my tail for weeks on this case. Cut me some bloody slack and tell me about the cat."

"What you have there is a female puma. She's an adult, probably a good two meters in length, weighs maybe forty to forty-five pounds."

"Any idea what it's doing roaming the countryside south of Durham?"

"If I had to guess, I'd say it was probably released back in the 1960's. Lots of folk kept things like that as pets before they passed the Dangerous Animals act. Then, when they had to turn them over to the authorities, some people just let them go into the wild."

"Could one have survived in the area for nearly twenty years without anyone seeing it before?"

"Probably not. In the wild, a cat like that would probably only live ten, maybe twelve years. That cat looks like it's a young adult, maybe five years old. Either someone turned it loose within the last couple of years, or there was a breeding pair around here not so long ago."

"Can we track it? Capture it perhaps?"

"Hard to say with pumas. They have a huge territorial range. That cat could be thirty miles away from where that picture was taken by now, or it could be half a mile away. Depends if she's got cubs."

"Great. So, about the attack on the livestock. Are you telling me that a puma couldn't kill all those sheep?"

Matt took another drag on his cigarette. "Oh, it could kill them alright. It could, but it didn't. Not those sheep."

"How can you tell?"

"Look at the way they've been torn up. Flesh ripped from the bones. Cats don't feed that way. They rasp the meat off the bones with those sandpaper tongues of theirs. What did this was canine, but I suppose your lads in forensics will work that one out eventually. Like I say, two different things."

"So, how many dogs would it take to do something like this?"

The old hunter laughed. "Depends on the dogs. A pack of Dobermans could do it a damn sight faster than a pack of Yorkshire terriers."

Steven felt his temper flare, but managed to maintain his composure; just. "OK, then let me put it another way. What kind of dog do you think did this?"

Matt frowned. "Well, Sergeant, that's where you've got me stumped. Whatever it was, it was a big bastard. Look at the bite marks. Its jaw must have been almost a foot across. Maybe some kind of cross breed. Great Dane crossed with a Bull Mastiff and a fucking Shetland pony? Whatever it is, it's big and it's got a nasty temperament. You wouldn't want that bugger to start humping your leg, I can tell you that. And if it did, you'd fake a feckin orgasm."

This wasn't what Steven wanted to hear. Inspector Franks was adamant the cat was the problem, but Matt was telling him otherwise. He wasn't sure what was worse: big cats breeding in the area, or some monstrous dog being let loose on livestock. He pushed a pile of papers aside and picked up the telephone. Better to break the news to Franks sooner than later. He'd dialled the first digit when the door to the office burst open. Constable Phillips stood in the doorway, sweating and out of breath.

"Sarge, you both better come with me. They've found a body. Torn apart like those sheep last month."

"What? Where?"

"In the woods, in High Moor. " Constable Phillips looked down at his boots. "And, Sarge,...it's a kid."

***

Graeme Reynolds

26th March 1986. King's Close School. 10.45.

The children marched into the assembly hall in single file and sat in rows on the hard wooden chairs in their respective classes; youngest at the front, oldest at the back.

An elderly television set stood at the front of the hall while Mr Jones, the third year teacher, fussed with a tangle of cables that led to the school video recorder.

The low hum of muted conversation filled the hall while Mr Jones attempted to tune the television into the video player. John glanced across the room and tried to catch Michael's eye, but the other boy just looked at his feet. Lawrence Mitchell glared back at John and slowly ran his finger across his throat.

"You are dead," he mouthed. John ignored him and waited for his moment.

The educational videos that they were forced to watch with alarming regularity were an ordeal that none of the assembled children enjoyed. They ranged from embarrassing old programmes from the depths of time about water safety with Rolf Harris, to newer, but no less dull, items about industry or road safety. The last one they had to sit through had been about rivers or something and it had gone on for over an hour. They'd missed play time because of that one. John, however, had a plan.

High Moor

Mr Jones stood up and beamed in triumph as the two white lines appeared on the TV screen. He turned off the tuning signal and retrieved today's video tape. Miss Watson and Mr Smith closed the curtains to the hall. Shafts of sunlight pierced the darkness, and dust motes danced in the beams before winking out of existence as they passed into shadow. John fished in his pocket and retrieved a small grey box.

During the last torturous video session, John noticed that the VCR at school was exactly the same model as the one he had at home. Over the course of the last week, a plan had formed, and now he was ready to put it into action.

"Quiet please," said Mr Jones, "That means you, Karen Burke."

The murmur of conversation faded. Mr Jones stood for a moment until he was sure that he had everyone's undivided attention. "Today, our video is about crop rotation in the seventeenth century. This will tie into your class projects, so I expect you all to pay attention." A chorus of groans rose from the children. Mr Jones ignored them and pressed play on the video recorder.

The television screen was filled with static and then turned black. White letters displayed the inspired title, "Crop rotation in the seventeenth century," and a feeble rendition of *Greensleeves* warbled from the elderly television's speakers. Then the tape stopped and rewound to the beginning.

Mr Jones looked confused, ran a hand across his bald head, and pressed play again.

The screen turned black once more and the first few bars of *Greensleeves* played, then the programme stopped and the tape ejected from the VCR.

Mr Jones made a show of examining the video cassette, then placed it back into the machine. "Er...we seem to be having some technical difficulties."

As soon as he hit play, the tape went into fast forward. The titles flashed by, and a man in a corduroy waistcoat, not unlike the one worn by Mr Jones, appeared on the screen. The man's arms waved in the air as if performing some sort of energetic dance. At the back of the hall, someone cheered.

Mr Jones stopped the tape and ejected it, his bald head going as red as the few remaining tufts of hair around his ears. He pushed open the flap at the front of the machine and blew into it, then switched the machine off and back on again.

He squinted at the VCR with suspicion in his eyes, put the tape back into the machine, and pressed play. The titles came up and the music started. He hovered near the VCR, but the titles and the music faded and the man in the corduroy jacket appeared once more, less animated than on his previous visit. Satisfied that the machine was now behaving itself, Mr Jones walked across the hall to his seat.

The second Mr Jones sat down, the VCR started to record over the program. He flew from his seat, arms flailing, and dove at the possessed video recorder. He slipped on the polished wooden floor and landed in a tangle of gangly arms and legs in front of the first year students.

The hall erupted in laughter as Mr Jones, still on his knees, hit the eject button and retrieved his precious tape from the demonic VCR.

He dusted himself off and tried to regain some dignity.

"There seems to be something wrong with the video," he said to the sniggering masses. "I'll call the repair man, but in the meantime you all might as well take an early break."

A cheer rose from the hall as the children, needing no encouragement, filed out to the playground. John grinned to himself, slipped the remote control back into his pocket, and looked across to Michael. His friend was still looking at the floor and didn't seem to have noticed the antics of Mr Jones.

Outside in the playground, John went over to Michael and Marie, who were standing alone in the corner of the tarmac play area. "Did you see Jones go flying? Man, I thought I was going to piss myself."

"Yeah, it was pretty funny," said Michael, without conviction.

"What's the matter?"

Marie looked up at John with tear brimmed eyes. "David didn't come home last night."

"What? I saw him go in the house with you two, for tea."

"Dad made him go back out and get the tools from the camp," said Michael. "Dad was mad...really mad. Not seen him go off like that in ages."

"Dave probably just stayed in the camp, out of the way, till he calmed down," said John. "We can go round there on the way home from school and see if he's there, if you want."

Michael looked up and the beginnings of a smile appeared at the corners of his mouth.

"Yeah, that's probably it, and Jones was funny as fuck back then. Don't know what was going on with that video, but we got extra playtime so I'm not complaining."

John rolled his eyes up and put on his most angelic expression. "Erm...I might have had something to do with that." He removed the remote control from his pocket.

"You did that? John, you are my fucking hero. That was genius, mate. Genius."

"John, that was brilliant," said Marie, "and thanks for cheering us up." She hugged him and then pulled away, her cheeks flushing scarlet.

"Oooh! John's got a girlfriend," shouted Lawrence Mitchell from across the playground. Heads turned to look at the three friends. Girls sniggered and whispered to each other. John felt his cheeks burn.

He balled his fists and strode forward to where Lawrence, Simon, and Billy stood. "What's it to you Mitchell? Looking like a giant panda not good enough? You want some more?"

"You better get in line if you want to fuck the little slag," said Billy Phillips, "I hear her brothers have first dibs."

Michael stood by John's side. "I've had enough of you arseholes," Marie joined him and the three friends faced their tormentors.

The playground erupted in cries of "fight, fight, fight," and the rest of the children formed a circle around the combatants, eager for the violence to begin.

Mr Smith pushed his way through the crowd, accompanied by two police officers, a man and a woman. "Break it up you lot. Michael, Marie? Can you come with us please? And John? I believe Mr Jones would like a word with you, about the school video recorder."

Michael and Marie exchanged confused glances as they were led away through the playground. What had they done now?

***

26th March. Mill Woods, High Moor. 11.34.

Steven lifted the blue tape and stepped beneath it. Matt Wilshire followed behind him and lit a cigarette. He offered one to Steven, who shook his head and made his way through the bracken to the crowd of men in white forensics coveralls. One of them was being sick in the undergrowth.

Another of the forensics officers put up his hand. "You might want to stop there, Sergeant."

"Why's that?"

The man pointed to the bracken. The vegetation was covered in congealed blood that stained the green leaves black. Swarms of flies filled the air. The forensics officer's white coveralls were bright red below the knee.

"Jesus," said Steven. "How far does this mess extend?"

"About ten feet in every direction around that tree," he said, pointing to an oak tree with the remains of a tree house high in its branches.

Steven tried to take in the detail of the scene, but found his eyes skipping away from the tree.

This is ridiculous. I'm a trained police officer. There's nothing here that I haven't seen before a hundred times.

He forced himself to focus and discovered that he was wrong.

Red tendrils hung from the branches of the oak. At first Steven thought he was looking at paper party decorations, until he realised that they were intestines. Blood oozed through the gaps in the wooden boards of the tree house and formed large dark red drops that spattered on the forest floor with sickening regularity like some form of perverse metronome.

He followed the path of the ropes that led from the tree house to the adjacent pine and saw the wounds in the tree where something had climbed up it. The scars oozed sap as if the tree was weeping for the dead boy. He started to get a picture of what had occurred here, and it didn't make a lot of sense.

One of the white-coated forensics officers held up a severed arm with a blood stained chisel clutched in its pale white hand. "Boss, I've found the other one." Then he placed it in a clear plastic bag.

Steven grabbed Matt's arm and guided him towards the officer and his grisly trophy. "Take a look, Matt. Is it the same as the sheep?"

The old man's face was white with shock. "Yes. Definitely canine, not feline. Same sort of bite diameter. I'd say this boy was killed by the same animal that killed those sheep."

Steven grabbed him by the shoulders and turned him around so that they were face to face. "So, Matt, you tell me. How many fucking dogs do you know of that can climb a forty-foot tree?"

The old man looked unsteady on his feet. He leaned against a tree for support and took several long deep breaths, then he pushed his way past Steven and moved towards the gore-covered oak.

He circled the tree, making deliberate, careful steps as he widened his search radius, eyes fixed on the soft, bloodstained ground. After a few moments, he stopped and crouched to examine something.

"Jesus, oh dear Jesus..." he said, his voice barely above a whisper.

Steven could see the old man trembling from where he stood. His face had become ashen, and his hands shook as he retrieved a cigarette from his pack and took a long deep drag on it.

"Matt? What's the matter?"

"Over here. You need to see this."

Steven cursed and tried to pick his way through the blood-soaked bracken to where the old hunter stood. By the time he reached him, he could feel the cold, sticky wetness soaking through his trousers. He tried not to think about it and focused on Matt instead. "So? What have you found?"

Matt gestured to the ground. Steven saw two large prints, just visible through the foliage. The prints were around two feet apart, and each was a foot long. Steven could make out impressions at the front of the prints, where claws had dug deep into the earth, and a rounded mark from the heels.

"This is where it jumped down from the tree," said Matt.

"What the hell? Those prints look more like a human footprint than anything else. Do you have any idea what could have made tracks like that?"

The old man shook his head. "I can't help you, lad. I'm sorry, but I just can't."

"Do you know what kind of animal did this, Matt? I need your help here because I don't have the slightest idea of what the hell is going on."

"I can't, Steven. That's all there is too it. Consider me off the case and unavailable for any consultation. In fact, I'm taking the wife and the grandkids, and I'm going on holiday. Today."

"What the fuck, Matt. Don't leave me hung out to dry like this. I've got a fucking puma stalking the area, which may or may not just have killed a child, and I have no-one else I can turn to for help tracking the fucking thing down and put a bullet in it."

Matt turned and walked away from the tree. Steven grabbed hold of his arm and turned him around. "Don't you walk away from me, Matt. Don't you fucking dare."

The old man fished in his coat pocket and pulled out his packet of cigarettes and a pen. He removed the cardboard insert and wrote down a number, then handed it to Steven.

"I can't help you, Steven. I'm not sure if anyone can, but this guy might. He's a yank called Carl Schneider. I met him about fifteen years ago, in Germany. If anyone can help, he can. Assuming he's still alive."

Steven took the card and looked at the number.

"Well, that's something I suppose," he said, but Matt had already started walking away from the crime scene.

He turned his head and said, "God help you, Steven. God help you." Then, without so much of a backwards glance, he headed off towards the path and his waiting car.

Chapter 6

24th April 1986. Newcastle Airport. 10:00.

The rain fell in sheets. It drummed against the metal roof of the police car and obscured the view from the windscreen, despite the best efforts of the wipers.

Constable Phillips turned to Steven. "Do you want me to come with you, Sarge?"

"No, take the car and park it up, then go get yourself a coffee or something. I have a feeling this might take a while."

Steven paused, willing the rain to let up. When the weather responded by raining even harder, he sighed and stepped from the car into a puddle. He cursed, pulled his hat down, and ran to the building. By the time he pushed open the glass doors, the rest of him was as wet as his feet.

He walked to the customs area, leaving wet footprints on the tiled floor in his wake. As he pushed open the door, he was met by a uniformed customs officer.

"Sergeant Wilkinson? I'm PO Michaels. Can I get you anything? Tea? Coffee?"

"No, thank you, Officer Michaels. You said on the telephone that there was a problem with Mr Schneider?"

Officer Michaels raised his eyebrow. "In a manner of speaking. Perhaps it's better if you see for yourself."

Steven followed him to a small room at the end of the corridor. The customs official unlocked the door and both men entered, then Officer Michaels locked it behind them. On the table were two large aluminium cases. Steven undid the clasps on one of them and opened the lid.

The case contained a heavy-calibre hunting rifle with a military grade starlight scope. Rows of ammunition nestled in the foam rubber interior. Steven removed one of the bullets and examined it under the fluorescent light. The round was about an inch and a half long with a silvered head. The end of the bullet had a deep cross carved into it.

Officer Michaels picked up the rifle. "What we have here is a Ruger .44, semi-automatic hunting rifle. The bullets are modified magnum rounds. The actual bullet appears to be made out of a silver/lead alloy. The cross on the end is especially nasty. When the round hits its target, it fragments. In essence, it will be like a small grenade going off inside whatever you shoot it at."

"Well, I knew Mr Schneider was going to be bringing his own weapons. I applied for the visitor's firearms permit on his behalf. Apart from the modified ammunition, I'm not sure exactly what the problem is here?"

"Take a look in the other case."

Steven popped the lid on the second case and stood for a moment in silence. "Jesus."

"Now you see why we called you."

The second case contained 9mm handguns, a number of knives, and what appeared to be a submachine gun, along with more of the cross-hatched silver ammunition.

"Is that what I think it is?"

"I'm afraid so. An Ingram Mac-10. It gets worse. Look underneath."

Steven was almost afraid to look. He removed the weapons and ammunition, then pulled back the protective foam. Six hand grenades were nestled beneath.

Steven massaged his temples and turned to the customs officer.

"Look, Officer Michaels, I understand that the automatic weapon and the grenades clearly aren't going anywhere, but the other items should be covered under the firearms permit. Mr Schneider was asked to come here to assist us with a delicate matter, and I would appreciate your help in resolving this situation as quickly as possible."

"There's another problem I'm afraid. The permit hasn't been approved yet."

"What? I applied for it almost a month ago. Do you know what the problem is?"

The customs official shrugged. "I called the Met, and as I understand it, the person that was supposed to rubber-stamp the application is on sick leave."

"Oh, for Christ's sake. Do you mind if I use your telephone?"

Steven spent the next hour being passed from department to department until he ended up back with the person that he spoke to in the first place. This did not improve his mood, and by the time he reached someone who could help, he was on the verge of yelling into the green plastic receiver. Eventually he slammed the telephone down and turned to the customs officer.

"They're going to fax through the permit within the next half-hour. In the meantime, would you mind if I saw Mr Schneider?"

PO Michaels led him from the room, through a maze of corridors, until they arrived at another door. The customs officer unlocked the interview room and Steven entered. The door closed, and the lock clicked once he was inside.

He'd not been sure what to expect from Carl Schneider. Their brief telephone conversation had left him with a mental image of an American version of Matt Wilshire. The arsenal locked in the evidence room had forced him to adjust his opinion, and he had been expecting a grizzled, Special Forces type. What he had not been expecting was the small, unassuming man sitting before him in a business suit.

Carl Schneider looked to be in his late fifties. He was almost entirely bald, with only a few tufts of grey hair remaining around his ears, and despite his slight build, the man seemed to have a presence about him, a quiet authority that was evident in his bright blue eyes and in the relaxed manner that he held himself, even while in custody.

Carl got to his feet and extended his hand. "So, you must be Steve. Pleasure to meet you."

Steven took his hand and winced as the older man crushed his fingers. "Nice to meet you too, Mr Schneider."

"Please, call me Carl. So, Steve, have you cut through all the bullshit with those idiots outside? Are we ready to get down to business?"

"More or less. We're still waiting for them to fax the permit through, and a few of your more exotic items won't be going with us."

Carl frowned. "Bloody bureaucrats, getting worked up over a few little details."

"I would hardly call hand grenades and machine guns a few little details."

"How do they expect a guy to do a job when you take away his tools?"

"What on earth do you need grenades and a bloody Ingram for? I would have thought the Ruger would stop anything short of an elephant."

"Son, the Ruger is for when we see it first and when it's at long range. The other toys are the backup plan, in case the rifle doesn't take it out first go, because if we don't kill it first time, we are gonna seriously piss it off."

"Well, if it's any consolation, you still have your knives and your handguns. Those should be enough to keep any angry pumas at bay."

"You think I came with all that crap for a puma? Son, I'd wrestle some mangy mountain lion into submission with my bare hands. We are after something a whole lot meaner than that."

"Matt said the same thing. He also said that whatever killed that boy was canine, but I don't know of any dogs that can climb trees, so why not let me in on the secret. What exactly are we dealing with here?"

Carl laughed, and then winked at Steven. "All in good time, all in good time. Now, let's get my gear, grab a burger and we can get ready for tonight."

"Why? What happens tonight?"

"What do you think you brought me here for, son? Tonight we go hunting."

***

24th April 1986. Mill Woods, High Moor. 19:30.

Steven gripped the wet surface of the tree trunk and hauled himself up towards the makeshift platform that he and Carl had spent most of the afternoon constructing.

The American located a clearing in the woods around a quarter of a mile away from where the Williams boy had been found and carried out his site preparation with an air of casual confidence. That should have made Steven feel better about the situation, but for some reason it had the opposite effect.

They built the platform on the intersection of two branches, almost thirty feet from the forest floor. They had trimmed the lower branches of the tree so that there were no obstructions to their field of fire. It had been cold, wet, unpleasant work, and every time Steven looked at the platform, he had visions of a similar structure where a boy had died the previous month. The thought did nothing to settle his nerves.

Steven reached the platform and hauled himself over the edge of the wood, praying that it would support his weight. The rain had stopped around an hour earlier. The only sounds were evening birdsong, and the sporadic patter of droplets of water falling from leaves.

Steven heard a rustling in the undergrowth, and his hand moved towards the flight cases containing Carl's weapons. A moment later, Carl Schneider emerged from the bracken holding a length of rope. At the other end of the rope was a goat.

Steven was puzzled. "Where the hell did you get that?"

Carl flashed him a knowing grin. "From a farmer on the outskirts of town. Cost me twenty pounds, which of course I'll be expecting back on top of my fee."

"Great. So now, Durham Constabulary is the proud owner of a female goat. Have you thought about what exactly we're going to do with it if your plan doesn't work?"

Carl tied one end of the rope to a metal stake in the centre of the clearing. "You could always keep it as a pet. Or eat it. Some good cuts of meat on a goat."

"Something tells me that the wife might object to my showing up with a slightly used goat. What makes you so sure that our mystery beast is going to take the bait?"

Carl finished his knot, walked over to the goat, and stroked the animal's head. Then he drew a knife and sliced the flesh across the goat's ribs. The animal squealed in pain and pulled at its tether. Carl walked away from the stricken creature and attached his tree climbing harness.

"What the fuck are you doing? I should arrest you right now for animal cruelty."

High Moor

The old man looked up at the police officer in the tree. All traces of humour had vanished from his face. "Steve, I do what I have to. Hopefully, this will save some lives. Now, the light is going, and soon the moon will be up. I don't want another fucking sound out of you until daybreak. No talking, no moaning. Don't even breathe loud. Both our lives depend on it. Do you think you can do that?"

Steven shrugged and pulled a pack of cigarettes from his coat pocket. "Sure, not a sound till morning. I think I can manage that."

"You can forget about the cancer sticks until daybreak, too. It'll smell the smoke half a mile away. We want the goat to be the bait, not us."

Steven sighed and put the cigarettes away just as the rain started to fall once more. This was going to be a long night.

Chapter 7

24th April 1986. St Paul's Church Hall. 20:15.

John and Michael peered through the glass door at the rain-soaked street outside. The water came down in waves, driven by the wind into ice-cold darts that hammered against the thin glass sheet.

John turned to Michael. "I thought your dad was coming to pick us up?"

"He's meant to do a lot of things, but mostly he just sits and gets pissed. He was always like that, but ever since..." said Michael, wiping his eyes with his Cub Scout neckerchief.

John put his hand on his friend's shoulder. "Sorry, mate, I really am. If you ever need anything..."

Michael moved away from John, glaring at him through red eyes. "If I need anything? I need everyone to stop looking at me like I'm some kind of freak. I need people to stop blaming me for the curfews and the Cub Scout camp being cancelled." Michael's voice cracked and the tears flowed. "Most of all, I need for my brother not to be dead. Can you do any of those things, John?"

"Mike, no one's blaming you for any of that."

"Really? Did you see everyone in that hall look at me when Mr Wilson cancelled the camping trip?"

"It's not like that. It's just that no one knows what to say to you to make it better. I don't know what to say, and I've known you all my life."

"How can anything make it better? It doesn't matter how sorry everyone is, John. My brother's still dead, my dad's still a useless fucking drunk, and everyone in town thinks I'm either some charity case, or that somehow it's all my fault."

The two boys stood in silence in the church hall entrance, watching the headlights of vehicles driving past, hoping that one of them was Michael's father.

The lights of the church hall flickered out as Mr Wilson, the scout leader, closed up for the night.

"Has your lift not arrived yet, boys? Do you need a ride home?"

"My dad will be here in a minute," said Michael, "He's just running late."

"Well, you'll have to wait outside for him. I'm locking the hall up now. Are you sure you don't need a lift home? The curfew's in effect, and I wouldn't want you to get into trouble."

John put on his best smile. "We're fine, thanks. See you next week, Mr Wilson."

The two boys stood in the porch while Mr Wilson locked the doors, got into his car, then drove away.

"Do you think your dad's coming?"

"Is he bollocks. Come on, let's walk and hope the coppers don't see us."

The boys hurried through the darkened streets, keeping close to the walls of the terraced houses in an attempt to avoid the worst of the rain. Within minutes, they were both soaked through, their thin jumpers and scout caps failing to offer any kind of protection from the elements. The boys ran on in silence and misery until they passed the comprehensive school, turning onto the lane that would take them home. As they crossed the road, a shout came from a bus shelter.

"Hey, losers! We want a word with you."

Michael and John turned to look. Malcolm and his gang were huddled under the metal shelter, passing a joint between them. The two boys exchanged glances, then broke into a sprint.

"The school field," said John, "cut across it. We can lose them in the dark."

They ran through the open gates, then took a sharp right turn off the tarmac road and across the wet grass. The main school building rose up to greet them as they cleared a rise; a dark monolith silhouetted against the reflected orange haze of the sky.

Michael risked a look over his shoulder only to find, to his dismay, that the four older boys were gaining on them.

"Go faster, they're getting closer," he gasped.

John opened his mouth to reply, but then tripped and fell down the embankment, sliding on the wet grass, to come to rest next to an ornamental rose bed. Michael ran after his friend and helped him to his feet. They got ready to run once more, but it was too late. The older boys had caught up to them.

Malcolm pushed John in the chest and sent him sprawling back into the muddy grass. "Hey, lads, where do you think you're going?"

Lawrence launched a kick at John. The blow caught him in his stomach, and he collapsed to the floor, struggling to draw breath. Simon grabbed Michael from behind and held his arms.

Billy walked over to him, an evil smirk on his face. "You owe me a quid, scumbag, plus interest."

Michael kicked out at the other boy, who stayed just out of reach.

"You still want to have a go? Not many brains in your family, are there? Especially now dear Dave's worm food."

John struggled to rise. Malcolm punched him in the face, and he fell back into the mud. Lawrence sat on his chest, pinned his shoulders to the ground, and rained a fusillade of blows onto his head. Malcolm turned his attention to Michael.

"By my reckoning, we've got a few scores to settle with you little shit bags. Number one..." he said as he punched Michael, "that little episode outside the shop last month."

Michael fought to hold back his tears. "The one where my little sister kicked your fat fucking arse, you mean?"

Malcolm ignored him. "Number two..." This time the blow connected with Michael's stomach, knocking the wind out of him. "This curfew. If your stupid brother hadn't got himself killed, we wouldn't have coppers coming round school, giving boring lectures on why we can't go outside after dark."

Michael sucked air into his lungs through sobs of pain and rage.

"Number three..." Malcolm's fist lashed out again, striking Michael in the mouth, splitting his lip. "Just because I don't like you and your stinking family."

"My turn, Mal," said Billy. "Number four,..." he said, bringing his foot up between Michael's legs, "you took my pocket money."

Michael screamed in pain and fell to the floor. John was still pinned under Lawrence, crying out with each blow that struck him.

Malcolm stood over the battered boy and pulled out a pocketknife.

"You see this, Michael? I'm going to cut your balls off with it." He tilted his head to John. "His too. Your sister will probably thank me."

***

The great beast moved through the shadows in search of prey. Water fell from the skies. It hid the moon behind a flat grey curtain and muted the scents of the creatures that huddled in their lairs, waiting for the predator to pass.

The moon called to it, her song rising and ebbing in the beast, a tide of blood, deep inside that it could barely contain. The pressure rose to a crescendo, setting its nerves alight with a furious ecstasy.

High Moor

The beast sniffed the air and tried to sort through the myriad scents. The sharp, acrid stench of the human settlement, the sweet stench of terror, from pets that trembled within their houses, the faintest tang of blood in the air, the cries of pain and alarm that accompanied it. Prey.

The monster dropped down onto all four legs and ran off through the undergrowth, into the night.

***

24th April 1986. Mill Woods, High Moor. 20:21.

Steven was not having a good time. The only sounds he could hear were the steady hiss of the rain and the mewling of the injured goat. The rest of the forest was silent. A drop of water made its way through his waterproof jacket, trickling down his neck, and his legs were cramping up. He adjusted his position to ease his discomfort. The platform creaked beneath him. Carl gave him a disapproving look. Steven responded with a shrug, then settled back to resume his vigil.

The goat got to its feet, straining against the tether. It bleated in terror and ran in a circle, rising onto its back legs as it struggled to be free.

Carl put his hand on Steven's shoulder and put his finger up to his mouth, then reached under the oilskin to retrieve his rifle and one of the pistols. He passed the handgun to Steven without a sound. Steven took the weapon from him, still unsure what good a pistol would be at this range. His heart pounded in his chest, and for a moment, he forgot to breathe as he searched the dark woods for any sign of movement.

77

***

24th April 1986. King's Close School. 20:23.

Michael struggled against Simon's grip as Malcolm brought the knife up to his face.

He glanced at Billy. "Get his pants off, then hold his legs down."

Michael screamed and lashed out with his feet, catching Billy square in the face. He fell backwards into the mud, blood and tears mingling with the rain. Malcolm replied with a savage kick to Michael's stomach that knocked the air out of the smaller boy's lungs. Michael folded over. Malcolm pulled Michael's trousers and shorts down around his ankles while Simon yanked him to the ground.

Malcolm turned to Billy. "Pin his fucking legs down. Sit on them if you have to, and stop crying like a bloody baby."

Billy got to his feet and sat on Michael's legs. Malcolm picked up his knife and kneeled beside him.

"God. Don't! Please, someone help!"

"There's no help for you, Mikey. Now lie still. This will be over before you know it."

John's face was a mess, but the pain had subsided to a dull throbbing, punctuated with sharp flashes of agony as Lawrence landed another punch. He heard Michael screaming for help and knew that he was next in line for whatever Malcolm had planned.

High Moor

John arched his back and brought both his legs up straight into the air, then hooked them around Lawrence's shoulders. The move surprised the older boy, who fell backward into the mud. John stumbled to his feet. He kicked out at his assailant and caught him in the jaw. Teeth flew from Lawrence's mouth. He fell back to the ground, unmoving. John didn't care if he was alive or dead. He just knew he had to help Michael.

He reached across to the flower beds, grabbing a smooth stone the size of a grapefruit. He ran up behind Malcolm, and hit him with the rock as hard as he could.

Malcolm screamed and fell to the floor, clutching the back of his head. Billy got to his feet and rugby-tackled John. The boys rolled around in the mud, throwing wild punches at one another. John managed to connect a blow with Billy's already broken nose, but although he cried out in pain, this only seemed to fuel his rage, and he soon overpowered John.

Malcolm stood up and put his hand to the back of his head. His fingertips were dark with blood.

"I was just going to neuter you little bastards, now I'm going to fucking kill the pair of you."

Simon pulled Michael to his feet, while Lawrence got up from the ground, holding his jaw. He tried to speak, but only a thin squeal of pain emerged from his bleeding lips. Malcolm picked up his knife and stood before Michael and John, silhouetted against the orange glow of the sodium streetlights.

He moved towards John. "Time to die."

Bright light illuminated the boys, and a voice rang out across the school field.

"This is the police. Stay where you are."

Malcolm looked up at the police car that pulled onto the driveway, then turned back to his friends. "Throw them in the bushes, and then let's get the fuck out of here. This isn't over, you two. Not by a fucking long shot. And if you say a word to the coppers, then we'll burn your houses down, with your scummy families still inside. Got it?"

Simon and Billy shoved Michael and John into the rose bushes before they ran off into the darkness. Thorns punctured the boys' skin as they landed in the flowerbed. John tried to rise, but felt his skin tear at the attempt. He fell back, sobbing in pain and rage. The police car pulled up alongside them and two officers got out.

One Officer ran over to the two boys and tried to free them from their thorny bonds. "Jesus, are you two OK?"

The rain had stopped falling, and the full moon appeared through a gap in the clouds as the boys were taken to the waiting police car.

Michael turned to John, the fury in his eyes mirrored by that in his friends. "This isn't over. I'm going to get those fuckers if it's the last thing I ever do."

"I'm going to kill them," said John. "Every single last one of the bastards. For you, me, Marie, and especially David. Even if it takes the rest of my life."

"Join the fucking queue," said Michael as the police car pulled out of the school to take the boys home.

***

High Moor

The beast drew closer to the prey. The sounds of panic were more frantic now as the goat became aware of its presence. The rain had stopped, and the scent of blood was pronounced, a sweet metallic odour over the underlying smell of the wet earth. The beast paused. There were other scents nearby. Human. Familiar.

The urge to rush forward to claim its prize was overwhelming, but the beast was old and experienced. It tried to place the familiar smell of the human. An image flashed across its mind. Darkness, then a flash of light. A searing pain across its chest. It snarled, remembering the human that had caused it that pain many years ago. It circled the scent, straining its ears for any sounds that would help it locate its quarry.

A creak in the branches above the forest floor. The sound of metal against metal. The click of a round entering the chamber of a firearm. The scent of fear and anticipation from the humans.

The moon emerged from behind the clouds. The urge to greet its mistress rose within the beast. It pushed the impulse down into itself and moved in silence through the bracken to where the humans lay in wait.

***

24th April 1986. Mill Woods, High Moor. 20:27.

The goat had stopped bleating and now lay flat on the ground as if resigned to its fate. Carl held the rifle against his shoulder and searched the undergrowth. Steven gripped the hilt of his pistol so hard that his knuckles turned white. The woods were silent.

Carl turned his head to Steven. "Something's wrong."

The tree that the two men were in shuddered; their platform creaked and shifted beneath them.

Steven felt his heart lurch in his chest. "What the fuck?"

"It's below us. Oh Christ, it knows we're here."

The tree shuddered again as something large crashed against it. The platform groaned in protest. One of the support struts fell to the forest floor.

"Climb," yelled Carl. "Get further up the tree before the platform goes."

Steven tried to haul himself up, but his hands and feet slipped on the wet branches. The tree shook once more, and another of the support struts splintered.

Carl clambered up amongst the branches like a monkey, but Steven was still struggling to gain a footing when the platform tore loose and plummeted down, taking most of their weapons and ammunition with it. Steven wrapped his arms around a branch and held on for his life.

"Climb, Steve, for Christ's sake climb, and whatever you do, don't look down."

Steven wrapped his legs around the trunk of the tree and tried to shimmy his way up to Carl's outstretched arms. The tree shook again. A monstrous howl reverberated through the forest. Steven couldn't help himself. He angled his head and looked down, regretting his action in an instant.

High Moor

Beneath him was something right out of his worst nightmares. The beast stood on two legs, almost seven feet tall. Thick white fur covered its entire body, apart from a line of scar tissue that ran across its chest. It had long, pointed ears and an elongated jaw filled with saliva-coated fangs. The creature's arms were heavily muscled and ended with razor sharp talons that it sank into the tree trunk as it hauled itself up to the two men.

"Fuck! It's coming, Carl. Shoot it. For God's sake, shoot it."

"I can't. I'll drop you. Now stop fucking about and get up here."

The monster was almost halfway up the tree now, closing the distance with apparent ease.

"Hold onto me, Carl. Don't fucking let go," said Steven, then he released his grip on the branch with his right arm as he tried to remove the pistol from his coat pocket.

Carl grabbed Steven's left arm in a two-handed grip and tried to pull him to safety. The branch that he lay on gave a small snap and shifted beneath him. The beast was now less than two feet away from Steven.

Steven's hand found the pistol in his pocket and pulled it free. The weapon slipped, and he almost dropped it before his fingers curled around the stock. Without taking the time to steady his aim, he pointed the weapon down and pulled the trigger.

A shriek of pain came from below, followed by a crash as the beast fell to the ground. It snarled at the two men, and nursing a wound to its shoulder, fled into the darkness of the forest.

Steven managed to find his feet and gripped the tree with leaden limbs.

"Fucking hell. That was... that was..."

"Yeah, that was a werewolf. A big one."

"A werewolf... a fucking werewolf? You could have told me, you bastard."

"Told you what? You'd have thought I was mad. Better to let you find out for yourself."

"Fucking hell," he said again. "So, now what do we do?"

"Well, Stevie, I don't know about you, but the Lord God Almighty couldn't make me get out of this tree until the sun comes up."

Chapter 8

25th April 1986. Mill Woods, High Moor. 05:47.

The darkness in the sky gave way to a dismal, flat grey. Shadows receded and then faded away. Sporadic bird song broke the silence as the world came back to life.

Steven had never been so glad to see the dawn. During the night, his mood had cycled between extremes of shock, terror, and misery. Carl had insisted on absolute silence to reduce the chance of another surprise attack. He hadn't even let Steven smoke, and the nicotine cravings had played across his already frayed nerves.

He turned to Carl and whispered, "Do you think it's safe to get down yet?"

"Probably."

"You getting down?"

"Nope."

"I thought you just said it was safe?" said Steven, a little too loudly. He winced at the sound of his voice.

"I said it was probably safe. I don't feel like testing the theory."

"I thought you were supposed to be some kind of expert on these fucking things?"

Carl paused and scanned the forest, listening for any sounds that were out of place, then looked down at the younger man and chuckled.

"Son, I've faced off with more than a few werewolves in my time. More than most people manage and live to tell about it, that's for sure. I wouldn't say I was an expert though. Not by any stretch of the imagination. What I am is the best you've got."

"Fuck this, I need a cigarette," said Steven, and reached inside his jacket. When he retrieved a sodden mass of cardboard, paper, and tobacco, he threw the pack to the forest floor in disgust. "Bollocks. So when did you start?"

"Start what?"

Steven rolled his eyes. "Collecting stamps. What the fuck do you think I mean? When did you start hunting werewolves?"

"That's a long story."

"You got anything better to do?"

The old man laughed. "OK, but it'll cost you breakfast. Deal?"

"Deal."

"It was October '44. Yugoslavia. The Yugoslav Partisans and the Red Army were doing a pretty good job at tearing the Nazis a new asshole. Belgrade was surrounded, and my bosses figured that the Germans would lose control of it within two, maybe three weeks. There were rumours of a research facility forty or fifty clicks south of the Jasenovac concentration camp, and they didn't want all that Nazi science falling into the hands of Mother Russia.

"So, they parachuted me and four of my buddies into occupied territory, with orders to grab anything interesting and then high tail it out of there before the Russkies turned up.

High Moor

"We were dropped in near the mountains and, once we got our shit together, we headed off towards our objective. Tino was our communications guy. He'd done a master's degree in physics before the war, so it was his job to try and identify the useful stuff when we hit the research station. Korky handled demolitions. Once we got what we needed, he was going to blow the place sky high. Harry was our close combat expert. Bad tempered son of a bitch, but I never saw anyone handle a blade the way he could.

"Our Sergeant was a big New Yorker called Pete. He was one of the hardest men I ever knew. Then there was me. A snot-nosed, ex ranch boy from Idaho. I'd been shooting things ever since I was big enough to hold a rifle. I was the team's sniper.

"Things started going wrong on the second night. We were probably around twenty klicks from our objective when we heard all hell breaking loose. There was a fire fight going down a few kilometres northwest of our position. It didn't last long. The woods echoed with automatic weapons fire for maybe four or five minutes and then just stopped.

The Sarge thought we should do a recon to see what was going on. The bulk of the fighting was a few hundred kilometres to the east, based on our last intel. Last thing we wanted to do was walk smack into a major offensive. We were going to get in, check it out, and if it looked like things were going to get hairy, then we'd get the fuck out of there and scratch the mission.

"It took us a couple of hours to make our way there. We took it slow and careful, making sure that no one could get the drop on us. It was Tino that found them in the end. A squad of Krauts; eight or nine of them, torn to shreds. Hell, I don't think there was any part of the poor sons of bitches left that was bigger than a football. There were plenty of empty shell cases lying around, but they were all German. No other bodies and no evidence of weapons damage on the corpses. Put the fear of God into us, I can tell ya."

Carl paused, reached for his handgun and clicked the safety off. Steven opened his mouth to speak. Carl shook his head. A twig snapped, off to their right. Both men raised their weapons, hardly daring to breathe. A badger shuffled from the undergrowth and regarded the two men with curious eyes, then continued on its way.

"Jesus, that thing scared the shit out of me," said Carl. "Where was I, oh yeah. We'd found the bodies and were on the verge of freaking out. The Sarge put a stop to that right away. Told us to get our heads back in the game. We moved out, weapons ready, back into the woods towards our objective. That was when the howling started.

"Now, I grew up on a ranch, and while wolves were pretty rare, I'd still come across one or two in my time. Loners that came down from the mountains, looking for food. Those howls didn't sound like any wolf I ever heard. There were at least three of them, to the north, south, and east of our position. We headed west, never thinking that they were driving us that way.

"They took the Sarge out first. He was bringing up the rear when he was hit. He got a couple of rounds off before the thing bit his fucking head clean off. In the darkness, all we could see was a big black shadow tearing into him. Tino opened up on it, but he might as well have been firing blanks. The bastard just ignored him and carried on ripping the Sarge to ribbons. The moon came out then, and I got a good look at the thing. It looked like a wolf, but much bigger. The size of a fucking grizzly. That was when the others attacked. They came running at us through the trees. The guys rained bullets at them, but they didn't even slow down. I'm ashamed to say that my nerve broke, and I ran. After a minute, the shooting stopped and the screaming started. After a while, the screaming stopped as well.

"I ran all night. I heard them howling, out there in the dark, but they never came too close. To this day, I have no idea why. All I know is that I came out of the forest into a village around midday; exhausted, dehydrated, and raving like a lunatic about monsters in the woods. Then I passed out, and the next thing I remember was waking up a couple of days later."

The sporadic birdsong within the forest was now a chorus. The first weak rays of the sun filtered through the branches, banishing the pre-dawn chill in the air. Steven had never seen a more welcome sight.

"I reckon it's safe to get down now," said Carl.

Steven raised an eyebrow. "Probably."

The two men laughed and clambered down to the forest floor, to the remains of their platform and the rest of their equipment. Carl sifted through the wreckage and swore as he retrieved his hunting rifle.

"The scope's got water in it, and the barrel's out of kilter. Ain't gonna be using this baby anytime soon. Damn, I really liked that gun."

"Do you think we got it? Last night?"

"I think you hit it, otherwise there wouldn't be enough left of us to fill a doggie bag. Whether it was enough to kill the bastard is another question."

"So, what do we do now?"

"Well, the rain has gotten rid of most of the tracks. After I get something to eat and take a shower, I'll come back here and see if I can pick up a trail. Maybe we'll get lucky. You should get onto the hospitals and see if anyone was admitted with a gunshot wound. You also need to think of a name for your goat."

"My goat? I..." said Steven, looking across to where the goat was tethered.

The goat looked at Steven, bleated at him in an accusatory tone, and then started eating the bracken.

"So was that it? Back in '44? You woke up in a village and it was all over?"

"Hell, no. I wish it was. Come on, I'll tell you the rest on the way back to the car."

The two men retrieved their equipment from the remains of the platform and untethered the goat.

High Moor

"Like I was saying, I woke up in a bed in the village. I'd turned my ankle pretty bad that night, even though I hadn't realised it at the time. It was swollen right up, and I struggled to put any weight on it. I'd lost my sniper kit, but I still had my sidearm and a full clip of ammunition, and I still had some of my standard issue field gear.

"The house belonged to a woman called Mirela. She was as beautiful a girl as I had ever seen. Dark, curly hair flowing down her back, curves in all the right places, and amber eyes that looked straight into your soul. To tell you the truth, I was surprised to see anyone of Romany origin in the area. Most of them had been rounded up by the Nazis and sent to the death camps at Jasenovac. She told me that her village had escaped the Nazis' attention because they kept to themselves. She wasn't kidding.

"The village itself was in a clearing, smack in the middle of the forest. There were no roads leading in or out, just a couple of trails. They had no power, got their water from a stream, and lived off the land.

"There were probably around twenty houses: log cabins with hardened mud interior walls, spread in a circle, around an ancient oak in the centre of the clearing. There was a blacksmith by the stream, one of the families kept pigs and chickens, and that was about it.

"I tried to talk to Mirela about what I'd seen in the forest, but she told me that some things were better left alone. I'd seen Lon Chaney Junior in *The Wolf Man* on my last leave though, and I had a pretty good idea of what I'd seen. When my ankle was strong enough for me to walk, I took my silver crucifix, melted it down, and replaced the lead bullet in one of my pistol rounds with a crude silver one. I had no idea if it would work on those things or even if it would fire, but I sure felt better having it.

"I stayed in the village for a couple of weeks. The others living there gave me a wide berth, and that suited me just fine. No one else except Mirela spoke English, and I sure as hell couldn't understand a word they were saying. I just waited for my ankle to heal so that I could get out of that god-forsaken country and back to the States.

"It happened one night. Mirela was away somewhere, and I went outside to take a leak. I'd just finished putting my guy away, when I heard a sound from the undergrowth behind her house. I pulled out my pistol just as one of those creatures emerged from the trees, carrying a rabbit in its mouth.

"For a second, neither of us did anything. I stood there, staring down this huge black wolf with amber eyes. I don't think it had expected to find me there and seemed to be unsure of what to do next. Then it dropped the rabbit, and I fired.

"The thing yelped and fell to the ground. All I wanted to do was run back to Mirela's house and barricade myself inside, but my legs wouldn't work. I stood there and watched the hair recede and the creature's body flow back into the shape of a person. Mirela, bleeding from a chest wound.

"The realisation hit me like a hammer. Mirela was a werewolf. Most likely, every single man, woman and child in the goddamn village was one too. A whole fucking pack of them. I could hear doors opening around the village, and raised voices. I didn't hang around to try and explain things. I took one of their horses and got the hell out of there. The next morning, I was picked up by a Nazi patrol and spent the rest of the war in a POW camp."

"Jesus. So, after that, you started hunting them down?"

"Hell no, not straight away. When the war was over, I went back to my folks' ranch in Idaho. I stayed there for a few years, but got restless and headed to Africa to hunt big game. Didn't hear about another werewolf for maybe ten years."

"Fucking hell. I'm surprised you wanted anything to do with it. I'd have run a bloody mile."

"Believe me, I thought about it. But, if I didn't do anything to help, then no one else was gonna. Sometimes you just have to do what's right. Anyway, changing the subject, you come up with a name for your goat yet?"

Steven smiled. "Yeah, I think I'm going to call it Lucky."

Carl laughed. "That it is, Steve, that it is. Come on then, I believe you owe me a breakfast."

***

25th April 1986. Traveller Camp, High Moor. 08:00.

Joseph lifted the pan of boiling water from the fire and carried it to his caravan. Despite the bright sunshine outside, the curtains were drawn, and the only light inside was provided by candles that flickered in the breeze as he opened the door. He placed the pan on a small table beside the bed and opened a leather pouch containing a set of surgical tools. He took the implements out, one at a time, and placed them into the hot water.

"Has there been any change?"

The dark-haired woman who knelt beside the bed looked up at him. "She's getting worse, Joseph. She's running a fever, and the wound won't stop bleeding." She placed a cold cloth onto the forehead of the semi-conscious old woman.

Joseph moved her to one side and leaned over. "Let me see, Yolanda." He removed the dressing from the woman's shoulder. Fresh blood welled up from the ragged wound and trickled down her arm. Joseph threw the blood-soaked cloth into the waste bin and applied a fresh dressing. Flowers of blood blossomed across the surface of the white fabric.

Yolanda put her hand on Joseph's arm. "Perhaps it's better this way. Better for all of us."

"She's my mother. I won't let her die. Not when there is a chance to save her."

"She's moonstruck, Joseph. Mirela has no control over herself anymore, and she is getting worse. She puts us all at risk."

Joseph ignored his wife, removed a set of tweezers from the hot water, then peeled back the dressing. "Hold her down. I need to get the bullet out."

Yolanda frowned, but complied with her husband's wishes. "You are not listening to me, Joseph. She has already killed a child, and now someone got close enough to shoot at her. How long before *they* track us here?"

Joseph's brow furrowed in concentration as he inserted the tweezers into the bullet hole. The old woman cried out in pain and shuddered on the bed. Her skin moved in waves. Thick white hairs sprouted and then retreated back into her flesh.

"Most of the bullet passed straight through, but it fragmented when it clipped her collarbone. I can feel it...there...got it," he said, drawing out a lump of blood-stained metal.

Yolanda looked at the remains of the bullet and put her hand to her mouth. "Joseph. It's silver. They know. We need to get away from here. Far away, where they will never find us again."

"We can't move her. Not yet. The silver will take time to leave her system. Later, when she is better, we'll leave."

She turned away from her husband, bitter tears running across her face. "You doom us all, Joseph. You doom us all." Then she opened the door and stormed out of the caravan.

Joseph removed a needle-and-thread from his pouch and sewed the wound closed. The old woman writhed on the bed and then was still. Joseph put his tools away. He was about to leave his mother to rest when her arm shot out and grasped his wrist.

"Joseph. Please, I beg you. Let me die."

He smoothed her hair back and kissed her forehead. "Mother, it's alright. Soon the sickness will pass, and you'll feel better."

"You're not listening to me, Joseph. I know that sometimes I am...elsewhere, but right at this moment I am here, and you will heed me. My heart cannot bear the pain any longer. I am responsible for the death of that child, and it destroys me. It eats away at me, even as my mind wanders. If you love me, you will let me die."

Joseph ran his hand across his mother's face. "You sleep, Mother. We'll talk more when you feel stronger." He blew out the candles and left the caravan, leaving Mirela to weep alone in the darkness.

***

25th April 1986. John's House, High Moor. 10.30.

"John? Michael, and Marie are here," yelled John's mother from the bottom of the stairs.

"OK, Mam," he shouted from his bedroom. He got up from his desk and ran downstairs to meet his friends, jumping the last three stairs to land with a thud on the hallway floor.

Mrs Simpson put her hands on her hips. Her face creased into a frown. "John! How many times do I have to tell you not to jump down those stairs? You'll go through the floor one of these days."

Michael and Marie stood by the back door, trying hard to keep their grins under control.

John rolled his eyes and gestured to his friends. "Come on upstairs, guys, before I do something else wrong."

"Do you want anything to drink?" said his Mother as the children filed past.

"No thanks, Mam, maybe later on," said John. Then the children left the kitchen and ran up the wooden staircase.

"For God's sake, you lot, you sound like a herd of elephants," said Mrs Simpson as the children stampeded through the house. Three muted apologies rang down from the top of the staircase. Mrs Simpson shook her head in mock exasperation and went back to preparing lunch.

John closed his bedroom door and moved a stack of comics from his bed to allow Michael and Marie to sit down. John sat on a swivel chair by his desk.

"You two look funny," said Marie, "like two giant pandas or something."

Michael made a face at his sister and winced at the movement. Both boys' faces were covered in dark purple bruises and small scratches. Michael's right eye was swollen almost shut, and John's nose was slightly crooked.

Michael punched his sister's arm. "At least we'll get better, you'll always look funny."

Marie giggled and stuck her tongue out at him.

"How was your dad last night?" said Michael, "I thought he was going to go mental when the police called him to the hospital to pick us up."

"He wasn't too happy with your dad. I think he might have hit him, if he'd been there. Did they ask you who beat us up?"

"Yeah, but I wasn't gonna grass. You heard what they said they'd do if we told."

"So, what are we going to do about them?" said Marie, "We can't let them get away with what they did to you."

John shrugged. "I don't know. They're older than us and there's more of them. We try anything, and they'll just give us another kicking."

Michael picked up one of John's comics and flicked through the pages. "We could get hold of them, one at a time, and beat them up for a change?"

"That's fine, but then they'll just gang up on us again and do worse next time. We need to find a way to get them off our backs for good."

"How about saving up our pocket money and paying some bigger boys to beat them up and act as our bodyguards?"

"Maybe, but do you know any older boys that'd do it and not just take our money?"

Michael thought for a moment and then shook his head. "No, all the older boys I know are arseholes."

"So that's it then. We might as well just stay inside all summer."

Michael shrugged. "Looks like it. Got any new games for your Spectrum?"

"Yeah, got a couple. Bring a tape over later on and I'll do a copy for you."

"I can't believe you two," said Marie. "You can't just give up like that. Malcolm Harrison and his little bum chums have to pay for messing your faces up."

"And do what?" said Michael.

Marie grinned at the two boys. "I've got an idea. Now listen up. This is what we're going to do."

Chapter 9

4th May 1986. Coronation Estate, High Moor. 14.22.

Malcolm scrawled his name on the glass window of the bus shelter with a black permanent marker. His ribs still hurt from the "discipline" that his stepfather had administered the night before, and he winced at every movement. Not that he'd ever admit his pain to the others. They'd be on him like a pack of hyenas. He needed something to take the edge off. Numb him until he could creep back into the house after his bastard stepfather had gone to bed. He finished his drawing and turned to his friends. "Billy, you got any smoke?"

Billy held up a black lump, wrapped in cling film. "Yeah, nicked this off my brother. There's about a quarter, and it's really good gear. Proper squidgy black hash. My brother's been tearing his room apart trying to find it."

"Give us a look," said Malcolm, and took the lump from Billy. He unwrapped the cellophane and sniffed the lump of cannabis. "This is good stuff," he said and broke the piece in half, put one in his pocket and passed the other back to Billy. "Better than that shit you got last week, Simon."

Simon looked offended. "That was good soap bar, that."

"It was a lump of dried dog shit. Are you telling me that you actually smoked it?"

"It wasn't dog shit. I paid three weeks pocket money for it from Geoff."

"It was definitely dog shit. It smelled of shit and looked like shit. Geoff was laughing about it after, up the park. And you put it in your mouth?"

"Piss off, Mal. I didn't smoke dog crap. I would have been able to tell."

"How? You know what dog shit tastes like? You been round to Pikey Mikey's for tea or something?"

Simon opened his mouth to respond when a milk bottle filled with yellow liquid arced through the air and shattered against the back of the bus shelter. Glass and stale urine rained down on the boys. They looked up and saw Marie sitting across the road on her push-bike. She smiled at them sweetly, then gave them the finger and pedalled off down the road as fast as she could.

Malcolm stood with his mouth open for a second, unable to comprehend what had just happened. When he spoke, his voice cracked with rage. "That little bitch. Get her. GET HER."

The four furious, urine-soaked boys jumped onto their bikes and took off in pursuit.

***

Marie was terrified. She couldn't believe she'd suggested this. The boys had argued with her, but she'd dug her heels in and eventually they'd agreed to her plan. She was regretting her stubbornness.

Malcolm and his friends were gaining on her. She risked a glance over her shoulder and saw the four boys pedalling down the hill, shouting abuse. She needed to slow them down if she was to have any chance of getting to her destination.

The main road into town was at the bottom of the hill, and she would have to get across it to reach the school. If she stopped, even for a second, the boys would catch her.

Just like playing Frogger. I'm ace at it on the computer.

She tried not to think about what happened to the frog when she got it wrong and increased her speed, trying to spot a space between the cars.

Here goes nothing.

Marie hit the junction and weaved to the right, passing just behind an old brown car. She turned left and saw a motorbike heading straight for her. Adrenaline surged through her, and for a moment she froze, hands locked in place and the bike free-wheeling.

Her speed carried her past the oncoming vehicle. She bounded over the kerb and turned left. A blaring of horns erupted from behind, and she grinned as she saw Malcolm being yelled at by an angry motorist. The four boys ignored the man and walked their bikes across the road. Marie pedalled away through the open school gates.

She dropped her bike at the front door to the building and tried the door. The top and bottom bolts had been undone. It was a simple matter to pull both doors so that they opened, despite the lock being applied. She could hear the yells from her pursuers and she ran off into the dark corridors.

***

"She's gone in the school," said Lawrence, as he passed the school gates and headed down the driveway.

Malcolm grinned. "Then we've got her. She can't ride her bike over the field, and she can't outrun us."

102

"No, Mal, she's gone inside the school. Through the front doors. Do you think there's a teacher there or something?"

"Who cares? If we see a teacher, we'll just wait outside for her. She's not getting away with that."

"What are we gonna do to her when we catch her?" said Simon.

"I don't know yet, but it'll make what we did to her brother look like nothing."

The four boys dropped their bikes on the floor next to Marie's and ran through the open doors into the dark, echoing corridors of the school.

***

John looked out from the bushes next to the school gates. "OK, they followed her. I still can't believe we let her do this. Did you hear those cars on the main road?"

"It was her idea. Anyway, she wouldn't take no for an answer. You go get her bike and lock the front doors again, I'll phone the coppers."

John nodded his agreement and both boys broke cover. John ran down the driveway. When he reached the doors, he loosened the bottom bolts and pushed them closed again. The bolts dropped into their holes and the door was again secure.

He then took a small plastic bag from his pocket and opened one end of it, gagging as the smell of the fresh dog turd hit him, and held the bag at arm's length. He pushed the handlebars of Malcolm and his friend's bikes into the bag, making sure that each grip was well and truly coated.

He then wiped the remains of the bag on the seat of Malcolm's BMX, picked up Marie's bike, and made a hasty retreat from the scene.

***

Marie crouched in the cupboard, hardly daring to breathe. In her panic, she'd taken a wrong turn. A window was open in one of the other classrooms where John had broken in earlier. Marie was supposed to escape through that window and join John and Michael before the police arrived. The fear of what Malcolm Harrison would do to her paled in comparison to the fear of how her father would react if the police brought her home again.

She could hear the boys in the other classrooms, yelling and breaking things as they searched for her. Then the door to the classroom she was hiding in opened.

Marie heard Malcolm's voice. "Where the fuck has the little bitch gotten to?"

The air was filled with sounds of tables being overturned and paper displays being torn from the walls.

"This is taking forever. We'll never find her at this rate," said Simon.

"I've got an idea," said Malcolm.

"What?"

Marie heard the distinctive metallic click of Malcolm's lighter.

"We'll smoke the bitch out."

***

John arrived back at the bushes with Marie's bike. Michael was already waiting for him.

"You do it?" he said to Michael.

104

"Yeah, phoned the police and told them I'd just seen Malcolm Harrison and his mates break into the school. Where's Marie?"

"Is she not back yet?

"No. You mean you didn't see her?"

"Oh shit. Maybe they caught her. We gotta go see."

"We can't. The police will be here in a minute."

"We can't just leave her there. God knows what those psychos will do to her."

John turned to look at the school, praying that Marie would come running around a corner. Instead, he saw black smoke coming from a classroom window.

"Oh fuck. Mike, go and phone 999 again. Tell them that there's a fire at King's Close School."

"What are you going to do?"

"I'm going to get Marie."

***

Marie crouched inside the cupboard, not daring to move. She could still hear Malcolm's gang running through the corridors. She could also hear the crackle of flames. Smoke seeped into the cupboard. She pulled her T-shirt up over her mouth and tried to open the door, but something was jammed against it. Panic rose in her chest. She threw herself against the door, over and over again. It opened a little more, then refused to budge another inch.

"Help, I'm in here," she yelled, no longer caring if the bullies found her. The effort filled her lungs with smoke and made her break out in fits of coughing.

Glass shattered in the room beyond. The sound of the flames grew from a crackle into a roar. Marie fell to her knees and sobbed. Her eyes burned and she felt dizzy.

"Help," she said, her voice barely above a whisper, and coughed again, each lungful of air sucking in more smoke, fuelling the coughs.

She was barely aware of the table being dragged away from her hiding place and the door being wrenched open. John pulled her to her feet.

"Come on, we've got to get outside," he said as he half dragged, half carried her to the broken window that he'd climbed in through.

The classroom was ablaze. Fire flowed across the notice boards and bookcases that adorned the walls. It licked at the polystyrene tiles on the roof, which melted. Droplets of fire fell to the floor and across the desks, igniting anything they touched. The heat was unbearable, and the smell of burning hair mingled with the thick black smoke that filled the room.

John pushed Marie onto the desk and she crawled out of the open window. She fell to the floor outside, coughing. John followed and helped her to her feet. They could hear approaching sirens in the distance, getting closer with each second.

"Come on Marie. We've gotta go."

Marie nodded. The two children made their way back to the bushes on the edge of the school field.

***

Simon's eyes were wide open and panic crept into his voice. "Mal, the doors are locked." Smoke-filled the corridors, and over the crackle of the flames they heard sirens.

Malcolm pushed Simon out of the way. "Let me see." He shook the doors, which remained shut. Malcolm kicked one of the door's glass panels out and crawled through. Billy, Lawrence, and Simon followed.

"We gotta get out of here, now," said Lawrence. The boys ran to their bikes, picked them up, and jumped on.

"What the hell? Oh God."

The boys dropped their bikes in unison and looked at their hands. Lawrence threw up. Billy joined him.

Malcolm looked at his friends in disgust. "Never mind that, we have to go."

Too late. A police car entered the school grounds at speed and squealed to a stop in front of the four boys. Two police officers got out of the car.

One of the officers grabbed Malcolm by the arm. "You lot, stay where you are."

The other officer grabbed Simon, and the two boys were manhandled into the back of the car. Once Lawrence and Billy stopped being sick, they too were locked in the rear of the police car.

Flames burst from the school windows, followed by a column of smoke, rising high into the air. The fire engines arrived. The crew's attempts to douse the flames met with limited success.

One of the police officers went through Malcolm's pockets and produced a small bottle of vodka and the piece of cannabis. "You boys are in a lot of trouble. Breaking and entering. Arson, alcohol, and drugs. I think we had better take you four back to the station."

"Bob?" said the other officer.

"Yeah?"

"Can you smell dog shit?"

***

John, Michael and Marie watched from the bushes. They saw Malcolm's gang bundled into the police car and watched as it drove away. Another fire engine arrived to try to contain the blaze, but it was too late to make much difference.

Michael turned to Marie. "What happened? You were meant to get straight out."

"I tried. I couldn't find the stupid classroom."

Michael threw his arms around his sister. "You could have been killed." Marie started coughing again.

"Anyway," she said, "what are you complaining for? The plan worked perfectly. Better than perfect."

"Apart from you two stinking of smoke, and John hardly having any eyebrows left, you mean?"

"Who cares about that? The police got them. They'll probably go to borstal."

"And did you see the look on their faces when they got on their bikes?" said John.

Michael grinned. "I know. I thought I was going to piss myself, especially when Lawrence and Billy started being sick."

John hugged his two friends.

"We got the bastards. We finally got them."

"Dave would have been proud," said Marie.

"Yeah, he really would," said Michael as he hugged his friends tighter. Behind them the school burned.

Chapter 10

7th May 1986. Woodside Farm, High Moor. 02.25.

The scream jarred Andrew Stott awake. His eyes snapped open in the dark and he lay motionless, listening for any sounds of intrusion. All he could hear were the staccato grunts of his wife next to him.

Damn, that woman can snore.

He looked at the alarm clock and groaned. He rolled over, putting the pillow over his head in a vain attempt to drown out some of the noise. His bladder ached. There was no way he was getting back to sleep. He threw back the covers and stumbled to the bathroom.

Andrew sighed with relief as he directed the stream of liquid into the porcelain bowl. He could still hear his wife upstairs. A bass rumble, interspersed with wet squelching sounds like a horse drowning in a bucket of jelly.

Maybe we should think about sleeping separately. She can sleep out in the fucking barn, and I'll stay in the house. On second thoughts, that would just piss the horses off.

Now that he was far enough away from his snoring wife, he could hear something else. Outside, the animals in the field were agitated. The sheep bleated their alarm, while the horses whinnied and snorted. He was about to run outside to see what the problem was, then he remembered the reports on the news. He pulled on his boots, grabbed a high-power flashlight, took his shotgun from the cabinet in the kitchen, and stepped out into the darkness.

High Moor

The night air was cold. The wind tugged at his dressing gown as he made his way across the farm yard. The sounds of distress were much clearer now. The temptation to call the police and retreat back to the house was overwhelming.

No. If it's just a bloody badger, then I'll be a laughing stock. Besides, if it is something else, God knows what'll be left by the time plod gets here.

He stepped out into the lane, shotgun raised to his shoulder. He held the flashlight in his left hand, under the barrel of the gun. The bleating from the sheep was frantic, and as he approached the field, he could see them packed against the barbed wire fence, trying to find a way through.

Andrew climbed over the gate and swept the torch around the field. In front of him, a pair of green eyes shone out of the darkness. His heart leaped and, for a split second, he almost ran. Then he pulled the trigger.

***

7th May 1986. Aykley Head's Police HQ. 10.00.

Steven Wilkinson and Carl Schneider walked side by side through the corridors of the police headquarters to Inspector Frank's office.

"You any idea what this is about, Steve?"

"Not a clue. Maybe the Inspector got your hotel bill."

The older man laughed. "Ha, can't expect to drag a man halfway around the world to do a job and then put him up in some fleapit. You Brits sure like to keep your hand on the purse strings."

They arrived at the Inspector's office. Steven knocked twice on the door. After a long pause, the Inspector's voice told them to enter.

Where Steven's office was a cluttered mess of paperwork and mismatched furniture, Inspector Franks' was pristine. A mahogany desk dominated the room, and matching bookcases adorned the walls. The Inspector looked up from his paperwork as the two men entered.

"Ah, Sergeant Wilkinson, Mr Schneider. Thank you for coming. Please take a seat, and I'll be with you in a moment."

Steven and Carl sat on the far side of the desk, while the Inspector examined the papers in front of him. Carl tried to catch Steven's eye, but the other man sat up straight in the chair and looked at the wall behind the Inspector. After a while, Inspector Franks signed one of the papers and put them in a tray.

"Sorry about that, Gentlemen. You know how paperwork can be. I'll get straight to it. We have some good news. The so called High Moor Beast was shot and killed by a farmer in the early hours of this morning."

Steven and Carl exchanged glances.

"Are you sure, sir?"

"Absolutely," said the Inspector as he pushed some photographs across the table.

Carl flicked through the pictures and shook his head. "This is a puma. A puma didn't kill that boy. You got the wrong critter."

The Inspector interlocked his fingers and rested his chin on them, then leaned forward in his seat. "If this animal was not responsible for the death of that child, Mr Schneider, then what was?"

Carl glanced at Steven. "I think it might have been a bear."

Inspector Franks raised an eyebrow. "A bear? You expect me to believe that, in addition to a large carnivorous cat roaming the area, we also have a man-eating bear on the loose?"

Steven put his hand up to silence Carl. "Sir, have the forensics reports on the boy come back yet? They should clearly show that the attack was not carried out by a big cat."

"The forensics reports were inconclusive, I'm afraid."

Carl sat forward in his chair. "Inspector Franks, I think you're making a grave mistake. I believe that whatever killed that boy is still out there and that lives are still at risk."

"Is that out of concern for the safety of the people of High Moor? Or are you more concerned about the continuation of your expense account, Mr Schneider?"

Carl's eyes narrowed. "What exactly are you trying to say here, Inspector?"

"I'm saying that, as far as I am concerned, this case is closed, and we shall no longer be requiring your services, Mr Schneider. Sergeant Wilkinson, you should resume your normal duties, effective immediately. After you drop Mr Schneider off at the airport, of course."

Carl got to his feet and leaned across the desk. "You can't do this, Inspector. People will die, and it will be all on you."

"That will be all, Mr Schneider. Unless, of course you would like to stay and discuss the matter of your attempt to smuggle illegal weapons into the country?"

Carl's face contorted with anger, and for a moment it looked as if he was going to reach across the desk and drag the Inspector over it. He exhaled, clenched his fists, and strode out of the office. Steven followed, allowing the door to slam behind him.

"Sanctimonious, officious, stuck-up little prick. Jesus, Steve, I don't know how you work for that asshole."

"There are days when it can be difficult. Like today. So is that it? You're going back to the States?"

Carl winked at him. "I think I might stick around for another couple of weeks and, you know, see some of the country. Gonna need a place to stay though, what with my expense account getting shut off. You up for having a lodger?"

Steven groaned. "My wife is going to fucking kill me."

***

7th May 1986. High Street, High Moor. 16.00.

Yolanda hurried through the crowded street, the newspaper clutched to her chest. She eased her way through the groups of schoolchildren that congregated outside the newsagent, and the lines of people with full shopping bags that waited at the bus stop.

She wanted to run, to get back to Joseph and tell him the news. Instead, she forced herself to walk, moving with grace and agility through small gaps in the crowd until she left the high street and started up the hill, past Coronation Park and the new housing estate that surrounded it.

When she reached the gravel road that led to the moor, her pace quickened. She was on the verge of running as she arrived at the gypsy camp.

Joseph sat by the campfire with two of the other men. A pot of water bubbled over the flame. Joseph looked up to his wife, his face a blank mask, devoid of any emotion or reaction to the casual observer. Yolanda, however, could read her husband like a book. "Joseph, I need to speak to you."

"Of course, dear." He got to his feet and walked to his caravan. Yolanda followed him and closed the door.

"What's the matter, Yolanda?"

She handed him the newspaper. "They killed a puma last night in a field near the town."

"And?"

"Well, don't you see? They'll blame the animal for your mother's activity. We move away. No one will think anything of it. We can be safe."

"And we will move away, Yolanda. When Mirela has recovered sufficiently to travel."

"And what if she changes on the next full moon, Joseph? What then?"

"She can't change. The silver won't be out of her system until after the full moon, and she won't be able to change until that happens. You know this."

"That may be the case in normal circumstances, but Mirela is hardly normal. She's moonstruck, and as you are very much aware, pack law requires all moonstruck to be killed. Do we really know if the same rules apply?

"One has never been allowed to live long enough for us to be sure. Not only that, but she's been shot with silver before. When we were still with the Pack, I heard rumours that Sebastian and the other enforcers dosed themselves with silver to build up a tolerance. What if the same thing happens with your mother? Can you at least take her out onto the moors?"

"We cannot move her, Yolanda. The stress could kill her. She is an old woman and has to be allowed time to recover. Once the full moon is passed, we'll leave. Not until."

"If you are wrong, Joseph, if she changes and it brings the pack down on us, then the responsibility will be on your shoulders alone. Will you be able to live with that?"

Joseph turned away from his wife, unable to meet her gaze. "I have no choice, Yolanda. I have no choice."

Chapter 11

23rd May 1986. High Moor. 15:20.

Marie crouched behind the tree stump, next to Michael and John, and screwed up her face. "It's not fair."

"What's not fair?" said John.

"You two get to go camping, and I have to stay at home."

An explosion rang out, and pieces of glass shrapnel flew over the children's heads. Michael peered over the top of the fallen tree, to where the remains of a milk bottle smoked around a patch of blackened grass.

"That was a good one. Let's do a rocket this time, John."

"Shall we do the big one?"

"Na, we'll set that one off last. Shoot a couple of the small ones off at once."

Marie folded her arms and puffed out her lower lip. "It's still not fair."

John removed two rockets from the box. "You could always join the Brownies. They sometimes go on camp with the cubs."

"No, she can't," said Michael. "She got a lifetime ban."

"Why? What did you do?"

Marie reddened. "It's not my fault. We were doing knots and it was boring so I tied up Lizzie Fletcher and locked her in the store cupboard and she was crying when Brown Owl found her and she said it was all my fault which it wasn't cos if Lizzie Fletcher hadn't been such a skinny dog and didn't smell like sick then I wouldn't have done it."

"And she called Brown Owl a God-bothering rug-muncher," said Michael.

"What's one of those?"

Marie shrugged. "I dunno. I heard Dad call one of those Jehovah's Witnesses it once. Seemed like a good idea at the time."

"Mam had to take her to Aunt Jean's every Monday night for six months, so that Dad didn't find out. Are you going to set those off or what?" said Michael.

John picked up the rockets and carried them over to the scorched patch of earth. "What's the target?"

"See if you can hit Mrs Smith's house. The old bag complained to Mam about me riding my bike on the pavement last week. Mam told her that I wasn't allowed to ride on the road and to mind her own fucking business."

John positioned the fireworks in the ground, lit the fuse, and ran for cover. The rockets shot into the air. One of them sailed over Mrs Smith's house and exploded in a shower of red sparks over the allotments. The second found its target and bounced off an upstairs window before blossoming into white light over her garden. A series of smaller explosions followed from Mrs Smith's vegetable patch. Cries of alarm could be heard. The children hid behind the fallen tree and laughed.

"That was brilliant," said Marie. "Where did you get fireworks from Michael?"

"They were Dave's. He got them last year from Baldie."

"The kid that had leukaemia?" said John.

"Yeah, his dad owns a shop, and Baldie was nicking stuff from the stock room. Dave got him to get fireworks, and he kept some back. Said it would be more fun to set them off in summer when no one else had any."

The children were silent for a moment. Marie wiped a tear from her eye and blew her nose.

"Come on, let's set the big one off now," said John. "Send it up right over the town. For Dave."

"Can I light the fuse?" said Marie.

"No. I found Dave's firework stash. I should get to set it off," said Michael.

"But it's not fair. You're going camping tonight, and I'm going to be stuck here by myself with nothing to do. You never let me do anything," said Marie, her voice increasing in pitch until it became a whine. Her face flushed. Tears were close.

John and Michael exchanged looks and shrugged.

"Alright, cry baby, but I want to aim it. You can light the fuse."

John waited behind the tree as Michael and Marie crouched over the large rocket. He heard muffled arguments over the aim that ended with Marie turning her back on her brother, with her arms folded and a face like thunder. When Michael was happy, he passed the lighter to his sister. Marie crouched down, quickly adjusted the trajectory of the missile, and lit the fuse. Both children ran and leaped over the fallen tree, landing beside John.

They waited for long seconds. Nothing happened.

Marie stood up. "Give me the lighter. The fucking thing's gone out."

John grabbed her arm and pulled her back down. "Wait for a second, sometimes they..."

He was cut short by a loud whoosh as the rocket took to the sky, leaving a rain of golden sparks in its wake. It sailed up into the bright afternoon sky, over the roads and houses of High Moor, and exploded in a cascade of green light. Secondary red starbursts erupted from within the fading green embers, which in turn faded into crackling white sparks that rained down on the rooftops.

"That was awesome," said Michael.

John grinned. "Yeah, it was great. We'd better get home and pack our stuff. Dad's taking us to the scout camp in an hour."

"Are you taking any fireworks with you, Michael?" said Marie.

Michael's face twisted into an evil smirk. "What do you think?"

***

High Moor

23rd May 1986. Fenwick Hall, High Moor. 18:00.

The car turned left, through the towering, wrought iron gates, into the grounds of Fenwick Hall. Trees hung over the road, forming a green canopy that wound its way through the woodland. Shards of late afternoon sunlight penetrated the heavy foliage and created brief flashes of light on the windscreen of the car.

John pointed to some old stone structures, encased within metal railings, set back from the road. "Dad, what are those things over there?"

"That's the Fenwick family mausoleum. The people who own this hall used to be buried there, instead of a normal cemetery."

Michael was appalled. "We're camping in a graveyard? They never said we were camping in a fu... in a graveyard."

George Simpson laughed. "I wouldn't worry, Michael. Those metal cages should keep any zombies safely inside."

"The whole ones, sure. What about the bits of them, though? Like crawling hands and stuff?"

"Or vampires. They would just turn into bats and fly through the gaps," said John.

George rolled his eyes. "I should never have let you two watch so many horror films."

"Na, we're fine," said John. "And remember, you promised to let us watch *The Howling* when we get back on Sunday."

"I said that I'd watch it first, and if it wasn't too gory, then I'd let you watch it. Don't get your hopes up."

"Is that really what those railings are for, Mr Simpson? To keep the zombies in?"

"No, Michael. It was to stop people digging up the bodies and selling them years ago. There aren't any monsters here, so you boys just enjoy your weekend."

The car passed out from under the trees, into a large clearing filled with a number of heavy canvas tents. Boys in Cub Scout uniforms ran around, while Mr Wilson, the scout leader, and Miss Hicks, his assistant, tried to bring some semblance of order to the chaos. Mr Simpson parked the car next to Mr Wilson's and got the boys' rucksacks out of the boot.

"I'll be back to pick you up on Sunday. Have a good time, lads. And boys? Be good."

John and Michael looked at George with a well-practiced, innocent expression on their faces. "Of course we will. See you on Sunday, Dad."

***

23rd May 1986. Weardale Industrial Estate. 19:00.

Steven turned into the industrial estate and parked his police car beside an empty unit. At this time on a Friday night, the estate was deserted. All of the workers finished at four then headed straight to The Sandpiper or some other local dive to blow half of their week's wages on booze. This made it ideal for Steven's purposes. The chances of being disturbed were minimal. Steven got out of the car, lit a cigarette, and waited.

Another police car entered the estate and parked beside Steven. Carl Schneider and Constable Phillips got out and walked over to him.

"Did you get them?" Steven asked.

Carl produced a plastic bag. "Yeah, three handheld CB radios plus two spare batteries each."

"Good, we'll use channel twelve for anything we want to keep off the police band."

Constable Phillips wore a confused expression. "Excuse me, Sarge, I still don't understand what we're supposed to be doing. Why the secrecy?"

"Because, Inspector Franks, in his infinite wisdom, thinks that the animal attack problem has been resolved. We think otherwise."

"There's not been any attacks in a month. What makes you think there'll be one tonight?"

"The pattern of the attacks, Constable. Each one was a month apart, so if there's going to be another one, it should be tonight."

"You'll patrol the south side of town," said Carl, "Steve and I will take the north side. You see or hear anything, then get us on the CB. Keep listening to your police radio as well. We're looking for anything that might be our beast."

Constable Phillips thought about this for a moment. "OK, got it."

"You know how to use one of these?" said Carl, handing the startled Constable a 9mm pistol.

The Constable's mouth fell open in shock. "We're not allowed to carry bloody guns. This isn't America you know."

Steven put his arm on his colleague's shoulder. "Constable, take the fucking gun, keep your mouth shut about it, and for the love of God, don't try to be a hero. If you need to use it, don't hesitate, but don't engage until Carl and I get there."

Constable Phillips took the pistol and looked at it as if Steven had handed him a venomous snake. He made sure that the safety catch was on and put the weapon in his pocket.

"OK, we know what we are doing. Let's get out there, and pray that we're wrong."

***

23rd May 1986. Traveller Camp, High Moor. 21:40.

Yolanda moved through the camp, carrying a plate of hot food. The moon was visible over the black outline of the mine buildings, covering the camp in a cool, silver light that dissolved into a dancing, orange glow as it got closer to the fire. The children were in bed, while the adults sat around talking. There was a nervous energy about the camp. Despite Joseph's reassurances about his mother, everyone was on edge. It was hardly surprising.

Yolanda climbed the steps and opened the door to Joseph's caravan. He sat beside his mother, who moaned and writhed on the bed.

"How is she?"

"See for yourself. Her beast tries to be free, but the silver holds it at bay. As I said it would."

"And if you had been wrong, Joseph? What then? There are children in this camp, or had you forgotten?"

He held up a silver knife. "If the worst had happened, then I was prepared. Do you really think that I am that irresponsible?"

"I don't know what to think of you anymore, Joseph. These past five years, running and hiding from the Pack. They have changed you. You are not the man I married anymore. I never see you smile and mean it. I can't remember the last time I saw you laugh. Was it really all worth it?"

"My mother loves you as her own daughter. How can you ask me that?"

"She hardly knows us anymore, Joseph. Her mind is leaving her. We run from our family, from the only place we ever belonged, for an old woman who is barely aware of us. Mirela was a great woman, but that woman is gone. All that really remains is the beast within her. So, I ask you again. Was it worth it?"

Joseph looked away from his wife, back to his mother. His shoulders tightened and he gripped the side of the bed, as if he might fall.

"Joseph, what is it?"

Yolanda looked past her husband. Mirela stopped thrashing and arched her back, crying out in pain. Her face elongated. Her teeth split her gums as they extended into long sharp daggers of enamel and bone. White fur bristled from her pores.

"Oh God, Joseph. She's changing."

Chapter 12

23rd May 1986. Fenwick Hall, High Moor. 23:40.

The full moon illuminated the clearing with a soft silver light as Mr Wilson, the scout leader, clambered out of his tent. Flickering shadows played across the rows of canvas, and muted fragments of conversation, interspaced with sporadic giggles, came from within.

"Lights out you lot, I mean it."

Instantly, the torches inside the tents flicked out and silence descended. Moments later, the whispering started again. Mr Wilson sighed. It was always the same on these camping trips. A ten-mile hike tomorrow would drain some of the boys' excess energy, but tonight he doubted if any of them would get much sleep.

He winced at a flash of pain in his abdomen. He should never have let the children help cook the evening meal. The fact that the chemical toilet had mysteriously exploded did not make his situation any easier. He had his suspicions as to the identity of the culprits, but a search of Michael Williams' and John Simpson's rucksacks had not yielded so much as a box of matches. Tomorrow he'd get the little bastards to clean the toilet out and see how funny they thought they were then. He picked up a shovel and a roll of toilet paper and headed off into the trees to take care of business.

His cramps intensified as he made his way through the woodland, and his stomach made tortured rumbling sounds. Once he was far enough away from the camp, he dug a small pit behind a towering sycamore, dropped his pants and sighed with relief as he released the pressure on his insides.

A twig snapped somewhere to his left. His sphincter tightened in a reflex action, and pinched off the half-expelled turd. He winced in disgust. His peripheral vision caught a blur of movement in the darkness. Another branch snapped.

"Get back in your tent, now. If I have to come over there, then whoever this is will be going home, first thing in the morning."

The woods were silent, apart from the soft rustle of leaves in the wind. Then another twig snapped, this time off to his right. Still crouched over the pit, he swung his torch up towards the source of the noise and caught a fleeting glimpse of white against the darkness.

"Do you think I'm joking? I can assure you this is not in the least bit funny."

A thick, guttural growl came from behind. He got to his feet, trousers still around his ankles, and span around, sweeping the torch like a searchlight. The woods were silent.

He wiped himself down and refastened his trousers. "Little bastards, we'll see who's laughing when I get done with you."

What if it's not the boys playing silly buggers? What if it's something else?

For the first time, Mr Wilson felt a small hard knot of fear forming in his stomach. He picked up the toilet roll and filled in the pit as quickly as he could, then set off through the trees towards the campsite.

The bracken at his feet erupted in a flurry of noise and movement. Mr Wilson let out an involuntary shriek before realising that he'd disturbed a family of pheasants roosting in the undergrowth.

He leaned against a tree. "Jesus." The fear started to subside, and he felt a mixture of relief and utter foolishness. He'd been coming to these woods for over fifteen years. There was nothing more threatening here than the occasional badger.

A branch snapped directly behind him. He felt hot breath on the back of his neck. He span around, waving the torch before him like a sword.

The torch light reflected off white fur. Sharp claws dug into his arms and sliced through flesh and muscle until they hit bone. Powerful arms lifted him off his feet. He looked into the slavering maw before him and opened his mouth to scream.

The beast's head drove forwards and dug its lower jaw under his chin, while its upper jaw clamped down on the top of his head. Flashbulbs of agony exploded across his head as fangs penetrated his skull. The pressure was unbelievable; he could hear bone crack, the sound echoing inside of his skull. His mouth was clamped shut, his scream locked inside him as the creature bit down.

His jawbone shattered, then was severed by razor sharp teeth as they cut through his flesh. He could smell the hot stench of the creature's breath, mingled with the metallic tang of his own blood as it gurgled in his throat. His skull splintered as the force of the bite increased, and Mr Wilson knew no more.

***

23rd May 1986. North Road, High Moor. 23:45.

Steven's CB radio crackled into life. "Hello, Sarge? Is there anyone there?"

He picked up the handset and pressed the talk button. "We're here. What's your status?"

"To be honest, I'm not even sure if I should be bothering you with this. A truck driver called in and reported that he'd seen a werewolf on the Durham road."

Carl and Steven exchanged worried glances. "Did he say where? Or what direction it was heading?"

"I'm sorry, but are you taking this seriously? I spoke to him and he's more than a little worse for wear from the drink."

"In the absence of any other reports of large predators, yes, I'm taking it seriously. Now where was it, and which direction was it going?"

"According to the driver, he'd gotten out of his truck to relieve himself and saw the thing burst through a hedge near the old railway bridge. He locked himself in his cab, and the werewolf took off across the fields to the southwest."

Carl unfolded a map and turned on the vehicle's interior light. Steven pointed to a road that ran from east to west.

"That's where we had the sighting. There's not really anything southwest of there for miles. Just open fields, the odd farmhouse, and Fenwick Hall."

"What's Fenwick Hall?"

"No one lives there now. It was a stately home, but was taken over by the county during WWII to house children from the cities. After that it was a special school. It's been closed for about five years. No one really uses it now, except for...oh no."

"What?"

"The boy scouts. They sometimes use the grounds for camping trips during the summer. If they're there this weekend, and that's where it's heading..."

Carl's face turned white. "It'll be a massacre. How far out are we?"

"It's clear across town. It'll take us at least ten minutes to get there."

The CB crackled and Steven realised that he'd been holding the handset in a white-knuckled grip with the talk button pressed.

"Sarge," said Constable Phillips, "I can be there in five minutes. I'll check it out and make sure that everything is alright."

"No, meet us on the road outside the hall, Constable. Don't go in there by yourself. Do you read me?"

Static answered Steven. Cursing, he turned on the siren and pushed his foot down hard on the accelerator.

High Moor

23rd May 1986. Fenwick Hall, High Moor. 23:47.

A long shrieking howl echoed around the clearing.

Lester Berryman sat upright in his sleeping bag and turned on his torch.

"What was that?"

Dylan Smith put his head under his pillow in an attempt to block out the light. "It's just someone's dog. Go to sleep fat boy, and turn that bloody torch off."

"That didn't sound like a dog."

"That's because it's the Fenwick Hall Werewolf," said Brian Morris. "It comes out on the full moon and eats fat cry babies like you."

"Piss off, Brian, there's no such thing as werewolves."

"No, it's true. It comes in the middle of the night and drags the fattest kid it can find out to the forest and then it eats him. That would be you."

Lester clutched his torch tighter and huddled down in his sleeping bag. When he spoke, his voice wavered. "There's no such thing. Now stop going on about it or I'm going to tell Mr Wilson."

"You better not piss yourself, Lester. I don't want to wake up floating in a lake," said Dylan.

"Maybe we'd better make him sleep outside, just in case. Grab his sleeping bag."

Lester kicked out at Brian as he leaned across and dragged the sleeping bag down.

"Have you seen his pyjamas, Dylan? They've got fucking bunny rabbits on them."

"Get off, you bastards. I'm telling Mr Wilson, and I'm telling..."

A dark shadow passed over the tent, and they heard heavy breathing outside. Lester's eyes widened in terror.

"It's come for you, Lester. It's going to get you," said Brian.

The dark shadow rose up and the canvas bowed as something pushed against it. Guy ropes snapped. The tent poles creaked.

"John, Michael, go fuck yourselves. You're not fooling anyone," said Dylan.

The only response was a deep, drawn-out snarl. Five huge claws punctured the heavy canvas sheet and slid down, slicing through the fabric with a terrible ripping sound. Lester pointed the torch at the gaping hole in the tent and screamed.

***

Andrea Hicks was less than impressed as she lay in the scout leader's tent, waiting for him to return. She had been seeing Colin Wilson for almost three years now and had even taken the assistant scout leader's job so that they could spend time together, away from his wizened shrew of a wife.

These camping trips were the closest thing that they had to spending a weekend away. Unfortunately, they had to share that time with twenty-five screaming brats who delighted in making her life as difficult as possible. Then, to top it all off, as soon as she'd crept into his tent, the stupid old bugger had gotten an attack of the shits and disappeared into the forest.

"Way to go and spoil the mood, Colin," she muttered, and pulled her jeans back on. The daft old sod could spend the night on his own.

A howl came from outside, so close that it seemed to be right outside of her tent. Then the screaming started.

She flung open the canvas door, ready to give the little bastards a good telling off.

A huge, white, muscular shape leaned into a tent and thrashed around inside. One of the poles had already collapsed, and the canvas rested over the rest of the creature as it fed. Dark stains spread across the fabric. Black viscous liquid dripped from the doorway and pooled on the ground outside.

A surge of adrenaline shot through her; her heart lurched as she took in the terrible scene.

Oh God! The boys. That thing's eating the boys.

She grabbed a hand axe and ran across the clearing, screaming Lester, Dylan and Brian's names, praying for one of them to answer. All she could hear was her own voice and wet tearing sounds from inside the tent.

She swung the axe at the white shape, and the blade bit deep into the monster's flank. It roared in pain and tore itself free of the tent to face its attacker.

The beast stood over seven feet tall. Ears lay flat against its head. White fur stained black with gore. Wet, glistening pieces of meat hung from four-inch talons. A tattered fragment of fabric, decorated with blood-soaked bunny rabbits was caught in its teeth.

"No," she screamed, and lunged forward with the axe, burying the blade deep in the monster's chest. It snarled in pain and swiped at her with a huge, blood-soaked paw.

***

The campsite was in pandemonium. Boys dressed in pyjamas ran screaming into the woods while others cowered in their tents, weeping in terror. John and Michael burst from their tent, fully dressed, in time to see Miss Hick's head sail free from her neck and land in the embers of the campfire. Hair ignited, and the head burst into flames, the skin melting like wax.

Michael pulled a firework from his bag, lit the fuse, and pointed it at the creature.

"You killed my brother, you fucking cocksucker," he screamed, as an incandescent ball of fire shot from the end of the firework and hit the werewolf square in the chest. It exploded with a thunderclap, and the monster fell back in shock. Michael reached for another firework. John grabbed his arm.

"For fuck's sake, Mike. You're just pissing it off. We've gotta go. Now."

The boys ran back along the trail toward the main road. The werewolf shook its head and, identifying its attacker, dropped to all fours and bounded across the clearing in pursuit.

"It's coming. Run, for God's sake, run."

***

High Moor

Constable Phillips turned into the Fenwick Hall estate and turned on the strobe light. Blue flashes illuminated the dark woods to either side of the vehicle as he drove along the gravel path to where the scouts camped.

He saw shapes on the road ahead. Two boys, sprinting towards him, their faces tear stained, contorted in terror and exhaustion. Behind them, something bigger--much bigger--was closing the distance with ease.

"Oh fuck..."

He slammed on the brakes, and the car skidded to a halt. He threw open his door as the boys raced past him, drew his pistol, and pointed it at the approaching monster.

OK, remember the training. Aim, breathe, squeeze.

He pulled the trigger. Nothing happened.

"Oh for fuck's sake, bloody safety catch."

Then it was on him. Claws like kitchen knives tore through his abdomen, spilling entrails into the dirt. Blood sprayed across the side of the car. The werewolf thrust its head into the gaping wound and bit down, snapping ribs like dry twigs, and emerged with the unfortunate police officer's heart in its fangs.

***

"The graves. Get to the graves," said John, panting with exertion and sheer terror.

Michael nodded and urged his leaden limbs to give him more speed. He risked a glance behind and saw the werewolf drop the dead police officer to the ground and resume the chase.

John reached the mausoleum first and squeezed through the iron bars, flattening himself against the cold granite tomb. Michael was halfway through when the werewolf caught up.

Michael screamed as he was dragged back through the railings. John grabbed his arm and pulled with all his strength, but he might as well have been trying to resist the pull of a truck. The werewolf plunged its head forward and closed its jaws around Michael's side. Ribs snapped and blood sprayed out from the wound. His scream turned into a wet gurgle as the fangs ruptured his internal organs.

"Get off my friend, you fucker," screamed John and thrust a lit firework into the creature's eyes. A shower of green sparks cascaded across the beast and ignited fur. It howled in agony and slashed out with its claws, slicing through the skin on John's arm, but releasing Michael.

Ignoring the pain, John dragged his unconscious friend through the railings to the relative safety of the old mausoleum.

The werewolf recovered in seconds, and threw itself against the metal cage. The iron creaked and started to bend. The monster swung its arm through the gap between the bars, slashing at empty air as it strained to reach the two children. John pulled another firework from the bag and then realised that he'd dropped the lighter. It lay outside, barely five feet away. It might as well have been on the moon for all the good it would do them now.

The bars creaked in protest as the werewolf threw itself against them again, bending slightly to extend the monster's reach by another inch.

High Moor

***

Steven was doing eighty miles an hour as he reached the entrance to the estate. He'd driven like a man possessed through the streets of High Moor, siren blaring. Drunks had staggered out of his path, yelling curses at the police car as it sped away.

Carl spoke into the CB handset. "Constable Phillips, respond. Pick up the goddamn radio."

Static.

Steven's face was locked in a grim mask as he hit the brakes and slid the car sideways through the gates into the estate. He saw flashing blue lights further down the road.

"Steve, over there. Stop the fucking car."

Steven's legs turned to rubber as he looked through the woods to where Carl pointed. The strobe lights illuminated the mausoleum and the beast hurling itself against the bars in what appeared to be slow motion. Two boys huddled against a granite tomb, while the werewolf thrashed against the iron railings, its talons mere inches from the children.

The car ground to a halt, and Carl leaped from the passenger seat, pistol in hand. He rested his arms against the top of the police car, aimed, and pulled the trigger.

***

A shot rang out. The werewolf stopped and stood up with what could have been a puzzled expression on its blood-drenched face. Another bullet slammed into it, throwing the creature back against the metal cage; then two more in rapid succession.

137

The werewolf slumped forward onto the earth, a glistening black pool forming beneath its prone body. Two more bullets slammed into it. White hair withdrew into the body. Bones twisted and snapped. Within seconds, the monster was gone and the naked body of an old woman lay on the ground.

John watched two men walk forward, weapons pointed at the naked corpse.

"Is it dead, Carl? Did we kill it?"

"I think so, Steve. Otherwise it just had the mother of all bikini waxes."

Steven shot the old woman in the face. Carl looked at him. Steven shrugged. "No harm in making sure."

Steven ran over to the mausoleum. John sat with his back to the granite tomb, with Michael in his arms.

"Son, are you hurt? Can you move?"

John stared at the old woman's corpse. The adrenaline that had fuelled him was spent, and he could feel the hot blood of his best friend soaking through his clothes onto his shaking body.

"Son, can you hear me?"

John looked away from the corpse and into Steven's face. His voice cracked as he spoke.

"My arm's sore, but my friend's hurt. He's hurt really bad."

"What's your name?"

"John Simpson. My friend is Michael Williams. Is it dead? Did you kill it?"

Carl stood by the corpse and rolled the old woman onto her back. Black, dead eyes stared up at the full moon.

"Yes, we killed it. You're safe now."

***

Carl leaned over the body. His brow furrowed. There was something familiar about the dead woman. As if he had seen her before. A memory flashed into his mind. A dark-haired, young woman, sleeping next to him, her face peaceful.

"Oh God, Mirela."

"So you recognise her then, Mr Schneider?" said Joseph, as he walked out from behind a tree, his arms raised. He was completely naked.

Steven raised his pistol. "Get on the ground, right fucking now."

"How do you know me?" said Carl.

"My mother spoke of you often. She never blamed you for what you did. After all, she had already taken what she needed from you."

"Taken from me? You mean...?"

"Why do you think you were spared? A closed community like the Pack occasionally needs some...fresh blood."

"So...does that mean?"

Joseph ignored him and turned to Steven.

"I have come to claim my mother's body so that I can bury her properly. I will leave here with her, and you will never see me again. You have my word."

"Bullshit. Your mother was a monster, and she's evidence. The body's not going anywhere."

"Are you sure about that, Sergeant?"

Carl lowered his weapon and put his hand on Steven's arm. "Steve, do as he says. Put the gun down. Slowly."

"Like fuck I will. The body's going in a meat wagon, and this fucker is coming down the station to answer some burning questions I have."

Carl nodded his head at the tree line. Over a dozen of pairs of reflective green disks stared back at them. "Seriously, Steve. Put the fucking gun down or I'll shoot you myself. We can't win here."

Steven's shoulders sagged, and he lowered the pistol. Two more naked men walked from the forest and gathered up Mirela's body then vanished into the undergrowth. Joseph looked at the mausoleum and the two boys within.

He pointed to the boys. "You have a problem, gentlemen. That one will not survive, his wounds are too great. The other one however, will live. He is the problem. It would be for the best if you let him come with us, where we can help him manage his condition."

"Like you managed your mother?"

"Mirela was old, and she could not control herself anymore. If the child is left as he is, then he will end up like her. Caught halfway between man and beast. I can help him."

"Excuse me for not handing an injured, traumatised boy over to a naked gypsy in the middle of the bloody night. The boy stays. Now I suggest you piss off before I lose my patience."

Joseph shrugged. "It's your decision, of course. Good luck, gentlemen. I would suggest that you don't try to find us. I am unlikely to be as civil if I feel I am being hunted."

He stepped back, melting into the shadows cast by the trees, until all that was visible were a pair of shining green eyes. Then he was gone.

Steven turned to Carl, his face ashen. "Is that it? Is it over?"

Carl looked at the two boys and shook his head. "No, Steve. It's not. Not by a long shot."

End of Part 1

Part 2

Chapter 13

24th May 1986. Fenwick Hall, High Moor. 00:30.

The woods were filled with light and movement. Blue strobes from the ambulances and squad cars flashed across the trees, the staccato effect diminished by the white headlights of the vehicles. Torch light danced through the undergrowth as police officers tried to locate the boys that fled the onslaught. Distorted voices and crackling static from the radios filled the air, the nervous calls of the search party members and barked instructions from the paramedics tending to Michael.

Steven leaned against his squad car and lit a cigarette. He offered one to Carl, who shook his head, but then took one anyway. He inhaled half of the cigarette in a single drag and coughed into his hand.

"Dirty fucking things. They'll be the death of me, I swear. Five years on the wagon, and now I'm letting them get their claws into me again."

"There are worse ways to die," said Steven, and nodded his head at the tarpaulin that covered what was left of Constable Phillips.

"You know we should have let it finish them, don't you? We didn't win here tonight. We made things worse."

"Could you have sat back and watched that fucking thing tear those two boys apart? Really?"

"No, Steve. I couldn't. Doesn't change the situation. Were there any others injured?"

143

Steven shook his head. "No, there were three dead boys in the tent, plus the two scout leaders. It looks like these two got its attention before anyone else was hurt. Did you know the younger one is the brother of the first victim? I don't envy the poor bastard that has to break the news to the family."

"The news that their kid is in the hospital, or the news that he's going to grow hair and fangs at the next full moon and kill everyone in the house?"

"Did you see the state of the poor little bugger? He'll be lucky to live till the morning, let alone until the next full moon."

"And if he does? What then, Steve? And what about the other one?"

Steven lit another cigarette. "Christ only knows. Are you sure that he's going to change? That he'll be like the woman was?"

"Hell, I don't know. That naked gypsy seemed pretty damn sure, but those boys are the only ones I've come across that ever survived an attack. They could be fine, or..."

"Grow hair, fangs and kill everyone near them. I get it. What I don't get is what the hell we do about it."

"Not many options, I'll grant you. We could talk to the parents, but they wouldn't believe a word we said until it was too late. We could hang around outside the house on the full moon, but that wouldn't save the families inside, and there might be a few questions asked if we shot two young kids full of holes.

144

We could walk away and leave things in the hands of God, but I don't think either of us could live with that. You got any bright ideas?"

Steven dropped his cigarette to the floor and ground it into the earth. "Yeah, maybe. Come on."

"Where we going?"

"We're going to talk to the kid."

The two men walked across the crime scene to the first of two ambulances. A paramedic sat in the rear of the vehicle, stitching John's arm. He looked up as Steven and Carl approached.

"How is he?" said Steven.

"He'll live. He's pretty shaken up, but the wounds don't look infected. We're going to take him to the hospital and shoot him full of antibiotics, just in case, but he should be OK."

"Any chance we could have a word with him?"

The paramedic frowned. "You lot don't hang around. You should probably wait until his parents are present before you conduct an interview."

Steven took a cigarette from his pack and offered it to the medic. "It'll be strictly off the record. We'll only be a minute."

The man took the cigarette and stepped out of the ambulance. "Five minutes, and not a word about this to my boss. Clear?"

Steven nodded. "As crystal."

John stared out of the ambulance with a vacant expression on his face. He didn't seem to notice the two men as they climbed in beside him.

145

"John? How are you doing?"

"I keep seeing it, over and over again. It's like when you get a song stuck in your head and it won't go away, no matter how hard you try." He raised his head and looked into Steven's eyes. "Why haven't they taken Michael to hospital yet?"

"They need to make sure that he's stable enough to move. If they don't do that, it might make things worse."

"You mean he could die?"

Steven nodded. "Do you know what happened here tonight?"

"Yes. I mean, I think so. It was a werewolf, wasn't it?"

"Yes, son, it was," said Carl.

"So, does that mean I'm going to turn into one as well? Like in the movies?"

Carl shook his head. "I don't know."

John thought about this for a moment. "Will you shoot me as well, when I change?"

"If we have to, then yes. I'm hoping it won't come to that."

"What about me mam and dad? If I change, will I hurt them?"

Steven nodded. "You might. If they are there and you change, then you might."

Tears streamed down the boy's cheeks, and for a moment he struggled to breathe through his racking sobs. After a minute, he brought his tears under control and looked up, an earnest expression on his face.

"Then you should shoot me now, just to be safe. I...I couldn't hurt my mam and dad. I wouldn't be able to live with myself if I did."

Steven put his hand on the boy's arm. "We can't, John. We could be wrong, and you might be fine. There's just no way that we can know."

"Until it's too late?"

"Yes, I'm afraid so."

John burst into tears again, and Steven put his arm around the boy's shoulder until his sobs subsided. He wiped his nose on his sleeve and turned to Steven.

"You're a policeman. What should I do?"

"I don't know, John. I'm sorry, but I just don't know. We just thought that it was important that you knew. What happens next is going to have to be up to you. Do you understand?"

The paramedic appeared at the rear of the ambulance. "OK guys, that's your lot. I need to get John here to the hospital. If you need to talk to him again, you can do it after the doctors check him out."

Steven tore the top off his pack of cigarettes and wrote a number on it. "This is my telephone number, John. If you need to talk to me, about anything at all, then call me. Day or night. OK?"

John nodded as the paramedic ushered Steven and Carl from the back of the ambulance. The doors closed and the vehicle pulled away, back down the gravel driveway to the main road.

"Do you think we did the right thing, Carl?"

"We did all we could, Steve. All we can do now is wait and hope."

***

24th May 1986. Bishop Auckland Hospital. 07:30.

"John? Are you awake, pet?" said a woman's voice. A soft, cool hand took his and pressed two fingers against his wrist.

John groaned and tried to turn over in the bed. "It's early, Mam. Let me sleep a bit longer."

The voice chuckled. "Come on, sweetie. I need to do some checks, and the doctor wants to see you, but you'll be able to go home later on."

As he rolled onto his side, he felt a painful tug on the back of his left hand. He smelled antiseptic and stale urine in the air, heard the old man in the next bed moan and break into a series of wet, painful coughs. Memories broke through the fog in his mind. Bright lights shining into his eyes. Something constricting his arm in the night, so tight that he felt it would burst like a water balloon, then relief as the pressure subsided. Trying not to cry as a man punctured his skin with a needle in the back of an ambulance and praised him for being a brave boy. Michael screaming as the monster ate him. He opened his eyes, and saw an old woman in a nurse's uniform standing over him.

"There we go, sleepy head. We didn't get chance to ask you last night, what would you like for breakfast?"

"Where's me mam and dad? Where's Michael?"

"Your friend is still in surgery. Your mam and dad will be along to pick you up later, after you've seen the Doctor."

John heard raised voices from behind the plastic curtain that enclosed his bed.

"I couldn't care less what time visiting hours are. Where the bloody hell is my son?"

"Sir, I've told you, visiting hours are from ten to two. If you don't leave now, I'll call security and have them escort you from the premises."

"Dad! I'm in here."

There was the sound of a brief scuffle from behind the curtain, then it swept open to reveal John's parents. His dad hadn't shaved that morning. Grey stubble covered his chin, and dark rings circled his eyes. His mam wasn't wearing any makeup, and her eyes were red rimmed behind her glasses.

John's father fixed the nurse with a glare. "If you don't mind, I'd like to see my son now."

The nurse looked around Mr Simpson to the matron, then nodded her ascent and left the cubicle, pulling the curtain closed behind her. John's mother threw herself against him, wrapping him in a tight hug that pulled on the IV in his hand.

"Mam, you're pulling the needle out."

His mother released him and sat in the seat beside the bed, dabbing her eyes with a handkerchief. His father stood next to her, his face a mixture of relief, concern, and anger.

"How are you doing, champ?"

"My arm itches, and the needle in my hand hurts. Other than that, I'm alright. Can we go home now?"

"Soon, mate. I think the Doctor wants to see you first, then we can go."

"Is Michael alright? The nurse wouldn't tell me."

"I don't know, son. I saw his mam in the waiting room with Marie. Do you remember what happened? The police say you were attacked by a bear."

"It wasn't a bear. It was a werewolf."

John's mother shot his father a murderous glance. "I told you not to let him watch those bloody horror movies, George."

"Caroline, give it a rest will you. John, there are no such thing as werewolves. They're just make believe for films. It was dark, and I can see how you might think it was one, but it was just a bear."

"It was a werewolf, Dad. When the policeman shot it, I saw it turn back into an old woman, then the other werewolves came and took her away. He told me that's what it was."

"The copper told you it was a werewolf? Do you know who it was? Did he tell you his name?"

"He gave me his phone number. Told me to call him if I wanted to talk."

Mr Simpson opened the cupboard beside the bed and checked the pockets of John's jeans. After a moment, he took out a small piece of cardboard.

"Is this the one? The policeman that told you that you were attacked by a werewolf?"

John nodded. "I might turn into one, next full moon. I don't want to hurt anybody, Dad. I don't want to hurt you and Mam. What should I do?"

"You just need to get a bit of sleep, see the Doctor, and then come home with us. We'll be back in a bit."

High Moor

John grabbed his father's hand. "Where are you going?"

Mr Simpson's face was like thunder, but when he spoke, his voice was low and even. "Your mam and me are going to go and have a word with the police."

Chapter 14

26th May 1986. Aykley Heads Police HQ. 09:30.

Steven's head pounded in time to the click of his shoes on the wooden floor. His mind cycled through the events of Friday night on a perpetual loop. It was worse when he closed his eyes. When there were no external distractions, he got it all played back, in glorious Technicolor. Sleep had become impossible, so he'd made do with an alcohol-induced coma for the past two nights. This brought its own problems, which were making themselves very evident this morning as he headed to Inspector Franks office.

He arrived at the heavy wooden door and knocked twice, wincing as the sound reverberated through his skull and triggered a brief twinge of nausea. For a moment, there was no answer. Steven prayed that his boss had been called away on some urgent matter, so that he could lock himself in his office with a mug of coffee and some painkillers. It was not to be.

"Come in," said Inspector Franks' disembodied voice from behind the door.

Steven sighed and entered the room. If it were at all possible, Inspector Franks looked worse than Steven. Dark rings circled his eyes, and he didn't appear to have shaved for at least two days. The room smelled of body odour, expensive aftershave, and stale tobacco smoke.

"Sergeant Wilkinson, please have a seat. I've been going over your report, but there are a few gaps and I was hoping that you could enlighten me."

"Could you be more specific, sir?"

The Inspector got to his feet and walked around the desk, until he was standing over Steven.

"Well, we can start with you explaining why you ignored my orders with regards to this case and carried on investigating it. Then we can get to the part where you used unencrypted, public communications to discuss an ongoing investigation."

"Sir, with respect, if I had not ignored your orders, then it's likely that every single one of those boys would have died on Friday night. The evidence had shown that the cat killed by the farmer was not responsible for the death of the Williams boy, but you chose to ignore that for the sake of positive headlines in the local paper. As for using the CBs, well, we didn't have a lot of choice. It's not like we could have used our police radios, given your objection to the case."

"So, instead you decided to broadcast the details to every amateur radio enthusiast in a five mile radius? Worse than that, you broadcast that you are following up on the sighting of a werewolf?"

Steven grimaced. "That was the description given by the truck driver who sighted the bear, sir. He was a little worse for wear at the time, as I understand it."

"Oh, I'm sorry. So, you are saying that you weren't looking for a werewolf? Then would you care to explain why Constable Phillips was found holding an unregistered firearm, that he was neither trained nor authorised to use, that contained silver bullets?"

"The weapon belonged to Mr Schneider, sir. He must have given it to the Constable. I can't comment on the nature of the ammunition. Mr Schneider is a little eccentric, but the weapon and ammunition were all covered by the firearms permit that you signed."

"I see. Mr Schneider gave the Constable a sidearm, but you had no knowledge of this. And when you arrived on the scene, Mr Schneider fired on the alleged bear, seriously wounding it and causing it to flee into the woods. Is that correct?"

"Yes, sir. That is correct."

"The statement from the Simpson boy stated, among other things, that two men saved him by shooting the 'bear'. Who do you suppose the other man was, Sergeant Wilkinson?"

"It was dark, and the boy was under severe duress, sir. It's easy to see how he may have gotten events confused."

"And was he confused when you and Mr Schneider told him that he'd been attacked by a werewolf, after the incident? When you gave him your personal contact details? Oh yes, I know all about that, Sergeant Wilkinson.

"I had the boy's parents in this very office on Saturday morning, demanding to know why a police officer would say things like that to a traumatised ten-year-old boy. I have to say, I'd love to know the answer to that one myself."

Steven shifted in the chair. His hangover was getting worse. Waves of gooseflesh and nausea washed over him.

"What exactly would you like me to tell you, sir?"

High Moor

"What I would like you to tell me is the fucking truth, Sergeant. Do you recognise this report?" he said, holding up a brown cardboard folder. "You should, it's the one you submitted on Saturday, and as far as I'm concerned, the whole thing is a complete pack of lies. From my perspective, you disobeyed a direct order and as a result, caused the death of a fellow officer. You then falsified your report, which is in itself, a criminal offence."

Steven got to his feet and stared straight into the Inspector's eyes. "As I have previously stated, sir. I ignored your orders because they were idiotic. If I'd listened to you, then we would be explaining why there were twenty-five dead boys found at that campsite, instead of three. You tell me, sir. How exactly would the press have portrayed you then? As an incompetent fuckwit that only sees the world in terms of his own career? Those children are alive despite your best efforts, and I would do the exact same thing again if I had to."

The Inspector retreated behind his mahogany desk, his face flushed with a combination of fear and anger. "Sergeant Wilkinson, I am left with no choice but to suspend you from duty without pay, pending a full investigation. That will be all."

"You jumped-up, pompous little shit. Do you think I'm going to put up with this? I'll have the union tear you a new arsehole."

"That will be all, Mr Wilkinson. Now get out of my office before I have you dragged out."

***

26th May 1986. Neville's Cross, Durham. 16:45.

Steven barely registered the front door opening. He sat in the front room of his two bedroom, terraced house, with the curtains drawn and the air hazy with cigarette smoke and the stink of stale alcohol. A children's program was on the television, some cartoon that he'd not been paying attention to, background noise to stop him going crazy in the silence. The click of heels on linoleum. The swirl of smoke in the beams of light that pierced the curtains as the living room door opened.

"You're home early, hon. Did they give you the day off?"

He placed his empty glass on the table with exaggerated care and turned to face his wife. He could sense the storm brewing. Any second now the thunderheads behind her eyes would break and the storm would unleash its full fury.

"In a manner of speaking."

"Well, it's about bloody time. No one should have to go through what you did and then go straight back to work. Did they sort out an appointment with the counsellor?"

"Not exactly. The Inspector was none too pleased that I disobeyed him, even if it did mean I saved the lives of all those children. He suspended me, pending an investigation."

"He did what? That little tosspot can't do that. Have you spoken to the union?"

Steven reached for the bottle of whiskey beside the sofa and poured himself another large glass. "The union aren't interested. There's a chance that charges could be brought against me, and that fat, useless union rep scurried back to his hole. Until the investigation completes, they don't want to know."

"Well, I hope you aren't just going to sit here on your arse, stinking the place up with smoke and drinking yourself to death until they sort this out. You haven't even done the washing up, and there's that shelf that needs putting up in the kitchen. If you're going to be around the house, you can bloody well make yourself useful."

"Franks suspended me without pay, Laura. I can't even go and sign on because I still technically have a job. After all I did, all I went through, and they just fucked me over."

Laura's eyes darkened. She strode across the room and yanked the curtains open. Steven winced as bright sunshine shone into his eyes.

"How long? How long are you not going to be bringing any money in?"

"Fucked if I know," said Steven, draining his scotch in a single gulp. "Could be a month, could be a year. Fuck em."

"Fuck them? What about me? I've put up with a lot of shit from you over the past few months. First, that bloody goat you brought home."

"That was only for a couple of days, until I could get it re-homed."

"Yes, a couple of days with it eating my flower beds, pulling the washing down off the line, and crapping all over the garden. Then you bring that bloody yank home without even consulting me about it. Do I not get a say over who stays in this house and for how long?"

"It was complicated, Laura. Franks wouldn't pay his accommodation anymore and..."

"And so we have to provide bed and board, do we? Where does it say that in your contract of employment? Do you know how many times I have found him walking out of the bathroom without any clothes on? I'll tell you. Every bloody morning. Every single one."

"I don't know what you want me to say."

"What I want you to say is that he's going. Today. I want you to say that you'll have your job back in a few weeks and we won't risk losing the house when we can't pay the mortgage. I want you, for once in your miserable, selfish, pig-headed existence, to treat me with some fucking respect, because I don't deserve this."

"Look," said Steven, reaching for the whiskey bottle again, "I've had a really shitty day. Can you wind your neck in, stop screaming at me, and let me get my head straight."

"Get your head straight? That's bloody hilarious. Your mate Johnny Walker's going to sort it all out is he? It'll all be alright once you finish the bottle, will it? Do you remember what we talked about, before all of this happened? We were thinking about bringing a child into the world, but now there's a naked fucking American living in what would be the nursery, and you're an out of work, alcoholic dosser. How could you look after a child, Steven, when you can't even look after yourself?"

Steven stumbled to his feet and knocked over the coffee table. The overflowing ashtray spilled across the carpet, along with the contents of his shot glass, turning the ash into a wet black stain on the cream fabric. His face contorted in anger.

"Do you have any idea what I've been through? The things I've seen? The things that I've had to do? You just go off to your little job, wiping people's arses and making them cups of tea, and then come home and criticise me for trying to unwind after I've just seen a bunch of kids get torn to ribbons."

Laura's mouth dropped open in shock, and Steven knew that he'd crossed a line. Then the front door slammed.

Carl's voice came from the hallway. "Hey, Steve, you home? Get your butt in gear, buddy."

The American threw open the living room door, then paused when he saw Steve and Laura's expressions. "Oh, sorry. Is this a bad time?"

Laura's voice cracked with barely suppressed tears. "No, Mr Schneider. Your timing is fucking perfect. The drunken prick is all yours. I'm not putting up with this shit for a second longer." She stomped out of the room and slammed the front door behind her. Moments later, her car started up and drove away.

"Shit, Steve. Didn't mean to interrupt anything. Anyway, what I wanted to tell you was that I got a lead on those gypsies. From what I can tell, they…"

"Fuck off, Carl."

"Hey, Man. No need to be like that. I thought you'd want to know where Joseph and his crew went."

"It's not my fucking problem, Carl. I got suspended today, which more or less means I'm unemployed. There are criminal charges hanging over my head, and now it looks like my fucking wife has walked out on me, so pardon me for not giving a shit about a bunch of Gypos."

"Look, Buddy, I'm real sorry about that, but you need to get your head back in the game. We've only got three weeks till the next full moon, and not only do we have a wandering pack of werewolves to worry about, but we have two kids that will, in all likelihood, kill their entire families and everyone around them. If we don't think of a way to deal with this, we could have an epidemic on our hands."

"Carl, I'm obviously not getting through that thick, fucking skull of yours, so let me make this as simple as I can. I am no longer an active police officer, so it's nothing to do with me anymore. I'm done with this shit, and I'm done with you. Now get out of my fucking house and don't come back."

Chapter 15

31st May 1986. John's House, High Moor. 10.22.

Marie closed the back door of her house with deliberate care. She smiled with satisfaction as the lock clicked and waited for a moment to see whether her escape had been detected. When no sounds of pursuit came from the house, she crossed the driveway and rapped on John's back door.

She heard her mother in the kitchen, washing the breakfast dishes. Marie was sure that at any second she'd open the door and usher her back inside. She'd just raised her hand to knock on John's door again, when the door swung open and Mrs Simpson stood before her.

Caroline Simpson looked tired. Her face had lost its colour, and her entire frame sagged as if carrying an invisible load. She looked down at Marie, and for a moment, said nothing. When she did speak, her voice was muted, as if the effort of speech was almost too much for her.

"Hello, Marie. What can I do for you?"

"Hello, Mrs Simpson. I was wondering if John was in?"

"He should be in his room. Please, come in. You'll have to excuse the mess. I'm just about to clean the kitchen."

Marie stepped through the door, feeling a surge of relief when it closed behind her. She headed through the kitchen, past a sink piled high with washing up, to the foot of the stairs.

"John," yelled Mrs Simpson. "Marie's here to see you."

Silence.

Mrs Simpson climbed the stairs, with Marie following behind, and tapped on John's bedroom door. "John, are you in there?"

When no reply was forthcoming, Mrs Simpson opened the door and entered John's bedroom. The room was a mess. Discarded clothes covered the bedroom floor, and books lay strewn across the bed and desk. Piles of cassette tapes containing pirated video games were stacked next to John's computer, which, along with the small portable television, was still turned on. A rope was tied to the bed and dangled out of the open window.

Mrs Simpson put her hands on her hips. "Oh, for God's sake, the stupid little bugger will rip his stitches out if he's not careful."

Marie edged towards the door. She felt a sudden need to be out of the house, before Mrs Simpson started asking questions about where John might be or what he might be up to. "I'll go and find him, if you like."

"I'll come with you, Marie. He might be hurt from climbing out the window, or something else might have happened to him. I'll just get my coat."

"It's alright, Mrs Simpson. Really. There are lots of places he might be, and some of them might be a bit tricky for a grown-up to get to. It's better if I go and look myself. I'll tell him to come straight back if I find him."

"Are you sure? Maybe I should check with your mother first."

Fear blossomed in Marie's stomach. Her parents would go mad if they found out she'd sneaked out.

"Mam's really busy, Mrs Simpson, and my dad's in a funny mood. It's fine, really. I'm allowed out as long as I don't go too far from the house."

"Alright, but you tell him to come straight back the second you find him. OK?"

Marie crossed her fingers behind her back and put on her most angelic smile. "I promise, Mrs Simpson. Straight back."

Marie fled through the back door before Mrs Simpson could change her mind and crept around to the front of the house. When she got to the road, she turned left and sprinted up the street. She climbed over the metal gate at the end of the road, into the fields that ran behind the strip of houses, and stopped to catch her breath.

Where would John go if he didn't want anyone to find him?

The possibilities ran through her mind. He wouldn't go to the playground behind the housing estate because there would be lots of kids there at this time on a sunny bank-holiday Saturday.

While Malcolm and his friends were under house arrest, awaiting trial, there were plenty of others that would make his life a misery. He wouldn't go into the woods because of what happened. No one went into the woods anymore. That only left one possibility. Marie checked over her shoulder to make sure no one was following, and then set off across the fields in search of her friend.

The tree stood at the intersection of four fields. A towering oak tree, surrounded at its base by a sprawling hawthorn bush. The farmer had, for the sake of pragmatism, fenced off the bush and cut a corner out of each field to accommodate it. The effort to remove the sprawl of vegetation was not justified, considering the small increase in available land it would yield. The hawthorn appeared to be an impenetrable mass of wood, leaves and thorns on the outside. However, a couple of years ago, the children discovered that if you could crawl past the grasping branches, the interior of the bush was almost hollow.

They had used it as a base of operations for two years until Malcolm Harrison and his gang had found out about it. The gang had destroyed the tree house constructed in the arms of the old oak and had trashed the camp inside of the hawthorn bush. Now Malcolm and his friends were out of the picture, and this was the only place that John could have gone.

Marie climbed over the wooden fence, taking care to avoid the rusty barbed wire along its top, and headed for the small entrance at the side of the bush. She got onto all fours and crawled through the tunnel of thorns. She felt them tug at her clothing and scratch her arms as she pushed her way through into the cavernous interior.

Sunlight illuminated the floor in patches where it penetrated the dense foliage, the beams of light dancing as the breeze shifted the canopy of leaves. John sat on an overturned plastic drinks crate, his back to her. He didn't seem to realise that Marie was there.

"John? Whatcha doin?"

John gave a start and put something into his pocket. "Nothing. I just wanted to get out of the house and be by myself. You go home, Marie. Leave me be for a while."

"I had to sneak out of the house as well. Mam and Dad won't let me go anywhere after what happened. Your mam's looking for you, by the way. She found the rope."

John shrugged. "Doesn't matter. Have you been to see Michael?"

"Every day. Mam and me go to see him in the morning and at night. It's boring as fuck, but I want to be there when he wakes up so I can slap him for making me so worried."

"He still unconscious? Have the doctors said anything?"

"Yeah. He won't wake up, but they say he's not getting any worse and that it's too early to tell anything for sure." Marie walked over to him and put her hand on his shoulder. "John, what happened at the camp? No one will tell me anything, except that it was a bear."

"It wasn't a bear, Marie. It was a werewolf. It killed Mr Wilson and Miss Hicks and Brian and Dylan and Lester, then it tried to kill me and Michael."

"Piss off, John. Just cos I'm younger than you, it doesn't mean I'm stupid. There's no such thing as werewolves. Mam said so after we saw that film."

John turned to face Marie, and she saw no trace of humour in his eyes. No hint of a trick.

"Really? A werewolf?"

"Michael thought it was what killed David. He shot it with fucking fireworks and it came after us."

"And then what happened?"

"The police shot it and it turned into an old woman. Then a load of other werewolves took the body away. The police must have covered it all up or something."

"What did it look like? The werewolf?"

"What do you think it looked like? Half man, half wolf. Fucking massive, covered in hair with teeth and claws like kitchen knives."

"All of them? How did the others carry the dead one away?"

"The others were different. They changed back to people, and I saw one of them through the trees. It just looked like a big dog. Like an Alsatian, but three times the size. Like if an Alsatian shagged a Shetland pony."

"That's actually pretty cool. Imagine if you could turn into a big wolf like that. I'd bite Malcolm's bollocks off."

John laughed in spite of himself. "But then you'd have Malcolm's balls in your mouth."

Marie looked shocked for a moment and mimed sticking her fingers down her throat. "Oh my God, that's gross. Never ever in my life will I have *any* part of Malcolm Harrison in my mouth. That's put us right off me dinner."

"Marie, can you promise me something?"

"Yeah, sure."

"No, I mean really. Cross your heart and hope to die."

"Well, what is it? I'm not crossing my heart until I know what you want me to promise."

"Keep away from Michael on 22nd June. If he's not out of hospital, then don't go visit him. If he's home, then go and stay with a friend that night."

"Fuck right off. You can't tell me not to be with my brother. What if he wakes up and I'm not there? What if he doesn't wake up at all?"

"Listen, Michael and me survived a werewolf attack. All the books and movies say that we'll turn into one on the next full moon. That's 22nd June. I don't want you getting hurt."

"Do you really think that'll happen? You're both going to turn into werewolves in three weeks' time?"

"Yes, I do. You didn't see the thing, Marie. It was worse than anything in the movies. Every time I close my eyes, I can see it. I wake up screaming every night to the same dream. When the moon comes up, Michael and me are going to change, and we'll hurt anyone that's near to us when we do. I don't want that to happen to you."

"What about you?"

"I'm going to take care of it. I won't hurt my mam and dad, or anyone else."

Marie sat down next to John and took his hand. It was warm. Sticky. She looked at her hand and saw that it was slick with blood.

"John, what did you do?"

"I was trying to end it. Kill myself before the full moon. I couldn't cut deep enough because I was scared. Then you turned up. I'm a coward. A fucking coward." John's eyes brimmed with tears and he sagged.

"John?"

He looked up at Marie. Her eyes blazed in fury and she punched him in the face as hard as she could."

"What the fuck?"

"How could you think of doing that? Kill yourself? You survive all that, and then just cut your wrists? You are a selfish fucking bastard, John Simpson. How do you think your mam will feel?"

"She'll be upset, but at least she'll be alive."

"OK, so what about me?"

"You?"

"Yes, me. One of my brothers is dead; the other is in hospital and might never wake up. Me mam wanders around the place in a daze all day, and Dad's done nothing but drink himself unconscious since Dave died. You are all I have left. Why would you leave me too?" She threw her arms around John's neck and sobbed.

"Marie. It's important. You have to promise to stay away from Michael on the 22nd. Promise me, Marie."

"You have to promise too. Promise you'll stay with me and don't do anything stupid. Then I'll do what you say."

John hugged the girl tight, tears streaming across his cheeks.

"OK, Marie. I'll find another way to keep everyone safe. I promise."

***

31st May 1986. Hamsterley Forest. 14:45.

Carl sat in his rented Ford Escort and lit another cigarette, disgusted at himself. *I keep off the fucking things for years, and suddenly I'm back to two packs a day.*

The bank holiday traffic had been as bad as expected. The roads were packed with vehicles, and the car park at the forest visitor's centre was completely full.

High Moor

Couples walked hand in hand through the shaded paths and tracks. Families talked and laughed as they made their way through the well-tended woodland. The forest was full of life and happiness as people took advantage of the sunny May afternoon.

The tourists and dog walkers had not, however, roamed too far along this track. The presence of the traveller camp in a clearing a quarter of a mile beyond where Carl was parked had made sure of that. Cars turned around in haste when they sighted the circle of caravans. People on foot decided that it was probably best that they take another route.

Carl didn't know if it was merely their natural suspicion of travellers, or whether it was something subconscious that screamed in the deepest, oldest parts of their mind. Beware. Predators are near.

He picked up his binoculars from the passenger seat and trained them on the camp. The gypsies seemed not to realise that he was there and went about their business. Pots of food bubbled over an open fire. Children played with an elderly Jack Russell terrier. Men returned from the forest with arms full of wood or the occasional rabbit. Women washed baskets of clothes in the stream that ran along the edge of the clearing.

Several of the men appeared to be injured. A large dark-haired man had white linen stretched over the left side of his face. Others wore slings. A young man, probably no older than seventeen or eighteen, hobbled to the fire on crutches. His right leg was missing below the knee, and fresh blood stained the dressing.

Carl stubbed the cigarette out in the overflowing ashtray and exhaled the last lung full against the windscreen.

"What the fuck are you doing here, Carl? What the hell do you hope to accomplish?" he said to himself.

"I was going to ask you that exact same question, Mr Schneider."

Carl jumped in his seat, startled at the unexpected voice. Joseph stood by the driver's door. He pointed a shotgun through the window at Carl's head.

"I wouldn't do anything stupid if I were you. Take your gun and put it on the passenger seat, then get out of the car."

Carl weighed up his options and didn't like any of them. With a sigh, he reached into his coat pocket and took out his pistol.

"And the other one. I don't recommend you do anything to make me nervous. This shotgun has a hair trigger, and I would hate to ruin the upholstery of your car."

Carl's shoulders sagged, and he withdrew his other pistol, putting it alongside its twin on the passenger seat, then he opened the door and stepped out onto the road. Joseph took a couple of steps back and motioned towards the gypsy camp with the barrel of his gun.

"After you, Mr Schneider."

The two men walked down the road to the parked caravans. Carl could see movement in the trees on either side of them.

"Why not just kill me now and have done with it? That's what you said you would do if I came looking for you, isn't it?"

"I say a lot of things. Some of them are even true. At the moment, let's just say that your fate is in your own hands and leave it at that."

Heads turned to regard Carl as he entered the camp. Up close, he could see that many of the people were carrying injuries, not only the men, but some of the women and children as well. Over twenty pairs of eyes followed Carl with suspicion and barely contained anger.

"What the hell happened here?"

"Mirela happened. She changed in the middle of the camp and attacked the first thing that she saw. Her family. Her friends."

"Why the hell did you keep her in the camp on a full moon? You must have known what would happen."

"Mr Schneider, you know almost nothing about us. Under normal circumstances, when we are poisoned with silver, we cannot change for more than a month. Not until the poison is out of our system. My best guess is that, as Mirela survived being shot with silver twice, she may have built up a degree of resistance. It was my error in judgement, and I shall bear the consequences of that for the rest of my days."

"How many people did you lose?"

"Seven, including my wife Yolanda. Some of us managed to change and drive her away before she could kill any more. Once we had tended to our wounded, we pursued her and, well, you know what happened then."

"I'm sorry, for what it's worth."

"It's worth very little, but thank you anyway." Joseph opened the door to a large mobile home and motioned for Carl to go inside.

"Take a seat, Mr Schneider. I'd like to talk about why you're here."

Carl moved a folded blanket from a chair and sat down. "I'm here because I couldn't understand why you hadn't left. I needed to know what you were up to and whether you were going to be a problem."

"You've seen those outside. They are the lucky ones. Most of the other injured are recuperating in their caravans. They are too badly hurt to move far."

"Then why not get them proper medical help?"

Joseph laughed. "You think it's that simple? Leaving aside the questions that would be asked with so many wounded, what do you think would happen if someone were to look at our blood through a microscope? The risk of exposing ourselves would be too great. If humans had definitive proof of our existence, then they'd hunt us down and exterminate us. This brings me to my second reason for staying."

"The boys?"

"Yes. Those children are infected. They will change on the next full moon. Whether they are like us when they change, or like Mirela, remains to be seen, but if I had to make a guess, I would say the latter is more likely."

Carl nodded. "That's what I was afraid of. So you're hanging around for what? To see what happens? Or are you intending to do something about it?"

"We haven't decided yet. There are other factors to take into consideration."

"What other factors?"

"The involvement of the Pack for one. When Mirela became afflicted, I fled the Pack to protect her. They order all Moonstruck to be killed. No exceptions."

"Why?"

"In part, it's to maintain secrecy. A moonstruck werewolf is a savage beast, incapable of rational thought. It is inevitable that, sooner or later, one would provide irrefutable evidence of our existence. The other reason is fear. We heal from most injuries very quickly unless the damage is severe. Not even silver is guaranteed to kill us, although it inhibits the healing process. The claws and teeth of another werewolf though? Well, you can see the results of that outside."

"You don't heal from injuries inflicted by another werewolf?"

"We do, but it takes time. It won't be until another lunar cycle has passed that our bodies will repair the damage."

"So, let me get this straight. You think the Pack are here? Now?"

Joseph shrugged. "I don't know, Mr Schneider. I would say that it's possible. Even likely. If they are here, they will stop at nothing to protect our secret. That puts everyone around those children in grave danger."

"Jesus. If I am honest, Joseph, I have no fucking clue what I'm supposed to do here."

"The solution is obvious, Mr Schneider. You need to kill both of those boys before the next full moon."

Chapter 16

21st June 1986. Neville's Cross. 13.00.

The sound of the telephone reverberated through the house, waking Steven, who was asleep on the sofa. The noise hurt his head as if the sound had solid spikes that caught against the inside of his skull and tugged on brain matter. His head span and he stumbled to his feet, kicking a plate across the floor. It broke as it collided with the coffee table. Steven swore and staggered to the hallway.

If this is some bastard trying to sell me something, there'll be hell to pay.

He snatched the handset from its cradle. "What?"

A child's voice answered. Small and uncertain. "Hello? Is that Sergeant Wilkinson?"

Steven rubbed his eyes with his free hand and tried to force his mind into focus. "Yes, this is Steven Wilkinson. Who is this?"

"It's John Simpson. You told me to call you if I needed to."

Steven felt like someone had just dropped him into a bath of ice. His mind cleared in an instant, and his hand tightened around the receiver until his knuckles turned white. "John. Of course. What's the matter?"

"I don't know what to do. The full moon's tomorrow night and I'm scared."

"John, calm down. We don't know for sure that anything's going to happen."

"I do. I know."

Steven pulled a stool out and sat down. "How do you know, John?"

The line was silent for a moment. "I...I tried to kill myself. I cut my wrists."

Steven was appalled. "You did what? Do your parents know?"

"It healed up. It healed up nearly straight away. I know you said that I had to take care of it, but I can't."

"I didn't...I mean, oh fucking hell. John, I didn't mean for you to try and hurt yourself. You're not going to try anything like that again, are you?"

John sniffled down the phone. "No, it's no use. It just hurts and then it's like I never did anything. I wanted to know if you could lock me up? Put me in prison so I don't hurt anyone."

"I wish I could, John, but I'm not a police officer anymore. Not really. I can't get access to any cells, and even if I could, the other policemen would never let me lock up a ten-year-old boy."

"But the healing. That means I'm going to change, doesn't it?"

Steven sighed. "Yes, it probably does."

"Can you take me away somewhere, then? Somewhere far away from anyone, so that I won't hurt anybody when it happens?"

Steven thought about this for a moment. "John, are your parents home today?"

"Yes, Dad's out in the garden and Mam's cooking."

"Alright, I'm going to come round and see you all. I'll be there in a couple of hours, OK?"

176

"OK. Thank you, Sergeant Wilkinson."

Steven put the phone down and ran a hand over three days of beard.

"Steven, you're a fucking idiot. You just couldn't stay away, could you?" he said to himself. He put the kettle on and made a cup of strong black coffee while he tried to think about what he'd say to John's parents.

***

21st June 1986. John's House, High Moor. 13.15.

Carl sat in the rear of the Ford Transit van and waited. He'd wound down the driver's side window not only to allow some air to circulate in the stifling heat of the June afternoon, but to allow him a clear line of sight on his target. He eased aside the blanket that hung behind the front seats with the silenced barrel of his rifle and focused the sights on the red telephone box down the street.

Can I do this? Can I really blow the head off a ten-year-old boy in cold blood?

Joseph's warnings ran through his mind, and he wiped the sweat from his brow. The door to the telephone box opened, and John Simpson stepped out into his crosshairs.

Just like any other shot. Concentrate on your breathing. Feel the target. Anticipate its movement. Breathe and squeeze.

His finger touched the trigger. Cold metal against warm skin. The finger curled around the trigger and tightened until he felt the pressure point. That final resistance before the weapon fired and a young boy lay dead in the street.

An elderly couple emerged from the house next to the telephone box and called to John. The man put his hand on the boy's shoulder while the woman took his hand and talked to him. The three of them walked away, past Carl in his hiding place, towards John's home. The boy reached the front door, waved to the old couple, and vanished back inside.

Carl hadn't realised that he'd been holding his breath. He exhaled with a whoosh of air, clicked the safety catch on his rifle, and put it down beside him.

Time was running out fast. The damn kid hardly ever went outside, and this had been a golden opportunity. Maybe the last clear shot he'd get. Carl cursed himself for not firing when John was in the telephone box.

He disassembled the rifle, placed the parts into a flight case, picked up a bottle of water, and got out of the van. He was exhausting his options. Short of marching up to the house and forcing his way inside, then shooting the kid at point blank range, there weren't many choices left open to him. There was just one more thing he could try. Carl locked the van and walked across the pub car park to gates that lead to the fields behind John's house.

***

21st June 1986. John's House, High Moor. 15.20.

John paced the floor in his bedroom, kicking clothes out of his way. Marie sat at his desk, playing a game on John's computer.

"Do you want a go, John? I've had loads of turns, and you haven't played once?"

"No, it's OK, Marie. You carry on."

"Well, can you stop doing that? It's doing my bloody head in."

John stopped walking and shoved his hands into his pockets. "I'm sorry. It's just...you know."

Marie nodded and paused the game. "Do you want to go outside, then? Just in the garden, like?"

John looked out of his bedroom window. The sun blazed down from a clear June sky. A light breeze moved the tops of the trees, and a wood pigeon called from somewhere across the fields. John tried to spot the bird, but a glint of light, like someone flashing a mirror caught his eye. He searched the field, but couldn't locate the source of the flash again. He shrugged. "Sure, it's too nice a day to be cooped up in here."

The children stampeded down the stairs, much to the disgust of John's mother, who complained vocally yet couldn't keep the smile from her eyes. She made the children a glass of lemonade each and sent them out to the garden after extracting a solemn promise from them both that they'd not go any further. John and Marie agreed in unison, and John winked at Marie when his mother turned away.

"I saw that, John," said his mother, still with her back to the two children. "You go outside of that garden, and you'll be grounded until you're thirty. I mean it."

John and Marie exchanged fearful glances and ran for the back door. They stood outside and burst into gales of laughter.

"How does your mam do that?"

"I dunno. She must have eyes in the back of her head or summit. She can hear a mouse fart from three doors down as well."

"I heard that, John," said his mother's disembodied voice from the kitchen.

John and Marie looked at each other and sprinted through the back gate into the garden, hands covering their mouths to hold in the laughter.

John's dad was at the bottom of the garden picking up dead wood from under the trees and chopping back the rampant brambles that were threatening to choke Mrs Simpson's expensive ornamental shrubs. He waved to the two children as they entered the garden, and they ran down to see him.

"Are you going to make a fire for that lot, Dad?"

"Yeah. Do you want to help?"

"I can make it. I learned how in Scouts."

George Simpson thought about this for a moment. "OK, just be careful. Fire's dangerous, and you need to treat it with respect. Those aren't your good clothes are they?"

"No, Dad," John lied, "I'll be really careful, and we can't go anywhere else and we're so bored. You'll be here anyway."

"Alright, but don't make it too big. I don't want the trees catching on fire."

John and Marie set about the building of the fire. John made a pyramid of larger pieces of wood while Marie, under John's instructions, filled the centre with smaller sticks and twigs.

Eventually, John declared that the fire met his standards and removed a box of matches from his pocket. He bent over and struck a match, cupped his hands around the flame, and held it beneath some of the kindling. The flame lapped around the wood, and after a moment, leaped to an adjacent piece, then another and another until it reached some of the larger sticks. John and Marie stood back from the roaring fire with their hands on their hips and satisfied smiles on their faces.

"Well done, you two. I'm impressed," said George. "Would you like a drink of anything?"

Marie smiled at him. "A glass of water would be nice, Mr Simpson."

John swatted at a mosquito that whined past his ear as he bent to retrieve his glass. "Can I have another lemonade please, Dad?"

"Of course you can. I'll be back in a second. Don't get too close to that fire," said George as he headed back to the house.

***

George made his way back up the garden and was surprised to find a man standing by the gate. "Hello? Can I help you?"

"Mr Simpson, I'm Steven Wilkinson, and we need to talk about your son."

George paused for a moment, unable to recall where he had heard that name before. Then the penny dropped and he stormed up the garden.

"You've got a fucking nerve coming here, you bastard. Give me one good reason why I shouldn't knock your bloody head off, right here, right now."

"Because you'd be assaulting a police officer for a start. Look, just hear me out, and I'll leave. There doesn't have to be any trouble. I saved your son's life. You owe me that much."

George put down the two glasses and opened the gate. "Come on then. You've got five minutes. We'll talk down here, away from the house."

The two men walked halfway down the garden and stood under a tree, far enough away from the children and the house that their conversation could not be overheard.

"Look, Mr Simpson, I don't blame you for thinking I'm a lunatic. Four months ago, I'd have thought the same. But I've seen these things on two separate occasions now, and there is absolutely no doubt as to what it was that attacked your son."

"Why don't you tell me what happened that night. Your version."

"OK. Well, we'd been hunting the thing since the first killing. I had no idea what we were dealing with, and my associate, Carl, didn't bother to tell me. Bastard let me find out firsthand, and it almost finished me. We heard about a sighting over the police radio, and I remembered that the scouts sometimes camped in the grounds of Fenwick Hall, so we drove over there to check on things. When we got there, we saw it trying to get two boys hiding behind the iron bars of a crypt.

"We shot it, and this seven-foot-tall, bipedal monster turned back into an old woman. Then a bunch of naked gypsies came out of the trees and took the body away."

"And you just let them?"

"There wasn't much choice. I got the impression that there were more of them than I had bullets left, and they didn't look like they were going to come quietly if I tried to arrest them."

George looked hard into Steven's eyes. "So, let's say for a second that it really did happen like that. What makes you think my son is going to turn into one of those things tomorrow night?"

"Carl has hunted these things all his life, and you've seen the movies. You have to at least consider it. Look, all I am asking is to keep an open mind and take precautions. If I'm wrong, then nothing happens and I'll happily let you punch my lights out. If I'm right though, then you and your wife are in terrible danger."

"Well, I'm sorry, officer, but it sounds like a load of bollocks to me. You've had your five minutes, now piss off before I lose my fucking temper."

"He's telling the truth, Dad."

George turned to face his son and realised John was holding a burning branch in his fist. Flames engulfed John's hand and the stench of burning flesh filled the air. George grabbed his son's arm and knocked the burning wood out of his grasp. He plunged John's hand into a nearby water butt.

"Oh God, call an ambulance, for Christ's sake."

"Dad," said John as he took his hand from the water and showed it to his father. "I'm fine."

George examined his son's hand for burns, but it was spotless, washed clean by the cold water. "Why the hell did you do something so stupid?"

"It was the only way to show you that he's telling the truth."

George Simpson hugged his son, tears running down his face. He turned to Steven, who was running his fingers around a hole in the trunk of a tree.

"I'm going to have to think about this, Sergeant Wilkinson. I really don't know what to do for the best."

Steven pulled out a flattened lump of silver metal from the hole and looked up, across the fields.

"Well, don't take too long over it, George," he said, his eyes never leaving the tree line. "If I were you, I'd get all of my thinking done well before tomorrow night."

***

Carl lined the crosshairs up on the centre of Steven's face. Steven glared right back at him. There was no way the police officer could see Carl from this distance, but he knew he was there, and the effect was quite unnerving.

He chuckled to himself as he disassembled the rifle and put it back into its case. "OK, Stevie. This one's all yours."

Chapter 17

22nd June 1986. John's House, High Moor. 19.15.

John hammered on the dining room window. "Marie. Marie, don't do it. You promised me."

Marie turned her head to look at John as her mother opened the car door. She shrugged her shoulders and blew him a kiss, then got into the back seat and closed the door. Moments later, the car started and pulled away, taking Marie and her mother to the hospital, to visit Michael.

John ran into the living room. "Dad, we have to stop them."

George was watching the football on the television. The world cup quarter finals were on, and England was playing Argentina. He didn't take his eyes from the TV set. "Stop who? What are you talking about?"

"Marie and Mrs Williams. They're going to see Michael, and it's the full moon."

"They will be fine, John. Nothing's going to happen. You'll see, everything will be alright."

"It's going to be dark soon, Dad. Shouldn't we be going?"

"Going?"

"You said that you'd drive me out onto the moors, before the moon came up."

"I know what I said, but that was just to calm you down. That copper got you upset."

"But you promised. Dad. You need to take me, now."

"John, there is no way on God's earth that I'm going to drive you out onto the moors in the middle of the night and leave you there. That copper has been through a lot. He's seen things that have messed with his head. I feel sorry for the poor sod, but I've had enough of his bollocks. Now, either sit in here and watch the match with us, or go and play in your room."

John burst into tears and ran from the room.

Caroline put down her knitting and glared at her husband. "There was no need to talk to him like that, George. He's upset enough without you making it worse."

"Well, the silly little bugger needed to be told. He'll see it was all nonsense after tonight, and we can get things back to normal. Oh my God, did you see that fucking handball? Come on, referee, he punched that in. That's never a goal. For fuck's sake! Cheating Argie bastard!"

***

22nd June 1986. Bishop Auckland Hospital. 21:00.

Marie ran along the corridor of the hospital, towards the stairs.

"Marie, for the last time, walk, don't run."

"But Mam, I want to see Michael."

"I don't care, young lady. Get back here this second or I'll put you in the car and take you straight home."

Marie shoved her hands into the pockets of her jeans and trudged back to her mother with a scowl on her face. "But if we don't hurry, we'll miss it."

"Miss what?"

"He's going to turn into a werewolf. It's going to be cool."

Joan Williams' expression turned hard. "You've been spending too much time with that John Simpson filling your head with nonsense. What do you think your father would do if he heard you saying things like that?"

"I don't care. It's the truth. John set his hand on fire and didn't get burned, so he must be a werewolf."

"Marie, that's enough. I don't think you should see John anymore. The boy's obviously not right in the head."

"But Mam, you can't..."

"I can, and I have. I don't want you hanging around with him anymore. Now be quiet. It's a hospital, and people are trying to rest."

Silent tears of rage ran down Marie's cheeks as they entered the ward and she ran off ahead to her brother's room. As she turned the corner, she collided with a man in a white coat.

"Marie, what did I tell you. Get here this second," said Mrs Williams, grabbing her daughter's wrist in a vice grip. She turned to the doctor. "I'm ever so sorry about that, Doctor..."

"Schneider, Miss," said the doctor in an American accent. "Doctor Carl Schneider, at your service."

***

22nd June 1986. John's House, High Moor. 21.10.

Steven drummed his fingers against the steering wheel and peered at the house. He saw the flickering glow of the television set through the curtains in the living room and, at the rear of the house, one of the bedroom lights was on.

To his keen detective skills, this indicated that George Simpson was a fucking idiot who'd ignored all of the warnings and decided watch the bloody football instead.

He checked his watch. The moon would rise in about ten minutes. He reached to the glove compartment of his car and took out a pistol. He checked the ammunition and stuffed the weapon into his jacket pocket.

"Fuck it," he said, and got out of the car.

***

22nd June 1986. Hamsterley Forest. 21:18.

Joseph stepped out of his Caravan and took a long drag from the cigar in his hand. The moon was rising. Already he could feel her tugging at his blood, energizing him until it took an act of sheer will to prevent him from changing right there and singing a joyful lament. The camp was quiet. The others moved around in silence, casting him sideways glances. Doubting his judgement. It made no difference. In the morning, the injured would have healed, and they could leave this place forever.

"She always did call to you more, Joseph. As if you were a little moonstruck yourself."

Joseph did not turn to face the speaker immediately. He inhaled another lungful of smoke, enjoying its taste as it rolled over his tongue and into his chest, savouring it. It would, after all, be his last. He wrestled with his fear and regret for control of his emotions, and when he won that battle, he turned to the source of the next.

"She calls to you, too, Sebastian. After all, you are Mirela's son, as much as I."

Sebastian stepped from the shadows and walked across to his brother. "I am surprised to find you here, if I am honest. I would have expected you to be out cleaning up your mess. Instead, I find you lazing around a campfire. Mother would never have approved."

Joseph shrugged. "Mother is dead. She no longer cares what I do. It would seem that my little brother at least still looks out for me."

"You are four minutes older than me, Joseph. It makes no difference."

"I know, but you will always be my little brother."

"Why did you let them live, Joseph? Bad enough that you defy your Pack once, but then to compound it like this? It's irresponsible, even for you."

Joseph picked up a piece of wood and raked over the embers of the fire. "The American is dealing with that particular problem. I thought it better that we stay far away, to avoid any suspicion."

"Schneider? Our father, the great werewolf hunter?"

"Can you think of anyone better? He's been slaughtering our kind for over forty years. Two young boys should not present a problem."

"He killed our mother. You should have torn his throat out there and then."

"You are upset about Mirela? Now? If we had not fled then, you and the rest of my 'family' would have killed her years ago."

Sebastian grasped the lapel of Joseph's jacket and brought him up close. "Vengeance demands it. I was not happy about the situation with Mother, but the law is clear. Moonstruck need to be killed. You violated that law, and worse, you allowed her to rampage through the countryside, killing innocents and putting every one of us at risk. Everything that has happened here is your fault."

Joseph nodded. "I know. I take full responsibility for my actions. I only ask that you let the others go. Return to the Pack."

Sebastian looked at his brother and shook his head. "You know I can't do that, Joseph."

The moon rose above the horizon, bathing the clearing in a cool, white light that contrasted against the warm flicker of the campfire. Joseph looked into the eyes of his brother as they turned into flat phosphorescent disks.

"I'm glad they sent you, Sebastian. It was good to see you again."

***

22nd June 1986. Bishop Auckland Hospital. 21:18.

Marie felt Michael's hand twitch in hers. She looked up at her mother, who was reading a magazine. "Mam, can you get me a drink from the machine please?"

"That's all the way down in reception, Marie. We'll be going soon, and I'll get you a drink on the way out."

"But, Mam, we've been here ages, and I'm really thirsty. Please?"

"OK, but if I go, you do not leave this room. Got it?"

"Got it. Cross my heart and hope to die."

Mrs Williams eyed her daughter with suspicion. She put down her magazine, took her purse from her bag, and started the long walk back to the hospital entrance.

Michael twitched again. His hand tightened on Marie's.

"Michael? It's me, Marie. Are you awake?"

The boy twitched again, a violent movement that jerked Marie's arm.

"Michael, stop it. You're hurting my arm."

Michael's eyes snapped open, and he looked at his sister with feral yellow eyes. Another spasm hit, harder this time. Michael arched his back and screamed in pain, gripping his sister's arm so tight that his knuckles turned white.

***

22nd June 1986. John's House, High Moor. 21:18.

John felt sick. His body oozed sweat and he was on fire inside, although his skin was cold, almost numb in contrast. He could hear his dad downstairs.

He'd been on the telephone to his friend, Alan, ever since the football had finished. John had been surprised to learn a number of brand-new curse words, despite having no idea to the meaning of most of them. A stab of pain shot through his stomach.

He tried to shout out to his parents, but the words came out as a croak. "Dad, it's happening. Please."

Another stab of pain lanced through him. He fell to the floor, catching the power cables of his computer and television as he fell. They slid from the desk and crashed onto the floor beside him. John heard footsteps on the stairs.

His insides twisted. He felt his internal organs rearranging themselves. Then the bones began to stretch and snap. He screamed in abject agony as his spine warped and bone knives burst through his gums. The scream became more guttural, then turned into a howl.

George and Caroline Simpson burst into John's bedroom, just as their son's transformation completed.

***

22nd June 1986. Bishop Auckland Hospital. 21:22.

"Michael, let go. Let go, you fuck-wad, that hurts." Marie cried and pulled her arm away.

Michael cried out. "Marie, run. RUN." His words ran into a long guttural scream. His face elongated. Fangs burst through bloody gums. Hands twisted and turned into talons. Hair grew from the pores on his skin.

Marie turned and ran from the room. She sprinted down the corridor, screaming for her mother, trying to block out the howling from her brother's room.

***

Carl saw the girl run from the room. "About fucking time, girlie."

He stepped from the storeroom into the corridor, then slipped into the boy's room and closed the door behind him. In all his years hunting werewolves, Carl had never witnessed the transformation from man to beast firsthand. The sight was distressing, even to him. The creature thrashed on the bed, howling in agony as its bones snapped and reformed. The transformation was almost complete. He didn't have much time.

High Moor

All doubts left him. This was no longer the cold-blooded murder of a comatose child. This was just another werewolf, plain and simple, and he knew how to deal with werewolves.

He removed a syringe from the jacket of his white lab coat and stepped around the bed, avoiding the thrashing talons and snapping teeth of the transforming creature.

"For what it's worth, kid, I'm sorry."

Carl injected the contents of the syringe into the IV and stepped back. He had no idea if the colloidal silver solution would work, but he figured it was worth a try, given the messy alternatives.

The werewolf stopped thrashing and opened its eyes. The transformation was complete, and the silver compound didn't seem to be doing a damn thing. It fixed its eyes on Carl and crouched, ready to attack. Carl cursed and backed away from the creature, fumbling in his pockets for his gun.

So much for the easy way.

Carl's sweating hand wrapped around the grip of the pistol. He tried to yank the weapon out from his coat, but it caught on the fabric. Carl tugged at the 9mm in desperation. The werewolf tensed its muscles and leaped.

***

22nd June 1986. John's House, High Moor. 21:24.

George stood transfixed in the doorway, as the creature that had once been his son got to its feet. His mind screamed at him that this couldn't be real, despite the evidence of his senses.

Caroline grabbed her husband's shoulder for support. "John? Oh God, John, is that you?"

The werewolf turned to face them. It stood over six feet tall and was covered in coarse, dark-brown fur. Its ears flattened against its head and it snarled.

George pushed his wife back, out of the room. Adrenaline flooded his system, numbing his limbs. He stumbled out of the room and slammed the door closed as the werewolf pounced. The pine door reverberated when the monster collided with it.

"Get up, Caroline. We have to get out of here."

She tried to shake off her husband and reached for the door. "But what about John. What about my baby?"

The door shuddered as the werewolf threw itself against it. A long crack appeared on its surface.

George dragged his wife back along the hallway to the stairs. "There's nothing of John in that room. Come on, woman, for fuck's sake. That door won't hold it for long."

A furious howl emanated from their son's bedroom as the werewolf redoubled its efforts to escape. The sound of wood splintering could be heard above the howl. Caroline regained her senses and hurried down the stairs, behind her husband.

George reached the back door as a loud crash from upstairs confirmed that the pine bedroom door had lost its battle. "Where the hell are the keys for the door, Caroline?"

"Well, if you put them where they're supposed to be, you'd know."

"Jesus Christ, Caroline. Not now. Where are the fucking keys?"

High Moor

George heard heavy footsteps on the landing above and the creak of the stairs. He scattered papers and jars from the work surface. "Where the fucking hell are the fucking bastard keys?"

Caroline reached over to the rack on the wall, where the house and car keys were kept, and handed them to George with trembling hands. George dropped them. While he groped on the floor, Caroline put her hand on her husband's shoulder. "George, it's too late. It's here."

There was no trace of John in the eyes of the creature before them. Only the kitchen worktop stood between them, and the beast that had once been their son. George hugged his wife as the werewolf tensed its muscles to pounce.

The back door flew open, the wood splintering around the lock as a result of Steven's kick. He raised his pistol and fired twice at the centre of the werewolf's chest. The creature fell back, and landed on the kitchen floor, behind the counter.

Caroline put her hands up to her face. "Oh God, you shot him. You shot my boy."

Steven ignored her and moved around the edge of the counter, pistol raised. When he got to the other side, he breathed a sigh of relief.

"Relax. I shot him with tranquilisers and paralytics. Stuck enough sedatives in him to knock out a rhino."

George and Caroline walked up to stand behind Steven and peered over his shoulder. The werewolf was flat on its back, with two darts protruding from its chest. It was snoring.

Steven took off his backpack and removed a long length of very thick chain. "I have no idea how long that stuff is going to take to wear off. George, would you mind giving me a hand, before we find out the hard way?"

***

22nd June 1986. Bishop Auckland Hospital. 21:25.

Carl grunted as he pushed the body of Michael Williams aside and got to his feet. That was a very close call. The silver solution kicked in when the werewolf was in mid-flight, and Carl was struggling to draw his weapon.

The effect had been instantaneous. Fangs and hair retreated, and by the time the boy collided with him, he was just a boy. A dead boy.

Carl picked up Michael's body and laid it out on the bed.

"I'm sorry, kid. Really, I am."

An alarm rang in the nurse's station. Carl was surprised that no one had come to investigate the noise before now. He closed the boy's eyes with his right hand, stepped out of the room, and walked away.

Chapter 18

23rd June 1986. John's House, High Moor. 04.44.

Steven walked to the window and pulled back the curtains. The faint glowing embers on the horizon an hour ago had burst into a conflagration that ignited the clouds and pushed back the night. The first glimmering fingers of sunlight danced through the branches of a sycamore tree. Steven let out a long breath that was one part relief and two parts exhaustion.

The tranquilisers worked for around half an hour, and then the werewolf had woken up. By this time, however, it was encased in ten meters of heavy chain. To be on the safe side, George then wrapped the chains with four rolls of duct tape, and Steven taped the monster's jaws tight shut with another entire roll. It worked. The werewolf thrashed in fury, but was unable to escape. After four hours of struggle, it curled up in the corner of the room and went to sleep. Steven and George stood watch in silence for the entire night. Caroline cried herself to sleep in the front room.

"The sun's coming up. How is he, George?"

George said nothing. His face had turned chalk white, and sweat beaded on his forehead.

"George?"

"He...he turned back. Oh God, I think I'm going to be sick."

Steven didn't turn to face the other man. His attention was on a car parked across the road. "Don't you think you should unwrap him then? I'm pretty sure there are laws against chaining up ten-year-old boys in their bedroom."

"Oh, of course. Aren't you going to give me a hand?"

The interior of the car glowed for a brief moment, then was dark once more. "No, George, there's something I need to do," he said and stormed out of the room.

Steven left the house and marched across the street to the parked car, then opened the driver's door and got inside.

Carl Schneider didn't bother to look up. He took a last drag from his cigarette and stubbed the butt out in the ashtray. "Morning, Steve, good to see you're still in one piece."

"Why are you here, Carl? To take another pot-shot at the boy?"

Carl looked up at the younger man. "He's still alive? What happened?"

"I shot the thing full of tranquilisers and chained it up in one of the bedrooms. Stop avoiding the question. Why are you...wait...what happened at the hospital?"

Carl reached for another cigarette. "Nothing happened. The kid was too messed up from the attack. Body couldn't cope with the change. He died mid-transformation."

Steven knocked the pack of cigarettes from Carl's hand. "You mean you had nothing to do with it? You just happened to be there?"

"Of course I was there. I was there with a loaded 9mm in the supply closet. Luckily, I didn't need to use it. Might have been tricky to explain a kid with a hole blown through him. As it was, he just died."

"Well pardon me if that sounds just a little bit too fucking convenient, Carl. I might have been inclined to believe you if you hadn't been shooting a high-powered rifle at a child playing in his back garden yesterday."

"Jesus, Steve. What do you want me to say? Would I have shot the kid if I had to? Of course I would. Can you imagine what a werewolf would do if it was loose in a hospital? The other kid, too. You can't keep him drugged up forever."

"I don't need to. His parents and I just need a way to contain him, every full moon."

The old hunter shook his head. "Steve, don't get involved anymore than you have. As a friend, I am suggesting that you might want to put some distance between you and that family."

"It's a bit late for me not to get involved. Anyway, I don't see the problem. The parents can't deny what's happening now. That will make containment that much easier."

"The boy's not the only problem. Like I told you before you had your breakdown, I found Joseph and the rest of them. They were hiding out in some forest, about twenty miles away. They caught me spying on them, and they told me that there might be more coming."

"More what? Werewolves? Why?"

"To clean up the mess. Hide the evidence." He looked up into Steven's face. "And to get rid of any witnesses."

Steven picked up Carl's packet of cigarettes without asking, took one, and lit it. "Jesus. Just when I think I've gotten things under control, something else happens. What did Joseph say exactly?"

"Not much. He's not one for straightforward explanations. I could tell he was scared, despite the bullshit."

"Then why don't you make yourself useful? Go back there and find out what's coming, and if there's anything we can do about it."

"I don't think he's going to be too happy to see me, Steve. He's pissed about what we did to his mother."

"I don't give a flying fuck. I've got enough to deal with here, so it's down to you. Stick a shotgun in the bastard's mouth if he doesn't feel like chatting. I want to be prepared for once, rather than just reacting."

Carl sat in silence for a moment, his brow furrowed. "OK, I'll go and ask. There's a good chance I'll end up as a chew toy, but don't let that worry you."

Steven stubbed out his cigarette and got out of the car. "I'm sure you can handle it. And Carl? If I find out you had anything to do with the death of the Williams boy, then you and I are going to have words. Am I making myself clear?"

Carl grinned at Steven, but the smile never reached his eyes. "As crystal."

Steven got out of the car and slammed the door behind him. He walked back to the Simpson's house, opened the front door, and went inside without so much as a backward glance.

Caroline Simpson was in the kitchen, washing the dishes. She turned to Steven and smiled. She looked like she'd aged ten years overnight. Fatigue and worry had pronounced the lines on her face, and her eyes were sunken, red-rimmed orbs that were moist with recent tears. When she spoke, her voice wavered, as if the simple act of speech was an effort.

"Is everything alright, Sergeant Wilkinson?"

"Yes, I just had to take care of something. And please, call me Steven. I'm technically not a Police Officer at the moment."

Caroline had the decency to look ashamed. "Alright. Would you like a cup of tea, Sergeant...I mean, Steven?"

"No, but thank you. How's John?"

She turned her back and started washing up again. Steven was about to say something to her, when George and John walked into the kitchen.

George's expression was a confused mix of fear and relief. John's hair clung to his forehead in damp tendrils. The boy's eyes stayed focused on the linoleum of the kitchen floor.

"John? How are you?"

A plate slid from Caroline's grip and shattered into the sink. She swore under her breath and fished the porcelain fragments from the water. She didn't turn to face her husband and her son.

"I'm alright. I just need a bath. How's Michael? Did he...?"

Steven looked up at George. The other man nodded in response to the silent question and put his hand on his son's shoulder.

Steven took a deep breath. "I'm sorry, John. Michael didn't survive the change. He was too badly hurt."

John closed his eyes and nodded. When he spoke, his voice cracked with emotions that he struggled to contain. "What about Marie and Mrs Williams? Are they alright? Did Michael hurt them?"

"As far as I know, they're fine. An associate of mine was watching Michael, and apparently he died before he finished changing."

John wiped his eyes with his arm as he fought back sobs of grief for Michael. He pulled free of his father and threw his arms around his mother. She flinched at his touch.

"Mam? Don't you love me anymore?"

Caroline's shoulders stiffened, and for a moment, she said nothing. Then her shoulders dropped and she turned to face her son with tears running down her cheeks.

"Oh, you daft little sod. Of course I love you. I'm sorry if I made you think otherwise. Come here and give your old mam a cuddle."

Steven smiled as mother and son embraced. It felt like it had been a long time since he'd smiled. He looked across to George and the smile faded. The other man's brow was furrowed with worry.

"So, Steven. What exactly do we do now?"

High Moor

23rd June 1986. Hamsterly Forest. 05.50.

Carl turned off the tarmac road, onto the gravel track that led past the empty visitor centre, to the heart of the forest. The woods should have been filled with birdsong. Instead, a brooding silence hung over the trees. Carl barely noticed.

"Ungrateful limey son of a bitch," he said for the fourth time. "If I hadn't come running when he called, he'd be knee deep in corpses by now. Who the fuck does he think he is, talking to me like that?"

He slammed his hand against the steering wheel. "I should turn this piece of shit car around, drive straight to the airport, and get the fuck out of this fleapit country. Let 'em sort their own mess out."

He'd toyed with the idea since the previous evening. Chances were that the hospital would only do a superficial post-mortem. They had no reason to expect foul play. If they did find anything, the silver solution was freely available at any chemist's. Steven would know, but would he do anything about it? Could he do anything? Was it worth risking arrest for murder?

"This is the last little errand I'm doing for that asshole. Once it's done, then so am I."

He felt better now that the decision had been made. Pangs of guilt blossomed at the back of his mind, but he crushed them before they could grow into anything that might make him reconsider.

He parked the car around the bend from the camp, retrieved a pistol from the glove compartment, lit a cigarette, and stepped out into the woodland.

The silence hung over the trees like a shroud. No animals rustled in the undergrowth. No birds sang in the trees. Carl chambered a round and moved along the track to the camp. He turned the corner to find the clearing empty.

"Hairy bastards hightailed it," he said to the forest. He wasn't surprised. Joseph had said as much. He just hadn't expected them to clear out so quickly.

He entered the remains of the campsite and gagged as he tasted the metallic tang of blood in the air. The grass was stained dark brown, except where dew had settled. The dewdrops were bright red, as if the ground were weeping blood. Carl's hand tightened on the pistol.

The tire tracks of the caravans did not lead onto the road. Instead, they vanished into the trees, where they were swallowed up by the foliage. A faint smell of smoke could just be detected over the heavy stench of blood.

Every instinct in Carl's body screamed at him to get away from this place. Small fragments of meat lay on the ground, buzzing with flies. Near the cold embers of the campfire lay a man's hand. A thick gold wedding band was on the third finger. Carl remembered seeing that ring on Joseph's hand the night before.

A howl carried through the trees and echoed around the clearing, making it impossible to determine the location or distance. Another howl answered. Then another. Then another.

High Moor

Adrenaline flooded the old man's system, and he fought to control the urge to run to the relative safety of his car. He knew that if he acted like prey now, he was as good as dead. He turned around and retraced his steps.

Branches snapped in the woodland to his left. Carl swung the pistol up as a pheasant burst from cover and flapped off into the high branches of a sycamore tree.

He rounded the corner, and his car came into view. The urge to sprint the last hundred yards was overwhelming, but he fought to retain his composure.

The undergrowth rustled behind him, and he brought the pistol to bear as a branch snapped to his right. Somewhere near, a deep growl came from the woodlands.

"Oh fuck this," he said and ran for the vehicle, as his last shred of self-control evaporated. He was aware of large, black shapes tracking him to either side, never showing enough of themselves to give him a target. He fired blind to his left. The car was close now. He would reach it in a matter of seconds. Without breaking stride he fished the keys from his pocket.

A short, middle-aged man stepped from behind a tree and blocked Carl's path.

Carl raised the pistol and pointed it at the man's face. "Get out of my fucking way, asshole."

The man smiled. "I hope you're not leaving just yet, Mr Schneider? I was hoping we would have a chance to have a little chat. Father to son."

Chapter 19

23rd June 1986. Hamsterly Forest. 06.10.

Carl narrowed his eyes and looked at the man before him. There was little in the way of family resemblance to Joseph. Where Joseph had been tall and broad shouldered, the newcomer was of medium height and build with short-cropped grey hair and bright blue eyes. Carl could have been looking at a younger version of himself.

"So, Mirela had another bastard. What did she do? Squeeze out a litter? Any more of you fuckers for me to worry about?"

The man's face twitched, and his eyes blazed with fury for a fraction of a second before the calm mask snapped back into place. "I am called Sebastian, and I am the last of Mirela's bloodline. There are no more...bastards for you to concern yourself over."

"Good. Not sure if my pension will cover all the child maintenance payments. Now, why don't you tell me what you want, before I blow your fucking head off."

Sebastian raised his hands and a thin smile played across his lips. "All in good time. There is no reason for us not to remain civil. Please, put down the gun, and we can discuss things like adults."

Carl nodded to the forest. "I'll put the gun down when you call off the dogs. Deal?"

Sebastian raised his hands. "Of course." He turned to the forest and called out, "All of you, return to the vehicle. I will be along in a moment."

Carl heard movement in the undergrowth and watched three indistinct forms move away through the trees. Once he was certain they were far enough away, he lowered the pistol. "OK, you want to talk, so talk."

Sebastian leaned against the bonnet of Carl's car. "I want to talk to you about two boys. I'm sure you know whom I refer to."

Carl shrugged. "They're dead. I killed one in the hospital last night. My associate took care of the other."

"I know all about the child in the hospital. Colloidal Silver solution, wasn't it? Very creative, I must say. How did your associate, the police officer, handle the other?"

"How do you think? The kid changed, and my friend shot him before he could hurt anyone. End of story. So, what happened here? Where are Joseph and the others?"

"They have been dealt with according to Pack law. They harboured a moonstruck and put our entire race at risk. The law is quite clear about the penalty."

"I keep hearing this word: moonstruck. I'm still not clear on what exactly that is. Care to enlighten me?"

Sebastian laughed. "My father, the great monster hunter. I would have thought that in the decades you have spend slaughtering my kind, you would have accumulated a little more knowledge about your prey. I'm not sure whether to be amused or offended by your ignorance. With most of us, the animal and human sides live in harmony. We change at will, and when we transform, we retain our intellect and reasoning.

"When one of us becomes moonstruck, the two halves are at war. The full moon forces the transformation, but the human side fights the change and the result is a creature caught half-way between man and beast.

"It knows only instinct, pain, and rage. It kills indiscriminately and draws unnecessary attention to our kind. That is why we put the afflicted out of their misery. For protection. Ours and yours."

"So you killed your brother for protecting your mother? That's pretty fucking cold. If Mirela had still been alive, would you have killed her too?"

The mask of calm on Sebastian's face slipped and his eyes took on a feral gleam. "If you had not murdered her, then yes. I would have put her out of her misery."

"Well, it's a goddamn shame you didn't get around to it sooner, or I wouldn't have had to come over here to clean up your mess. Are we done here?"

Sebastian smiled. "Yes, Mr Schneider, I'd say we are."

Carl raised his pistol and fired. Sebastian flew back against the car and rolled over the bonnet, lying prone on the other side of the vehicle. Carl groped for his car keys with trembling hands and unlocked the driver's side door.

As he reached for the handle, his peripheral vision caught movement to his left. He turned to face the threat too late. A huge black werewolf crashed into him, sending him sprawling to the ground.

Carl rolled to his right and brought up his pistol. The werewolf lunged forward, jaws gaping. He felt his arm slide past the open jaws, into the creature's throat.

Oh God.

High Moor

The jaws clamped down, through flesh and muscle, into bone. Carl squeezed the trigger. The sound of the firearm was muffled by his scream. The werewolf's brains blew out of the back of its skull as its fangs sliced through the skin and bone of the old hunter's wrist, severing his hand.

Carl wrenched his tattered stump free. The arm was ruined. Ribbons of flesh draped over shattered bone and shredded muscle.

He gritted his teeth and pulled his belt free of his pants. He wrapped the leather around his arm and tightened his makeshift tourniquet, then stumbled to the car door.

Howls erupted from the forest on all sides as he wrenched the door open and threw himself into the vehicle. Pain lanced through his arm, and he struggled to stay conscious. With his left hand, he tried to get the key into the ignition while he hit the central locking with his right elbow.

Shapes moved in the undergrowth, and three werewolves emerged from cover, onto the track, two ahead of the car and one behind.

He turned the key in the ignition, grateful that he'd chosen a hire car with automatic transmission. When the engine spluttered into life, he put the vehicle into reverse and slammed his foot onto the accelerator.

The car flew backwards, slamming into the werewolf that had been ready to leap at the rear window. Despite the agony in his arm, Carl couldn't help but take some satisfaction from the crunch of metal impacting bone as the creature was knocked aside.

He locked the steering wheel, and as the vehicle span around, he put the car into drive and accelerated away along the gravel path to the main road.

***

Sebastian got to his feet and dusted himself down. Three naked men stood beside him, while a fourth lay dead on the ground with a gaping hole in the back of his skull and the barrel of a 9mm protruding from the torn flesh of his throat.

One of the men stepped forward and looked at his leader with concern. "Are you alright, Sebastian? Are you hit? "

"Yes, but it is not serious. It seems that Gregor was not as lucky. Do you have his scent?"

The man nodded. "Gregor managed to take a bite out of the bastard before he died. The blood will make it easier to track him. What do you want me to do?"

"Wait until nightfall, and then follow the trail. He will lead us to the other child. When you find them, keep your distance. Don't engage them, just report back to me."

"And then what?"

Sebastian grinned. "When the moon is full, and the silver has purged itself from my system, we'll kill every last one of them."

***

23rd June 1986. John's House, High Moor. 07.00.

Steven felt exhausted. The events of the previous evening were catching up with him. Fatigue clouded his mind, and not even the strong black coffee had the desired effect anymore.

He felt jittery and nauseous, wanting nothing more than to go home, have a shower, and sleep for the next fourteen hours. He looked up from his mug at George and Caroline Simpson.

"I don't know what else to tell you. We need to get you and John out of here and find a place that we can safely contain him on the next full moon."

George ran his hand through greying hair and sighed. "It's not that easy, Steven. It takes months to move house. Even if this one sold straight away, it takes the bloody solicitors at least two months to sort the paperwork out. Can't we just do the same thing we did last night?"

"We could, George, but what if John builds up a resistance to the tranquilisers? What if the chains aren't secured properly when it comes round? We need to find a more permanent solution."

Caroline frowned and put her hand on her husband's wrist. "We don't want to leave our home. Is that so hard to understand?"

Steven rubbed his eyes and bit back the sarcastic comment that had formed on his tongue. "Look, there's something else. I didn't want to tell you earlier, in case it was too much to take in, but I think you should know. There might be more of them."

George glanced at his wife. "More what?"

"Oh for Christ's sake, George. More kittens. What the fuck do you think I mean? More bloody werewolves."

George's face fell. "Werewolves? Here? What do they want?"

"From what I've heard, they came to clean up the mess. Get rid of any evidence. That includes both of you, John, and me. All of us need to get out of here and lie low somewhere."

Caroline's hand tightened on her husband's. "If they're werewolves, then surely we have another month before we have to worry?"

"I don't think it's like that, Caroline. If they are anything like the others, then they can change any time they like. Even if that wasn't the case, they'd still be able to do plenty as men. It's too dangerous to stay here."

George and Caroline were silent for a moment. When George spoke, his voice had resolve that had not been there before. "My parent's house. It's been empty since Mam and Dad died. It's out of the way, and there's a basement. We could go there."

Caroline folded her arms and glared at her husband. "George, I don't want to live in your parent's old house. I want to live here, in the home that we made for ourselves."

"It's not forever, love. Just until we work out what to do next."

"I don't care, George. I'm not..."

Caroline's objections were cut short when the back door flew open and Carl Schneider staggered into the kitchen. The old American's face was ashen and he covered in blood. His right arm was an oozing stump, wrapped in the remains of his shirt and his leather belt to stem the blood flow.

He looked at Steven, eyes glazed with pain and terror. "You have to go. You have to leave now. They're coming. They're..." he managed before he succumbed to the blood loss and fell to the floor unconscious.

Chapter 20

23rd June 1986. John's House, High Moor. 08.45.

John stood in the shattered doorway of his bedroom with his hands on his hips. "Mam, I don't want to go to Gran and Grandad's house. It feels weird without them there."

Caroline's stance matched her son's. She fought back the angry response on the tip of her tongue and took a moment to compose herself before she responded. "John, I know. I don't want to go either, but you saw what happened to Mr Schneider. We have to go away for a while, just until this blows over."

"What about Marie? David and Michael are both...both gone. She's got no one left."

Caroline's demeanour softened. She put her arm around her son's shoulders as he fought back tears. "Marie will be alright. She's got her mam and...well, she's got her mam to take care of her. It's going to be hard, but she'll get through it."

John wiped his nose on the sleeve of his shirt. "At least I'll see her at school. Maybe she can come over for tea one night as well?"

Caroline took a deep breath. She'd been dreading this conversation. "About that, John. About school and...things. Your dad and I were talking, and we don't think you should go back. To school, I mean. I'll teach you from home from now on."

John eyed his mother with suspicion. "What? I mean, seriously? You don't want me to go to school anymore?"

Caroline frowned and fought the butterflies in her stomach. The next part was not going to go down well. "Not just school, John. You can't go to scouts anymore. You can't have your friends over. It's not safe."

"Well, I know it's not safe now, but when Dad and the Sergeant shoot all the bad werewolves, it'll be OK."

Caroline shook her head. "John, it's not safe for them. Your friends. You've got something wrong with you, and we don't know how else it can spread. Can you imagine Marie having to live with what you have? After everything else she's been through? Or one of your friends at scouts?"

John looked at his mother for a moment, mouth open in shock. "You're saying that I can't even see my friends again. Any of them? Ever?"

Caroline reached out for her son, only to find her outstretched hand slapped aside.

John backed away from his mother, into the ruins of his bedroom, tears flowing down his cheeks. "Don't touch me. You might catch something."

"John, please. We don't have any choice."

"You should have let him kill me. Better that than spending the rest of my life stuck inside with you."

John slammed what remained of his door, which was more than the last surviving hinge could stand. The shards of broken wood crashed to the floor.

Caroline fought for control of her emotions and pushed the tears deep inside until she'd done what she had to. When she spoke, her voice was firm and authoritative. "I know it's not fair, John, but we don't have any choice. Now pack your bags and get your arse downstairs and in that car. Don't make me get your father."

Caroline turned and walked away without waiting for a response. She made it downstairs and into the kitchen, before the wall inside her crumbled and the tears came.

John trudged downstairs ten minutes later. His face was red and swollen, and he struggled with two large rucksacks stuffed with the entire contents of his bedroom.

The back door opened and George entered the kitchen. He picked up two suitcases and was about to take them outside to the car when he noticed John. "I thought I told you to only get the essentials, John?"

"If you're really making me move away, and never see anyone ever again, then my computer, books, and comics are essential."

George looked at his son and sighed. "OK, fair enough. Now come on and help me get these things in the car."

"Can I at least say goodbye to Marie?"

George and Caroline exchanged glances. "No, John. I'm sorry, but Marie lost her brother last night. Her parents don't want you going round there and upsetting her more. They have enough to deal with."

John trudged after his father and helped load the car. Once the cases were in the boot and his mother checked that the gas was turned off for the fourth time, he was ushered into the back seat and locked in.

As the car pulled away, John looked back at Marie's house. She stood in her bedroom window, palm against the glass. She mouthed something to him that he didn't understand. John raised his hand in a mirror image of her pose. Then the car turned the corner and drove away.

***

24th June 1986. Bishop Auckland Hospital. 14:45.

Steven pushed back the thin curtain and stepped into the cubicle. Carl Schneider lay asleep on the bed, flat on his back and snoring.

Steven was shocked at his friend's appearance. His skin was off-grey, and the lines on his faced seemed more pronounced than before. A cocktail of intravenous drugs entered his system through a long, clear tube that disappeared beneath the blood-spotted bandage on the stump of his right arm. Steven was about to say something, but thought better of it and turned to leave.

"Where the hell do you think you're sneaking off to?"

Steven turned to face Carl. "I'm sorry, I thought you were asleep."

The old man regarded him with dull, flat eyes. "Well, I was until you came trampling through here like an elephant with a bee up its ass. Do you know how hard it is to get any shut-eye in this place?"

"Hey, I'm sorry. I just wanted to see how you were."

Carl raised his stump. "How the fuck do you think I am? It's your little errand that did this."

Steven bristled with a mixture of guilt and anger. "Well, I didn't expect your chew toy reference to be taken so literally. I thought you were supposed to be able to take care of yourself, you miserable old bastard."

Carl let out a weak, half-hearted laugh in spite of himself. "Ain't that the fucking truth. Shows how much I know. So, no flowers? No chocolates? I'm offended."

Steven grinned. "I didn't take you for a flowers-and-chocolate sort of bloke. Don't worry, I'll take the bottle of scotch I brought back to the shop and change it."

"If you do, I'll crawl out of this bed and shove your flowers and chocolates up your ass. Come on, don't leave an old man in suspense."

Steven produced a small bottle of whiskey from inside of his jacket pocket and put it on the bed.

"Bells? You brought me blended shit? You cheap fuck."

"It was the best that they had at the shop. Unless you would rather have had the own brand stuff? That was almost two quid cheaper. Again, I can change it if you like?"

Carl grabbed the bottle from the bed and held it to his chest. "I suppose I'll have to make do." He raised his right arm and moved it towards the bottle, then stopped and looked at the screw cap. "Ah fuck, for a moment I forgot about that. Don't suppose I could ask a favour?"

Steven took the bottle and removed the cap, then handed it back. "Are you supposed to be mixing that stuff with the drugs?"

Carl took a long swig from the bottle. "Do I look like someone who gives a shit? What's the worst that could happen?"

"Well, you could have a reaction and drop dead."

"Like that's a bad thing. You should have let me bleed out."

"Oh come on, Carl. Like I would have done that? People lose limbs every day. They make adjustments to their life and move on."

"Losing the hand ain't the problem and you know it. It's what took the hand. It's what the bite is going to do to me on the next full moon."

"Look, we can manage it. We're managing the boy, we can manage you. You just need to sort your head out and stop feeling sorry for yourself."

Carl glared at the younger man. "Feeling sorry for myself? Bet your sweet ass I'm feeling sorry for myself. I'm a fucking cripple, and in a little under four weeks I'm going to turn into the very monster that I've been hunting for nigh on four decades. I can't live with that, Steve. I just can't."

"Oh come on, Carl. That's bollocks. We'll find somewhere secure and lock you in for the night. Problem solved."

"Steve, I'm serious. When the time comes, I want you to take care of business. Can I count on you to do that?"

Steven looked at the floor. "I'm not going to kill you in cold blood, Carl. I'm sorry, but I won't."

"Then we have nothing more to say to each other. Get the hell out of my room, Steve, and don't come back."

12th July 1986. Castle Hotel, Durham City. 22.10.

The steady patter of rain against the window was punctuated by a pounding, bass rhythm from below and the sounds of raised voices. Sebastian got out of the bed and steadied himself against the bout of dizziness that swept through him. Sweat beaded on his forehead, and for a moment, he thought that he might pass out again. Then he regained control of his wounded body and walked across the room to the window.

Two police officers stood in a shop doorway across the street. One spoke into his radio, while the other looked on with visible apprehension. The sounds of glass breaking drifted up, and the younger officer said something to his companion. The other man put his hand on his colleague's shoulder and shook his head. After a few moments, the cacophony of noise from the bar subsided, and the only sounds were the bass thump of the music and the hiss of the rain.

The door to Sebastian's room opened and a large man with dark hair stepped inside. "It's madness down there. Why could we not have booked into a nice country hotel instead of this place?"

Sebastian didn't turn to face the newcomer. "Did you not enjoy your evening, Ivan?"

"These people are lunatics. The rain is coming down in sheets, and yet they walk around, half-naked, as if oblivious. There was another fight downstairs, and as far as I could tell, it was the top floor fighting those on the ground floor.

"They looked like they wanted to kill each other, and then they all just stopped and carried on drinking as if nothing had happened. I saw one of them buying a drink for someone that had punched him not two minutes earlier and congratulating his assailant on how hard he had been hit."

Sebastian chuckled. "It does no harm to spend time among the humans. If you can understand them, then it becomes easier to blend in. The ones in this place do seem a little stranger than some of the others I have encountered, I will admit."

"What is there to understand? They are animals."

Sebastian laughed out loud. "Ivan, if you do not see the irony in that comment, then there is no hope for you. Anyway, enough of the lessons on local customs. Have you heard from Dmitri?"

"Yes, I got his message earlier. He made it across the Austrian border and expects to be with the Pack in three days."

Sebastian nodded. "Any problems?"

Ivan shrugged. "There was an incident in France. Two customs officials with an overactive sense of curiosity. Dmitri made it look like an accident."

"It used to be so much easier to smuggle a corpse across borders. I miss the old days, Ivan. Things are becoming so much more complicated than they once were."

"You should have gone with him, Sebastian. The rest of us could have finished up here, and you could have gone back to recuperate."

"I'm fine, my friend. This is not the first time I have been shot with silver, and I doubt if it will be the last. I need to see this through."

"Because of Mirela? Or Joseph?"

"Yes. I loved my brother, and I miss him more than you could know, but it doesn't change the fact that he was a fool. My mother's situation was tragic, but if Joseph had not run with her, she would have been able to die with dignity, surrounded by those she loved, instead of being gunned down in the dirt. My big brother made a mess, and it falls to me to clean it up."

"I know that it's important to you, Sebastian, but why wait another week for your system to purge the poison when I could take Boris and end this tonight? We could be on the ferry first thing in the morning and home in a few days, instead of hiding out in this cesspool until the full moon."

Sebastian walked across the room to Ivan, grasped his shoulder, and moved his face to within inches of the other man's. "We need to know whether the boy is moonstruck. If he is not, then we will take him back with us. I appreciate your concern, Ivan, but the matter is not open for discussion." Sebastian released his grip and stepped back. "Are they all still there?"

"Yes, hiding out like rats. The policeman comes and goes, and the American did not return when he left the hospital. The boy and his parents never leave."

"Good. Have patience, my friend. This will all be over in a few short days. Then we can go home."

Chapter 21

21st July 1986. Treworgan Farm. 18.55.

Steven turned off the main road and drove through a maze of narrow country lanes. The evening sun flashed between the tall hedges, and the air was heavy and humid with the earthy scent of impending rain. He slowed the car and turned off onto a narrow gravel track. Dust clouds trailed his Ford Escort. He had to brake several times to avoid pheasants that leaped from the hedgerows and ran along the track ahead of him before darting away into the fields.

He passed between two parallel rows of horse chestnut trees that bordered the road, their limbs entwining to form a thick canopy. Then the house came into view.

The building was once a farmhouse. George's grandfather had owned most of the land around the property, but over time sold off the majority of the surrounding fields to neighbouring farms. By the time he died, only fifteen acres of woodland and pastures remained with the family. George had been trying to sell the place for six months, since his parents died. With the nearest neighbour over a mile away, it was a perfect place to hide, although the isolation made Steven nervous.

He parked the car next to George's Toyota, grabbed a canvas holdall and a large cardboard box from the boot, then walked up to the front door and let himself in. George walked from the kitchen to meet Steven, and took the cardboard box from him.

"Jesus, George. How many times do I have to tell you to keep the bloody door locked? I could have been anybody."

"I'm sorry. I could have sworn I locked it. Did you get everything?"

"Yeah. I got everything on your shopping list. No luck on the ammunition though. There's not many places around here making silver bullets, and even if there were, they wouldn't sell them to a suspended police officer with no firearms certificate. We'll have to make do with what we have and hope it'll be enough."

George carried the box of supplies into the kitchen and put it down on the worktop. "Are you sure that they'll come tonight?

Steven shrugged. "No idea. If it's going to happen, then the night of the full moon seems a likely candidate. Our attention will be split between John and them, and Carl wouldn't be able to help, even if he was still around."

"What makes you say that? Even one-handed, I'm a better shot than you'll ever be." said a voice from the hall. Carl Schneider stood in the doorway with a heavy pack slung over his back. "You should lock this door. Anyone could walk in."

"Carl? What the hell are you doing here?"

"That's gratitude for you. I'm here to save your sorry ass. Again."

"That's not what I meant. What's going to happen when the moon comes up?"

Carl winked at Steven. "Don't you worry yourself about it, Steve. I got it all under control."

"Meaning?"

"Meaning, I got it all under control. Now, are you going to stand there gawking, or are you going to give me a hand with this stuff? I seem to be one short."

Steven took the pack from the old man and almost dropped it due to the weight. "Jesus, what the hell do you have in here?"

"Just a couple of essentials."

Steven thought about opening the bag and changed his mind. Some things he just didn't want to know. Instead, he hefted it into the living room and laid it next to the faded sofa. "So, you think they'll come tonight?"

Carl regarded Steven with a curious expression. "What do you think?"

Steven felt as if he were in an examination. He thought about his response for a moment before speaking. "I think they'll come. It makes sense, and if you can track us down, then the chances are that they have as well."

Carl slapped Steven on the back with his stump. "Go to the top of the class, Steve. Now let's get this gear unloaded and get ready. We only have a few hours until dark."

***

21st July 1986. Castle Hotel, Durham City. 19.38.

Sebastian stepped out of the front door of the hotel and walked across the street to the waiting car.

Ivan got out of the vehicle as he approached. "Let me help you with that, Sebastian."

Sebastian glared at the other man. "I'm fine. Stop fussing like an old washer woman."

Ivan shrugged. "As you wish. Yuri reported in an hour ago. The American has arrived, as you predicted. The cattle are all in the trap. All we need to do now is spring it."

"Your confidence does you credit, but I would advise you not underestimate our quarry. Schneider has been slaughtering our kind for years, and the policeman survived an attack by a moonstruck. Even the boy's parents could get off a lucky shot."

"Bah, the American has one arm and will be in the midst of his change when we kill him. He will offer no resistance. The others are of no consequence. The policeman stinks of alcohol and fear, and the other two are frightened little rabbits."

"Have you forgotten the boy? Moonstruck werewolves, even as young as this one, can be quite formidable."

"The family will have him restrained. Once we kill the others, we can wait until dawn and kill him as he sleeps. You worry too much, Sebastian. We have faced worse odds than this before. Remember that fucking moonstruck outside of Prague in eighty-two?"

"Ha! Now that one was a handful."

Ivan grinned. "I thought I was going to shit myself when it came over the wall. You saved my life that day."

"Well, your distracting it by letting it eat you helped an enormous amount. I was most grateful."

Ivan laughed and made to slap Sebastian on the back but hit empty air. Sebastian was a blur of movement, almost too fast for the eye to follow. He grabbed Ivan's arm and forced it around his back, into a painful lock, and slammed him against the car door. Sebastian leaned in close, and when he spoke his voice was soft, almost a whisper. "I need you to remember who is the designated Alpha of our little group, Ivan. Your patronising comments and your false concern over the past weeks have been nothing but a clumsy attempt to make me look weak in the eyes of the others. Do you think of me as weak, Ivan?"

Ivan grunted in pain as his arm was forced further up his back. "No, Sebastian. Of course not."

"If you wish to challenge me for leadership of the team, then once this is finished, I will look forward to it. But be warned. If you say or do anything to belittle me again, I'll tear your throat out where you stand."

Sebastian released the other man and stepped away from him. Ivan stood on the pavement, red-faced, and balled his fists as if preparing to attack, then he relaxed his posture and got into the driver's seat. Satisfied, Sebastian climbed into the passenger's side and closed the door.

"Night will be upon us soon. Let's meet up with the others and put an end to this, once and for all."

***

21st July 1986. Treworgan Farm. 20.34.

Steven watched the sky. The final golden sliver of light from the sun had vanished beneath the western horizon ten minutes earlier, and the clouds had gone from white to orange and finally took on a deep crimson glow, as if filled with blood instead of water. Heavy, black storm clouds raced in from the southeast like a rolling blanket of malevolence. The scent of ozone hung in the air, and a faint rumble of thunder rolled across the countryside. He nailed the final plank of wood in place and turned to the group.

George and Caroline sat on the old sofa with their arms around John, who wept on his mother's shoulder. Carl was in the kitchen, doing something that he declined to share with the others.

"George, Caroline. It's almost time. You need to take John downstairs now."

George nodded his assent, and Caroline hugged her son tight. After a moment she released her hold and took the boy by the hand.

George took John's other hand. "Come on, son. We have to go and get you somewhere safe."

John sniffled and looked up at his mother with tear-filled eyes. "I don't want to, Mam. I don't want to change again."

"I know, pet, and maybe you won't if you try really hard. Better to be safe than sorry though."

Caroline led her son out of the room, and they descended the stone steps to the basement, with George following behind.

Steven put his hand on George's shoulder as he passed and held out a pistol. "George, take this. Just in case."

George shook his head. "No. No guns. You honestly can't expect me to shoot my son, no matter what happens."

"It's a fucking tranquiliser gun, you muppet. Better to have it and not need it, than need it and not have it. Now get downstairs and don't open that door no matter what happens. Got it?"

George took the weapon. "Thank you, Steven. For everything."

Steven nodded. "Go, see to your son. He needs you down there more than I need you up here. Carl and I will take care of everything else."

George nodded and followed his wife and son, then closed and bolted the heavy steel door behind him.

***

The basement had been a fruit cellar. At one point, George's father had subdivided it into several storerooms. It was in one of these that John would spend the night. They'd replaced the old wooden door with a reinforced steel one. The room was bare inside, and the faint smell of bleach and new paint permeated the air.

Sweat beaded on John's forehead. He shivered. He'd felt unwell for the last hour and, as the moon rose, his condition worsened.

"OK, son, it's time. Get undressed and we'll lock you in for the night."

John wiped a lock of hair from his eyes and looked embarrassed. "Do you have to watch?"

Caroline let out an exasperated sigh. "It's nothing I've not seen before a hundred times, John Simpson. Now stop messing about and get out of those good clothes before they get damaged."

"Dad? Please tell her."

George put his hand on Caroline's shoulder. "Come on, luv. He's a big lad now. Give him a second's privacy, eh?"

Caroline let out an annoyed tut and turned around so that her back was to her son. George did the same. Caroline angled her head a little to the left.

"Mam, stop looking! It's not funny."

"Alright, alright. Just get a move on."

After a few moments of shuffling, John announced that he was ready. George and Caroline turned to find their son wrapped in a blanket, with his clothes in a heap on the floor.

"Oh, John. You could have at least folded them up."

John fell into a crouch and screwed his eyes tight closed. "My stomach. It hurts."

George ushered his son into the storeroom and closed the door behind him. He slid the steel bolt into place and looked through the small viewing window at his son. "John, you've got to fight it, son. Don't let it beat you. Its mind over matter. Stay with us."

***

As soon as George closed the basement door, Steven went to the kitchen to find Carl. The old man sat at the kitchen table. He wore a heavy overcoat, and sweat ran across his face.

Steven sat down opposite him and leaned forward across the table. "OK, Carl. Time for you to fill me in on the plan."

Carl looked up at him through bloodshot eyes. "Plan? Who said anything about a plan?"

"For fuck's sake, Carl. Look at yourself. You're going to change any bloody minute. Are you just planning to sit here and wait for it to happen?"

"No, of course not. I'm waiting for the right time to come, before I act."

"Well, I hope for my sake that it comes before the moon rises. Where did you put the rest of the ammo? I've only got one clip for this pistol."

Carl shook his head. "There is no more ammo. I needed it. With any luck you won't need to use that pop gun at all."

"What the hell are you going on about? Will you just tell me what you're up to?"

Carl laughed and showed him.

Steven stepped back from the old man, a look of horror on his face. "Oh fucking hell, Carl. You can't be serious?"

***

21st July 1986. Treworgan Farm. 20.52.

Sebastian crouched in the undergrowth and suppressed a grin. The moon was rising, and he felt it in every cell of his body, a rush of power and ecstasy that made his limbs tingle. He knew that the others felt it too. Ivan, Yuri, and Boris stood beside him, stripped naked and eager for the hunt. Sebastian remained clothed. There would be time later to enjoy the slaughter.

With regret, he pushed his other self down into the recesses of his mind, where it growled and whined like an over-eager puppy. "Ivan, I want you to take Boris and Yuri. Circle the property, evaluate their defences, but remain silent and unseen."

Ivan's eyes shined as he struggled to retain his human form. "Why wait? We could be on them before they know what hit them."

"Have patience. At the moment there are two pups in that house that are feeling the moon, as we are. Before the moon rises, they will have to be restrained or they will kill everyone in that building. Once that happens, we will only have the three humans to worry about. Once we finish them, we can deal with Schneider and the boy at our leisure."

Ivan nodded and crouched down, with Boris and Yuri following suit. Hair flowed from their pores like a black tide. Bones snapped and reformed. Fangs burst from gums. After less than a minute, the transformation was complete. The three huge beasts turned and vanished into the thick foliage, leaving Sebastian alone.

"What are you thinking, Father? Will you hide and wait for your fate to claim you, or will you go down fighting?" He chuckled. "As if I didn't already know."

The first drops of rain fell from the sky, bursting onto the parched ground in a sporadic patter. The air smelled of wet earth, and Sebastian felt the hairs on his arm rise.

High Moor

The pull of the moon intensified until, combined with the anticipation, it was almost more than Sebastian could bear. Then the front door of the house opened, and Carl Schneider stepped outside.

Sebastian could see the old man sweating, even from this distance. He watched as Carl walked away from the house into the yard, then stumbled and fell to the floor. Carl's grunts of agony filtered through the steady patter of the rain and sporadic claps of thunder. The American got up onto one knee, and after a moment got to his feet.

"Come on, you fuckers. I know you're out there," he screamed into the oncoming storm. "Come out here and face me, Man to Mutt."

Carl opened his mouth to yell another challenge, but all that came out was an agonised wail. The moon had risen. His change was upon him.

Sebastian stepped from the undergrowth and walked over to Carl. "Do you feel it, Schneider? The power? The fury? Are you beginning to understand?"

Carl looked up at Sebastian with gleaming yellow eyes. The fangs burst forth, slicing open his gums in a spray of blood and foam.

Sebastian laughed. "You should know that I'm going to tear your head off before you complete your transformation, then I'll let Ivan eat your heart. Tell me, Father, while you still have the capacity to speak, do you have any last words?"

Carl smiled at Sebastian with a mouth full of razors and pulled open his coat. Three bricks of plastic explosives were strapped to his body. Those bricks were wrapped in layers of duct tape. Beneath the tape, dozens of bullet-sized lumps covered the surface of the explosives. Carl held a detonator in his clawed left hand. When he spoke, his voice was more animal than human. "Last words? Sure. How about, 'Who's the fucking daddy now, bitch?'"

Chapter 22

21st July 1986. Treworgan Farm. 21.00.

Steven watched the scene outside unfold through a gap in the boards that covered the living room window. He'd tried to reason with Carl, but couldn't find a convincing argument. If Carl stayed in the house, he'd change and kill them all. If they locked him in with John, then the two of them would tear each other apart. Carl knew this, and he knew that Steven had no choice but to go along with his plan. With barely suppressed tears in his eyes, Steven watched him connect the dead man's switch to the detonator. They shook hands and the old man went outside to his death.

The moon shone through the clouds, an indistinct silver glow that had an unmistakable effect on Carl. He stumbled and fell to his knees as the change swept through him. He screamed out in defiance, and then a short, grey-haired man walked from the tree line and stood just out of arms' reach, a mocking smile on his lips. The man's expression changed in an instant, from scorn, to disbelief, and finally horror. He backed away from Carl. The detonator fell from Carl's clawed hand. Steven threw himself to the ground and clamped his hands over his ears.

The explosion shook the walls of the house and blew the windows in. The expanding fireball illuminated the room with a bright orange light. Silver shrapnel punched holes in the door and window boards. Ornaments shattered into thousands of pieces. The television exploded.

Steven grabbed his pistol and got to his feet, with the blast wave ringing in his ears. He peered through one of the holes at the carnage outside.

Small fires burned around the yard, despite the rain. Holes riddled Steven and George's cars. The windscreens were blown out by the explosion, and shrapnel shredded the tires.

The ruined corpse of the werewolf lay in pieces back toward the tree line. Entrails stretched out behind the mangled torso, and the man's head had blown apart. Remnants of the dead werewolf's face draped over the shattered fragments of skull like a discarded rubber mask. There was not enough left of Carl to identify. Burning pieces of meat and bone covered the yard. The stench of burned flesh mingled with the sharp metallic tang of blood, the sulphurous reek of the explosion, and the heavy earthen scent of the falling rain. Steven said a silent prayer for his friend and looked around for any sign of life.

Maybe Carl got them all. Maybe it's all over.

A long, mournful howl resounded around the house, echoing around the yard and between the outbuildings. Two further howls, from different locations, answered the first; one from the rear of the house and another to the left hand side, by the sitting room. After a moment, a fourth howl replied. From the basement.

Steven checked his pistol. He had six rounds remaining and at least three hostile werewolves to deal with. He suppressed a rising wave of nausea, and as he chambered a round, his hands trembled. Fear threatened to crush him.

His fight or flight instinct pulled him in two different directions, paralysing him. He rubbed his eyes and strained his ears, alert for the slightest sound, trying to filter out the snarls of rage from the basement and the howl of the wind as it tore through the broken living room window.

A branch snapped outside. Claws clacked against the concrete of the footpath that circled the house. Then silence.

A shadow passed across the front door, gone before Steven could bring the gun to bear. A barely suppressed tide of panic rose in his chest. He caught movement out of the corner of his eye and swung the pistol round, but it was only the dancing shadow of a tree silhouetted against fire and moonlight.

He heard breathing. Heavy, regular, with the faintest hint of a growl held in check.

Then the lights went out.

Steven dropped into a crouch and backed against the living room wall. The only illumination was a flickering orange glow from the fires outside. His heart raced, and his sweating hands struggled to keep hold of the pistol. His limbs felt numb. He realised he was hyper-ventilating. He took a deep breath and tried to bring his terror under control.

Something collided with the living room window. A dark shape loomed outside. The wooden boards splintered as something chewed its way through them. Steven raised the pistol and fired.

The bullet blew a hole in one of the boards. The shape outside vanished.

Silence hung like a shroud, broken only by the pounding beat of his own heart and his ragged breathing. The back door shuddered in its frame when something slammed against it. The sounds of splintering wood from the sitting room and the kitchen followed.

Steven realised his mistake. All of the rooms led into one another. He couldn't defend all sides of the property by himself, especially with only five silver bullets. He moved across the living room towards the cellar, gun held out in a rigid double-handed grip. Each step felt like he was walking underwater.

He stepped into the hallway and searched the dark corners for any sign of life. Satisfied the way was clear, he sprinted to the basement door and grabbed the handle. Then one of the werewolves threw itself at the boarded-up window in the sitting room.

The boards shattered under the impact, showering the room in shards of glass and wood. A huge hulking figure, outlined in firelight, looked at him with glowing green eyes and snarled.

Steven sensed the impending attack. He raised his gun and fired at the malicious iridescent disks. The bullet tore a hole in the doorframe. He backed away until he hit the wall. Then the werewolf leaped.

Time seemed to slow. The creature's eyes dipped for a fraction of a second before the attack. Steven tried to steady his aim as the darkness of the room gave birth to a nightmare. The creature was massive. Coarse, black fur covered its muscular body.

High Moor

It regarded the man with intelligence and absolute loathing. Steven heard himself scream, and he pulled the trigger twice in rapid succession, more a reflex of his terror than an intentional act. The first round caught the airborne werewolf in the stomach and blew a fist-sized hole out of the creature's back. The second struck the monster in the head, splattering bone and brain across a picture of John's grandparents. The werewolf smashed into the wall beside Steven and lay still. Bones snapped and contorted. Hair receded into pores. Within moments, all traces of the wolf had vanished, leaving the ruined corpse of a naked man behind.

Steven stood frozen for a moment, too shocked to move. Then he regained his senses.

"Oh fuck this." He leaped to his feet and hammered on the basement door. "George, open the fucking door. For Christ's sake, open the door."

Steven heard John roar and renew his assault on the cell door below. Stairs creaked. The wind howled around the house, and the sporadic patter of rain turned into a steady hiss. He hammered on the door again. "George, get a bloody move on."

A flash of lightning illuminated the darkness of the sitting room. Another werewolf crouched on the carpet, ears flat against its head and teeth bared. A blur of movement came from the window, and a second creature landed beside the first. The monsters curled their lips and snarled. The bass growl merged into the low rumble of thunder from outside.

The door swung open. Steven threw himself inside, colliding with George. Both men rolled down the wooden stairs and landed in a heap on the concrete floor. The gun slipped from Steven's hand, skittered across the room, and came to rest in the far corner.

Steven looked up. The cellar door was still open. He untangled himself from George and started back up the stairs. Too late. The enormous form of a werewolf filled the door frame.

Where John and Mirela were bi-pedal, this creature moved on all fours. Long, pointed ears lay flat against the monster's head. The long, tapered snout was wrinkled into a snarl, lips pulled back to reveal two rows of razor-sharp fangs. Muscles moved like liquid beneath the layers of coarse, black fur. Terrible clawed feet, each toe ending with a black, curved talon that wrapped around the stairs, splintering the wood.

It tensed its muscles, ready to pounce. Steven held his breath and prepared to die.

The thunderclap retort of the pistol and the smell of gunpowder filled the cellar. The werewolf's head exploded in a cloud of hair, blood, and brains. Another shot rang out, shattering the foreleg of the already dead monster. The creature slumped to the floor.

Click. Click. Click.

Caroline stood against the back wall, the gun held in front of her. Tears of terror and rage streamed down her cheeks.

She walked towards the foot of the stairs, with the gun trained on the dead werewolf, and continued to pull the trigger of the empty weapon until Steven took it from her.

George got to his feet and put his arm around his trembling wife. "Is that all of them?"

A dark shadow filled the doorframe. Steven felt his heart sink. He had no more silver bullets. They were all as good as dead.

Unless.

The final werewolf looked at the terrified people with triumph in its eyes. It descended the stairs at a slow, measured pace. The clack of claws on wood counted down the last few seconds of Steven, George, and Caroline's lives. After what seemed like an eternity, it reached the bottom. It snarled and tensed its muscles to pounce.

Then Steven unlocked the door to John's cell.

The door burst open as John hurled himself against it. No trace of the ten-year-old boy remained in the creature standing in before them. It stood on two legs, well over six and a half feet tall. Coarse, brown hair covered sheets of rippling muscle. It sniffed the air, snarled at the three cowering humans, and then leaped at the other werewolf.

Claws flashed out as he swung at the silver-grey monster. It jumped back, only just avoiding the blow. It bared its fangs and snarled, then circled around to his left. John crouched and matched his opponent's movement. Then the silver werewolf pounced. Fangs flashed at John's throat, but he jerked his head back at the last instant and the teeth sank into the flesh of his shoulder.

Caroline took a step forward, reaching out her hand. "Oh God, John."

Steven grabbed her wrist and pushed her towards the cell. "Both of you, get inside while they're distracted. Move."

George couldn't tear his gaze away from the two werewolves. "But the door only locks from the outside."

Steven nodded. "I know, George. Now move your bloody arses before they remember us."

"Steven, you don't have to."

"I do, unless you have a better idea."

George shook his head and looked at the floor, unable to meet Steven's gaze. "No, I don't."

Steven ushered them both into the cell, closed the door, and slid the bolt home. "Don't be sorry, George. Take care of your family."

The fight intensified. The beasts crashed against the walls and smashed a wooden chair in the corner of the room into pieces. John lashed out with his claws and tore four ragged wounds in the side of the silver werewolf. The creature yelped and ducked under a follow up blow, then dove forward and bit a chunk of flesh from John's thigh. John roared in agony, slammed into the other werewolf, and they careened across the basement, towards Steven.

Both creatures were wounded. Whereas the silver werewolf was showing visible signs of weakness, the pain only seemed to fuel John's rage. His attacks became more brutal and frenzied.

Claws sliced through fur and muscle, fangs tore pieces of flesh from the silver werewolf's body until its fur was soaked with blood. The silver werewolf feinted forward, as if to return the attack, and then retreated from the enraged moonstruck. John pounced on it when it tried to flee up the stairs, and clamped his huge jaws around its neck.

The werewolf thrashed and snarled, but failed to break John's hold. The jaws tightened. Bones popped. Veins and arteries sprayed blood. Clouds of red mist filled the air and covered the walls. Then John's jaws closed. The severed head of the silver werewolf hit the floor with a wet thud before rolling down the stairs and coming to rest at Steven's feet.

Steven backed away until he came up against the stone wall. He watched as John tore the now human corpse into shreds of blood-soaked meat. John sniffed the air and turned around to face Steven. Scraps of torn skin hung from the side of the snarling beast's mouth. It began to descend the stairs, cautious at first, but growing in confidence. The wounds on its body were horrific. Ragged slashes across its abdomen oozed thick, crimson blood. Chunks of flesh had been torn from its shoulders and thigh, deep enough to show the bone. None of this seemed to bother it, as it stalked the former police officer.

Steven had nowhere left to go. He closed his eyes and waited for John to start eating him.

Ten seconds passed. Steven opened his eyes in time to see the werewolf slump to the floor with four darts sticking out of its right side. George peered through the small barred window with Steven's tranquiliser pistol in his hand.

Relief flowed through him; he fell to his knees. He looked up at George and managed a weak smile. "Oh fucking hell, George. You did it. You saved me."

George grinned back. "Well, it was the least I could do. It would be rude if I let our son eat you alive after everything you've done for us. Now get off your arse and let us out of this bloody cell before he wakes up."

***

22nd July 1986. Treworgan Farm, High Moor. 06.17.

The storm had passed. The rain first eased, then stopped altogether. The black clouds moved away, and the first glimpses of the early morning sun glimmered through the trees to the east. Steven stood on the porch and lit a cigarette. After he took a long drag, he coughed until he was almost sick. He looked at the cigarette, dropped it onto the muddy ground, and crushed it under his heel.

Picking up the shovel, he walked out into the yard. The rain had washed the blood into the earth and put out the fires during the course of the night, but the front of the house was still like an abattoir. Burned lumps of unrecognisable meat were strewn over the entire area, but it was worse when Steven saw something that he did recognise. A hand, or a scrap of tattooed skin, or part of Carl's head. He steeled himself and shovelled the remains of Carl Schneider into black plastic bags.

He worked in silence for more than half an hour, filling one bag, then another, then another, until he was satisfied that he'd gathered all of Carl Schneider's earthly remains. Then he leaned against the shovel and wept in silence.

George walked out of the house and across the yard. Steven didn't look up until he put his hand on his shoulder and said, "I've taken the ones from the house to the back yard. Dug a pit like you said."

Steven choked back his tears and turned to look at George. "How's John?"

"He's hurt pretty badly, but I don't think there's anything fatal. Caroline cleaned him up and bandaged him as well as she could. He's in a lot of pain, but I think he's going to be alright. The wounds were already clotted over when he changed back."

Steven nodded. "That's good. I'm glad."

George motioned to the black sacks. "Are they going with the rest?"

"No. The others we burn, but Carl gets a proper burial, or at least as close to it as we can manage. We owe him that."

***

22nd July 1986. Treworgan Farm. 09.30.

The bonfire had died down over the last couple of hours until all that remained in the fire pit were smouldering embers and charred bones. The stench of burned meat hung in the air like an oppressive cloud.

Steven, George, and Caroline stood next to a hole in the ground at the far edge of the property, near the woods. John sat on a wooden chair, his face pale. Three plastic sacks lay at the bottom of the hole.

George looked at Steven. "Do you want to say anything?"

Steven nodded. "Carl Schneider was a lot of things. He was a brave man, a complete pain in the arse, and he was my friend. He came over here to save us from the monsters that we didn't even know were among us, and gave up his life so that we might survive.

"There's a passage in the Bible about that kind of sacrifice, but for the life of me, I can't remember it. Hell, I don't even know if Carl was religious. What I do know is that, if there is a God, then Carl will be up there with him now, drinking his whiskey and laughing at me for being such a sentimental idiot." Steven took out a silver hip flask, undid the top, and poured the amber liquid into the grave. "Here's to you, Carl. I saved you some of the good stuff. Goodbye, my friend, and thank you. You will be missed."

Caroline and John wept while Steven and George shovelled earth back into the hole. When the task was complete, Steven stuck his spade into the earth as a makeshift headstone.

John looked up at his father and the ex police officer. "It's over then?"

Steven nodded. "For now, yes. There might be more of them out there, but for the time being, I think we're safe."

"What if more come?"

"Then we'll be ready for them, but I hope it won't come to that. If you're careful and stay hidden, then with any luck, this is the last we'll see of them."

"So what do we do now?"

End of Part 2

Part 3

Chapter 23

30th October 2008. A1 Motorway. 11.36.

The rain started to fall as John passed the Scotch Corner services. A thin damp mist condensed on the windscreen and fogged the interior of the car. He flicked the windscreen wipers on and turned the heater up to full. The warmth cleared the windows but did nothing to lift the dark mood of the car's occupant. He turned the radio on and listened to the news broadcast. More nonsense about someone resigning over a radio practical joke that went too far. He snorted and hit the scan button, skipping past classical music and people with stuffy voices talking about something irrelevant. He eventually settled for a classic rock station and relaxed back into his seat.

Flashing amber beacons lined the side of the road and stretched off into the distance where the drizzle imbued the lights with a pulsating orange corona. A lorry, three cars ahead, honked its horn in frustration. The traffic moved forward fifty feet and then stopped again. John drummed his fingers on the steering wheel in time to the music and played things over in his mind.

Someone had sent him a message. The appearance of a werewolf in High Moor, and the encounter with Malcolm Harrison, couldn't be a coincidence. It could be a trap. But if it was a trap to flush him out of hiding, why now, after all these years?

More to the point, why the hell am I walking straight into it?

He knew the reasons. If this was just a coincidence, then High Moor had a werewolf. Unless Steven was still around, he was the only one who knew about it. The only one who could do anything about it. Then there was Michael.

Michael's body was stolen from the hospital morgue the day after he died. Steven and his Father assumed it was the Pack removing evidence, but John always hoped that his friend had somehow survived. If it was Michael sending him a message, then he had to go back. Michael would have done the same for him.

The traffic started to move once more, and after a few miles, John cleared the road works. The landscape changed, becoming familiar yet strange. Wind turbines dotted the horizon, and the landscape of his childhood was eaten away by the grey and orange cancer of new housing estates until only sporadic patches of green were visible on the distant hills.

After John left the motorway, the changes became more pronounced. Dual carriageway bypasses replaced old, barely remembered roads. Houses and shops on the outskirts of town had been torn down, only to be replaced with orange brick-and-glass monstrosities that imposed themselves on their surroundings and matched neither the older buildings, or one another.

He passed the school, rebuilt after the fire in 1986. Where once, the school fields were surrounded by low wooden fences, they were now encased in a ring of seven-foot-tall steel railings with vicious spikes at the top and a yellow notice stating "Trespassers will be prosecuted." The place was more like a prison than a school.

The market place in the centre of the town was gone. In its place was an ornate paved square with a bandstand in its centre. Its false grandeur contrasted against the faded squalor of the shopping precinct beyond, with its abandoned, graffiti-daubed shops and litter-filled walkways. Those shops still open were either charity shops or discount chain stores with names like "Poundsaver". Most of the town now shopped in the large supermarket, built on the site of the old fire station.

Only a few establishments that John remembered from his youth remained. An old hardware store with a hand-drawn sign that had been faded when his father was a boy. A bakery where his mother once worked. A photographer's studio with paint peeling from the doors and window frame, and a thirty-year-old plastic sign bleached from exposure to the elements.

An old lady, wrapped up in a knee length overcoat and headscarf, pushed a tartan shopping trolley along the uneven concrete pavement. Her face was a creased mask of regret and cynicism, and she hunched her shoulders as she walked in an attempt to stave off the rain and biting cold.

High Moor

An overweight man in his early twenties, wearing jeans, a Newcastle United football shirt and little else, despite the rain, emerged from a bakery with a large pasty in one hand. He shot John a glassy stare and shoved the greasy food into his mouth. Chunks of filling fell to the floor and splattered across his trainers. The man seemed not to notice.

A gang of youths in hooded tops stood in the doorway of an empty shop, casting nervous glances along the street. A young child, no more than ten years old, cycled past on a BMX and, as he passed the group, he handed them a clear plastic bag containing white powder, then pedalled away as fast as he could. The gang moved out of the doorway and crept away, around to the back of the shopping precinct and out of sight.

John turned off the high street, towards the moor itself, only to find that the once-open expanse was gone. Now, a new housing estate covered the entire area. Even the old mine had been demolished and new properties erected on the site. John wondered if that had been such a good idea.

He drove past the moor and out of the town until the urban sprawl thinned and the tight-packed houses were replaced by open fields and small patches of woodland. John felt butterflies in his stomach. He hadn't been back to the house since the day after his seventeenth birthday, the day after he killed his parents.

A sudden wave of regret, loss, and guilt surged in his chest, and he pulled the car into a lay-by until the tears subsided and he was able to drive again.

He missed the turning and had to backtrack once he realised he'd gone too far. Thick weeds choked the track. The only indication that it existed at all would have been the overgrown hedges that flanked each side, if not for the fresh tire tracks in the mud and the flattened vegetation.

John reversed the car back onto the main highway and drove another half a mile before he stopped and parked on the side of the empty road. He got out of the car and put on a pair of thin leather gloves. He walked around to the rear of the vehicle, opened the boot, and after checking that he was alone, produced a thin metal torch and a 9mm pistol from one of the bags. He checked the ammunition, chambered a round, and tucked the weapon into the waistband of his jeans. Then, he crossed the road and set off across the fields toward his old home.

He kept close to the hedges and made slow progress, pausing often to listen for any sounds that were out of place, until the woods that marked the boundary of the property came into view. He removed the pistol from his jeans and crouched behind an overgrown hawthorn bush. The air was filled with the sickly sweet scent of rotting leaves. The steady patter of the rain and the distant hum of traffic were the only sounds that he could distinguish. There was no birdsong, only a brooding silence. John took a couple of deep breaths in an attempt to bring his racing heart under control, and then crept through the trees, around to the rear of the house.

High Moor

The years of neglect had taken their toll. Grasping brambles had overgrown the garden. A mountain ash had sprouted in the centre of what was once a neatly maintained lawn. His mother's vegetable beds were all but invisible beneath the encroaching weeds. Most of the glass in the greenhouse was gone, and ivy wrapped itself around the aluminium frame until it resembled the green skeleton of a building.

The house was worse. Slates were missing from the roof and the chipboard sheets covering the doors and windows had swollen with exposure to the elements until they burst free from the rusted nails that had held them in place.

The grass was flattened in a single track around the house. Someone had been here in the recent past. One person, judging by the tracks. John stayed low and listened for any telltale noises. Any indication that he was not alone, but again, heard nothing out of the ordinary. He picked his way through the overgrown garden and followed the path around to the side of the house. When he reached the edge of the building, he stopped and checked his weapon before he craned his head around the corner.

The front of the property was in no better condition than the rear. A sea of weeds had buried the gravel driveway. A pair of tire tracks led from the lane into the middle of the yard, and then the vehicle had turned around and gone back the way it had come.

Two cigarette ends lay next to the tracks. Whoever had been here was gone, for now at least. John put the pistol back into his pocket and walked up to the front door of his childhood home.

He took out his key fob and selected the tarnished brass key to the front door, still on his key ring after so many years, a constant reminder of where he'd come from and what he'd done. The front door had expanded in its frame and required several strong tugs before it creaked open for the first time in a decade and a half.

It took a moment for John's eyes to adjust to the gloom. The only light within came from the open door and shards of light entering through gaps in the window boards. Fifteen years of dust swirled in the air currents and danced in the light before winking out of existence as it entered the shadows. A small pile of letters and old newspapers were scattered across the faded carpet. John picked them up and checked the dates on the postmarks. None were more recent than 1995. He placed them on a table and headed into the living room.

The scents of rot and mildew, mingled with the faint ammonia tang of rodent urine, filled the damp air. The wallpaper was peeled back from the bare plaster and covered in black mould spots. The carpet squished underfoot. He entered the hallway that connected the rooms of the ground floor. The door to the kitchen was open, and he could see piles of washed dishes that had waited to be dried and put away for over a decade.

High Moor

A recipe book lay open on the worktop, the words buried beneath a layer of dust. His father's jacket was draped over a chair next to the kitchen table. John remembered his father's cursing when they got out of the car on that cold February day, and he realised that he'd forgotten it.

Long repressed memories flooded back. His mother sitting with him at the kitchen table, trying her best to teach him mathematics and science from old textbooks. His father coming in from the garden with dirty feet and the subsequent tongue lashing that he got.

John left the kitchen and walked to the basement door. He paused, his hand hovering above the doorknob. Annoyed at his hesitation, he grasped the handle and turned it. The stairs descended into pitch darkness. The air was heavy with a musky animal odour, even after so many years. There was no sign of rodent infestation, however. Rats and mice knew that this place had been the lair of a terrible predator and had stayed well away.

He descended the wooden staircase, testing each board before putting his weight on it. The door to his old cell lay open. Cleaning materials: a mop and plastic bucket, along with several bottles of bleach, stood against the wall. John bit back the tears, remembering his father's face at the window for each and every change, telling him to fight it, to keep control. The last thing John ever remembered when he turned was the disappointment in his father's eyes as the beast broke through and the change began.

He checked the door and was glad to see that it still functioned. He would need this place in a few weeks, unless he could finish his business here before the next full moon. Satisfied, he turned around and climbed the staircase.

He emerged from the dark, into the hallway, and turned to leave when a shape stepped from the shadows and blocked the open front door.

"You should really lock that door, John. Anyone could walk in."

"Yeah, it looks like they just did. Is that a gun in your pocket, Steven, or are you just glad to see me?"

Steven took a step forward and shrugged. He reached into his pocket and produced a 9mm pistol that was the twin of the one John carried. He put it on the table, next to the pile of post. "I'm glad to see you. What the fuck do you think? So, John, how have you been? It's been what? Fifteen years? You don't call, you don't write. I was beginning to think that you'd forgotten about me."

"You know how it is. Time gets away from you. It's good to see you, Steven. You're looking well."

The older man laughed. "That's bollocks, but thanks anyway. I know I look like crap. Cancer will do that."

"Is it bad?"

"Only if you consider terminal to be bad."

John nodded. "How long do you have?"

"No idea. Six months to a year, maybe. Two at most. Truth be told, I just don't think about it." He removed a pack of cigarettes from his coat and lit one, then broke into a coughing fit.

"Should you be smoking those, considering?"

"Stopping won't make much difference at this point, and I don't want to spend my last days pissed off because I'm craving a cigarette. Better to die happy. Anyway, what about you, John? Where the hell did you go?"

"I left straight after the funeral. The police weren't interested in me as a suspect, and I couldn't stand to be around here anymore. Not after what I did. And, if I'm honest, I thought you might decide to take matters into your own hands."

A wry smile played across Steven's face. "Well, I can't say that it never occurred to me. I know you didn't intend to kill your parents and the rest of those people, but the fact remains that you did. There was one slip up, and seven people were torn to pieces as a result. I wasn't sure whether letting you live was worth the risk."

"And now?"

"I'll reserve judgement. Has it happened since?"

John looked at his feet. "Twice. Once in Germany in ninety five, the other in Scotland in ninety nine."

"Deaths?"

"A few, but only people who deserved it. After ninety nine, I did my best to disappear. I bought a place in the middle of nowhere and stayed there. After that, no more problems."

"Fair enough. So what exactly are you doing back here?"

"Same thing as you, I imagine. I saw the news reports. I thought I might be able to do something."

"Like what? If it's another werewolf, and he's like you, then until the full moon, he's just going to be another person walking around in a town of forty thousand. When he changes, you'll be no bloody good because you'll be locked in your basement, howling at the fucking moon. What the hell do you think you're going to accomplish here, except for bringing another bloody werewolf into the equation?"

"I...I honestly don't know. I thought that I might be able to sense it, or something. Find out who it was before the next full moon."

"You can do that? Sense other werewolves?"

"I don't know. I thought I felt something, years ago, but I'm not sure. I thought it might be worth trying. Besides, I get the feeling that it'll find me first. The whole thing seems like someone is sending me a message."

"How do you mean?"

"The man that survived the attack, Malcolm Harrison. I knew him when I was a kid. He used to pick on us: me, Michael and Marie. The fucker made our lives hell. It seemed like too much of a coincidence. I thought it might be Michael."

"John, you're a fucking idiot. Michael died in 1986. I saw the body. If this is a message, then it's The Pack trying to flush you out. You shouldn't be anywhere near this place."

"I have to know, Steven. If it's The Pack, I'll deal with them and then get as far away as I can, but until I know for sure, I'm staying right here."

Steven picked up his pistol and put it back in his pocket. "I'm only going to tell you this once, John. Go home. Get back in your car and then piss off back to wherever you came from. Let me handle this."

"Sorry, Steven, but I can't."

"Your choice. Just be warned. Anything running around with fangs and claws on the next full moon is fair game. That includes you." Steven turned and walked out of the front door.

John stood in the doorway. "It really was good to see you again, Steven."

The old man nodded. "You too, John. You too." He turned and walked away into the rain.

Chapter 24

31st October 2008. Treworgan Farm. 19.45.

John was despondent after Steven's visit. Doubts clouded his mind, and he felt as if he were being watched from every shadow. In an attempt to distract himself, he assessed the damage to the house and set about trying to make it habitable once more.

He purchased two rolls of roofing membrane and a box of replacement tiles from a local builder's merchant and managed to repair the worst of the damage to the roof. Some of the supporting beams were rotten and would need to be replaced, but the hasty repairs had at least made the building watertight. He hired a petrol generator and four industrial dehumidifiers, which he positioned around the house in an attempt to dry the place out. Finally, he removed the boards from the windows and doors, to allow sunlight into the darkened rooms for the first time in years.

He ate a takeaway pizza in his old bedroom, which had escaped the worst of the water damage, and fell asleep on the same sheets that he'd slept in on his seventeenth birthday.

His sleep was troubled. Claustrophobic dreams of being trapped in an elevator filled with blood plagued him, and he awoke sticky with sweat several times during the course of the night. When the dawn came and the light woke him, he felt as if he hadn't slept at all.

High Moor

John drove around the town for hours and walked the length of the high street at least four times, hoping he would feel something, any indication at all that there was someone like him nearby, but he felt nothing. Nothing of another werewolf, and nothing for the small town where he had grown up. He walked in anonymity through the streets, visiting childhood haunts. No one recognised him, and he saw no familiar faces in the crowds that rushed past in the street. He was an intruder here. He didn't belong.

He returned to the house at four in the afternoon, thoroughly depressed, and began the mammoth task of cleaning over a decade of filth and neglect from the place. After four hours' hard work, the house began to look habitable. He scrubbed the kitchen work surfaces and floor until all trace of dust and mould had been removed. Then he tackled the bathroom, living room, and his bedroom. He hadn't managed to get the electricity and gas reconnected, despite several irate calls to their call centre. Instead, he cooked a simple meal on a portable gas stove and ate it off his mother's best china by candlelight, with a glass of cheap red wine.

He sat at the table, his meal completed, and thought about his next move. "Think, dammit. You're not going to get anywhere by wandering around the town with no clue. So come on. What's the plan?"

He poured himself another glass of Merlot and thought about his options. There wasn't much to go on. One attack, three weeks ago. One witness. Realisation dawned on him, and he groaned. "Oh bollocks, I'm going to have to talk to Malcolm bloody Harrison."

31st October 2008. The Sandpiper, High Moor. 21.00.

John looked up Malcolm's home number in the phone book and called, posing as a reporter doing a follow-up on the attack. A woman with a harsh northeast accent answered, and informed him that "The useless fat bastard's down the pub with his waster mates. Again." John thanked her, hung up the telephone and then called a cab.

The taxi driver dropped John off in the pub car park. The building was a casualty of nineteen sixties architecture, flat roofed with corroded aluminium window frames and pebble dashed render covering the concrete walls. Paper pumpkins and witches decorated the windows, and strobe lights flashed against the glass as they pulsated in time to the music from within.

A group of people gathered by the entrance, smoking cigarettes, forced to congregate outside in the bitter wind after the smoking ban the previous year. Witches in short skirts mingled with vampires and zombies. An argument broke out between a short girl dressed as a nurse, and a shaven headed young man in a monk costume.

The girl's friends dragged her away as she kicked and screamed obscenities at the monk. The monk shrugged and lit another cigarette as John stepped past him, into the pub.

John felt light headed and sweat beaded on his palms as he stepped into the crowded, noisy building. People stood five deep at the bar and screamed conversations at each other, in an attempt to be heard over the pounding music.

High Moor

John pushed his way through the dancing crowds and found a space next to a concrete pillar, where he could stand without being shoved or jostled. He usually did his best to avoid people, and he didn't feel comfortable being in such close proximity to this many. He realised something. This was the first time he'd ever set foot in a bar on a Friday night. It didn't look like he'd been missing out on much.

He tried to relax. He was here for a reason. The sooner he found Malcolm Harrison, the sooner he could get out of here. He scanned the area, but there were too many people packed around for him to see much from his current position. He stepped away from the protection of the pillar and squeezed through the gyrating throng, around to the other side of the bar.

This side of the pub, while busy, was nowhere near as crowded as the area around the dance floor. People sat around stained wooden tables, sipping their drinks and trying to hold a conversation over the relentless bass beat of the disco, or stood in small groups around the walkways between the seating area and the bar. John scanned the faces around the tables and grinned when he located his target.

The years had not been kind to Malcolm. The last time John saw him, he'd been a stocky boy, with thick brown hair, and sunken pig like eyes. Now that stocky frame had swollen into rolls of flab that protruded from under his t-shirt. His head was shaved in a vain attempt to hide his encroaching baldness. His small, beady eyes were red-rimmed and staring.

Apparently Malcolm had started the evening's celebrations early. John moved closer and made a show of putting a couple of pounds into the one-armed-bandit next to Malcolm's table, while he listened in to the conversation.

A small, grey-haired man in an old t-shirt and stained jeans leaned across the table. "So, come on then, Mal. Tell us what happened, again."

Malcolm took a swig from his pint glass and puffed himself up. "Fuck's sake, Billy. How many times you have to hear it. I was walking the dog, when something got hold of him in the park. I ran over and chased it off, but by the time I got there it was too late."

Billy sniggered. "That's not what I heard, mate. I heard you ran like Usain fucking Bolt all the way back to your house, crying like a big lass the whole way."

Malcolm's faced turned beetroot and he got to his feet. "Who the fuck told you that?"

Billy grinned. "Your Karen. She told everyone. Well, she told Lizzie Fletcher, so she might as well have."

The other men around the table, a tall, thin man with dark greasy hair and a fat red faced man with blond hair burst into laughter. Malcolm slammed his fist into the fruit machine that John was pretending to play. "Fucking bitch! I'll kill her when I get home." He looked at John and his piggy eyes narrowed. "Do I know you, mate?"

John stepped back, surprised. "Erm...no, sorry."

"Then why are you so fucking interested in our conversation?"

"I'm a freelance journalist, looking into what happened here. Sorry if it looked like I was listening in. I was just trying to work out the best way to approach you."

Malcolm turned his head to his friends. "You see that, you fucking losers. I'm famous." He looked back to John. "So, how much we talking about?"

"I'm sorry? How much...?"

"Money. For the story. What the fuck do you think I meant?"

"Ah, right. Well I've got to sell the story on, but how about I get a few rounds of drinks in and we just have a chat?"

The thin, dark-haired man regarded John. "Are you sure we don't know you? There's definitely something familiar about you. You been on TV or something?"

"No, nothing like that. I grew up around here, but I've not been back for years."

"What's your name? I might remember you?"

"It's John."

The blond man's eyes widened in recognition. "John Simpson? Are you John fucking Simpson?"

John felt his stomach lurch. He hadn't counted on being remembered. He thought about lying, but realised that, at this stage, it probably wouldn't do much good. "Yeah. I'm surprised you recognised me after all this time. Sorry, but your name is...?"

Malcolm's hand slapped down onto John's shoulder. "Don't you remember my friends? Billy, Simon and Lawrence? We definitely remember you."

"Look, I don't want any trouble, lads. I'm sorry for bothering you on your night out. I'll leave you in peace."

Malcolm shook his head. "Don't talk shite, man. Stay and have a drink with us, and I'll tell you everything you want to know, so long as you tell us what happened to you."

"What happened to me?"

"Fuck, yes. You're a bloody urban legend around this town. All that shit happened, and then you just vanished, never to be heard from again. Until now. Come and have a couple of pints and we'll swap stories. OK?"

John relaxed a little. The red wine he'd had earlier was having an effect, but he was still a long way from being drunk. "Alright. I'll stay for one. Pints?"

The men at the table nodded their agreement and John pushed his way through to the bar. He returned ten minutes later with five pints of lager, precariously balanced on a metal tray. Billy and Lawrence got up from their seats to make space for John and then sat back down beside him.

Malcolm raised his glass. "Cheers, John. Sorry if we were a bit hard on you back then. Kids can be cunts."

John raised his glass to Malcolm's impromptu toast. "That's alright. Like you say, we were kids. No hard feelings."

Malcolm exchanged a brief, furtive glance with his friends, and took a long swig from his pint, downing half of it in a single mouthful. "So, you first. Where did you disappear to?"

John sipped his drink and tried to work out exactly what to tell the other men. He hadn't been prepared for this conversation. "Well, after what happened, my parents decided that we should move away. So, we moved into my grandparents' old house, my mother gave up work and home schooled me until I was seventeen. Then I moved away. Went to college, did some travelling and ended up doing what I'm doing now. When I read about your encounter, I thought there might be something that the Nationals had missed, so I thought I'd come up here and poke around for a bit. It gave me an excuse to fix up the old house and get it sold as well. I've been putting it off for fifteen years and if I didn't do anything with it now, the chances are it would have fallen down."

Billy picked up his beer and took another mouthful. "Is that it? Everybody thought there was something more...interesting going on."

John smiled. "Sorry to disappoint. The truth hardly ever lives up to the stories, I'm afraid. You see that all the time in my line of work. You spend weeks chasing down a lead, only to find that it's a lot of bollocks. So, what about you, Malcolm? What happened last month?"

Simon sniggered. "Yeah, Mal. Seeing as we're on the subject of bollocks."

Malcolm's face flushed, but he didn't rise to the taunt. "Not here. Too many nosey bastards listening in. Come on, we'll go outside. I need a smoke anyway."

Malcolm, Billy, Simon and Lawrence downed the remainder of their pints and got to their feet. John put his half full glass down on the table and started to stand.

"You not finishing that?" said Simon. "Fucking waste of a good pint, especially considering how much the bastards in here charge."

John shrugged and finished the rest of his beer, then stood up. He immediately wished that he hadn't. The room span for a second, and he had to grab the table to steady himself. He didn't drink often, and he never did to excess. Two glasses of wine and a pint of lager seemed to be his limit. He took a deep breath, and when he was happy that he retained at least some basic motor function, he followed the others out of the busy pub.

The cold hit him like a hammer, although the others didn't seem to notice. He'd forgotten how bitter the wind could be in North East England. The climate of his Welsh mountain home seemed mild by comparison.

The cold was like a living thing, biting his flesh and penetrating his clothing. He opened his mouth to comment on it, when Billy and Lawrence grabbed his arms, while Simon grabbed him from behind, and forced his arm across his throat in a choke hold.

"What the hell?"

Malcolm stood before him, all pretence at friendship gone from his beady eyes. "Do you have any fucking idea, John, how long we've been waiting for you to show your face around here?"

High Moor

John struggled to catch his breath and cast a beseeching look at the bouncer, standing just inside the doorway. The man smiled and closed the door. Somewhere within his mind, his other half growled as it awoke. He pushed it deep down inside. "What the fuck's going on? What did I ever do to you?"

Malcolm's red face turned a deeper shade of scarlet. "What did you do? You hear this, lads? What did he do? I'll tell you what you did, John." Malcolm's fist flashed out and struck John in his solar plexus, knocking the wind out of him. "You ruined our fucking lives, is what you did. You and that gobshite friend of yours, and his little slag of a sister. You remember now? Setting us up with that school thing? We did five years in Borstal for that, and when we came out, no one would give us any kind of job worth a shit."

John struggled to breathe. The growl within turned into a snarl as his beast reacted to the assault. He lifted his head to look at Malcolm and for a moment, the feral look on his face caused the other man to take a step backwards.

"If I remember right, it was you fucking geniuses that burned the school down. I didn't give you the matches, or the pot, or the vodka. You fucked up your lives all by yourself."

Malcolm's fist lashed out again, and connected with John's mouth. His upper lip burst under the impact, shredding against his teeth. Malcolm shook his fist and stepped up close. "That's right, you clever bastard. But you were the ones that lured us there. You were the ones that called the police."

Malcolm's knee came up and struck John in the stomach. The air was forced from his lungs and he sagged against the grip of Billy, Simon and Lawrence.

John tried to focus, using every scrap of willpower to keep his beast in check. The monster inside him raged against the brick walls in his mind. He could imagine darting forward and clamping his teeth onto Malcolm's throat, feel the hard lump of the other man's Adam's apple crunch beneath his teeth. The taste of hot salty blood in his mouth and the satisfaction as the prize was swallowed. He struggled to regain control, knowing that it was all but useless. He was losing it.

Malcolm leaned in close. Close enough for John to smell the foul stench of his halitosis. "You got something to say, fuck-flaps? "

John could feel himself slipping away. The alcohol had been a big mistake. It weakened the walls he'd spent decades constructing, and the beast was throwing itself against them. He imagined cracks starting to appear. In moments it would be free.

"For Christ's sake, Malcolm. We were bloody children and it was almost thirty years ago. What the fuck is your problem?"

"What's my problem? Right now, my problem is you. I'm going to sort that out right now. You're going to leave here in an ambulance, you wanker. I'm going to make sure you never walk again."

A female voice called out from over Malcolm's shoulder. "Malcolm? Malcolm Harrison?"

Malcolm paused and turned his head. A bright red pointed shoe appeared between his legs, followed by the sickening thwack of leather meeting testicles. His eyes crossed and he slumped to the ground.

A tall woman with light brown hair stood behind him. She spat on his prone form. "Even after all these years, you're still a fucking twat."

The beast raged within John, giving him new strength. He flung Billy and Lawrence away as if they were children, and slammed his head back into Simon's nose, which shattered under the impact.

The woman winked at him and held out her hand. When she spoke, it was with a bad, fake Austrian accent. "Come with me if you want to live."

John couldn't believe what he was seeing. The woman standing before him was Marie.

Chapter 25

31st October 2008. High Moor Town Centre. 21.55.

John and Marie ran down the alley between the pub and the shopping precinct, out into the car park. Without breaking stride, they reached the edge and leaped over the low brick wall that separated it from the road, then turned the corner onto the high street and left their pursuers far behind. Lawrence and Billy gave chase for a couple of minutes before they gave up and stood yelling breathless threats.

They ran for another two-hundred yards, then stopped to catch their breath. John checked the street, but there was no sign of Lawrence and Billy. Malcolm and Simon were in no state to follow. He turned to look at Marie. When John had last seen her, she'd been an eight-year-old girl, crying at the window. The woman beside him was almost unrecognisable. Only the colour of her hair, the slight tilt of her nose, and the mischievous twinkle in her green eyes remained of the little girl from so many years before. She was tall, maybe five foot ten, slim, and wore a short, black evening dress. Gooseflesh prickled across her arms.

John took his coat off and handed it to her. "Here, you must be freezing."

Marie shook her head. "No, you're alright. You know what it's like around here. People catch you wearing a jacket on a Friday night and they'll start to think you're a southerner."

John laughed. "Marie? It is you, right?"

She smiled. "Got it in one. I recognised you as soon as I saw you. That was Malcolm Harrison and his little friends trying to re-live the good old days wasn't it? What did you do to piss them off?"

"Seems like they've been holding a grudge over that whole burning school thing, back in the day. I could have handled it."

Marie raised an eyebrow. "Yeah, right. Whatever you say. Are you OK? You've got blood all over you."

John wiped his face. "I'm fine. It's just a little cut, and it's clotted over now. Anyway, enough of that. I can't believe it's you. How the hell are you? It's been how many years?"

"More than I care to remember. I'm alright, though. Life didn't turn out quite the way I expected, but it's all good."

"How do you mean?"

Marie rubbed her arms. "Listen, John. We could stand here, in the middle of the street, freezing to death, or we could go and grab something to eat, a couple more drinks, and talk in the warm. What do you say? Wanna take a girl out to dinner?"

"What? Oh, yes, of course. Where should we go? Is anywhere around here even going to be serving food at this time of night?"

Marie grinned. "Don't worry. I know just the place."

***

The Monsoon Indian restaurant was just around the corner. John opened the door for Marie, and was enveloped in a blanket of warmth laden with the scent of exotic spices. Only one other couple sat in the window, waiting for their empty plates to be taken away. A waiter tried to seat John and Marie next to them, but Marie insisted on a table at the back, well away from the window.

The restaurant was decorated with red flock wallpaper and complex pieces of Indian parchment artwork. An ornamental fish tank, filled with tropical fish stood in the centre of the room. When John walked past it, the fish darted to the other side of the tank and bashed themselves against the glass. John hoped no one had noticed.

The waiter showed them to their table and passed them a menu. "Would you like anything to drink while you wait?"

Marie settled into her seat. "Yeah, I'll have a pint of Kingfisher and a bottle of...what's your house red like?"

"The house red is very good." He turned to John. "And for you, sir?"

"Just a glass of water and a black coffee for me, please."

Marie raised her eyebrow. "You not drinking?"

"No. I think I've had enough for tonight. Don't mind me."

Her eyes narrowed, and her lips tightened over her teeth. "You trying to get me drunk?"

John felt his cheeks flush. "Oh, God, no. Nothing like that. I meant..."

She laughed. "Don't worry, John. I'm just messing about. So, what we having?"

He looked at the menu, perplexed. "I have no idea what any of these things are. This is my first time in one of these places."

"Seriously? You've never had a curry before? Oh, you have no idea what you've been missing. How can you get to your age and never have an Indian?"

He shrugged and looked embarrassed. "I suppose I'm not much of a restaurant person."

"You don't get out much then? What's she like?"

John looked confused. "What's who like?"

"The woman who keeps you locked inside? She must be doing something right."

He shook his head. "No, there's no one. I just don't get out much."

"Well, this is going to be a new experience for you. Are you a veggie?"

"No, far from it."

"Good. How hungry are you?"

John hadn't realised before, but he was starving. Their close escape had sent his metabolism into overdrive, and the meal he'd eaten not two hours before was a distant memory. "I could eat a bloody horse."

She raised her hand. "Alright, mate? We're ready to order."

The waiter made his way to the table and took out his pad and pen. "Yes, madam?"

"Two chicken madras, two pilau rice, one sag aloo, one aloo gobi, two keema naan's, and some poppadoms."

"Thank you. Is there anything else?"

Marie looked across at John and smiled. "Yeah, better bring a jug of water instead of a glass for my friend."

The waiter smiled out of the corner of his mouth and took the menus. "Very good. Would you like ice in the water?"

Marie nodded and the waiter disappeared into the kitchen. Then she turned back to John. "So, where the hell did you disappear to all those years ago?"

John looked at the table. "I wasn't given much choice, Marie. My parents made the decision that we were moving to my grandparents' house and that was it. We packed up and went. I wanted to say goodbye, but they didn't let me. I'm sorry, for what it's worth."

"Do you have any idea how I felt back then? I was crushed. I lost the three most important people to me inside of a couple of months. Two of them within twenty-four hours of each other. It tore me apart."

"I don't know what to say. I didn't want to go, but there wasn't anything I could do about it."

Marie flicked her hair out from her eyes. "Pff, you could have at least written. Or looked me up on bloody Facebook for that matter." She looked at John's guilt-ridden face and chuckled. "Don't worry about it, John. I've wanted to have that rant for more than twenty years. It's out of my system now, I promise. So, come on then, tell me about what you've been up to for the last couple of decades."

John relaxed a little and took a sip from his water. "There's not much to tell. I lived at my grandparents' house until I was seventeen, and when my parents died I moved around a lot. Did some travelling in Europe and eventually settled in Wales. I'd invested the life insurance in some properties before I left. When the house prices went crazy I sold them off and had enough to clear my own mortgage and set myself up a small business designing websites. That's about it. How about you? You still living here then?"

Marie took a sip from her pint and wiped the froth from her lips. "Only for the last few months. My mother's been in a care home for years, and she got ill a while back, so I took a leave of absence from work and came back to be with her. Dad's been dead since I was thirteen, and there just wasn't anyone else."

"Oh, I'm sorry. Is she going to be alright?"

Marie shook her head. "She passed away a couple of weeks ago. I've just been sorting out her affairs since then. It's a horrible thing to say, but in some ways it's a relief. She didn't really know anyone was there towards the end. Her mind had been gone for a long time. The only thing left of my mother was her shell, carrying on because it didn't know any better. It's strange and sad really. I'm the last member of my family, and I'm a girl. The family name dies out with me." She took a long drink of her beer and looked up at John with an apologetic smile. "God, this is depressing. Can we change the subject?"

John felt a wave of relief sweep over him. This was not how he'd expected the conversation to go. "So, you said that you'd taken some time off work. What do you do?"

"Nothing too interesting. I'm in recruitment. You meet some interesting people once in a while, but usually it's the same old, same old. I enjoy it though, so it's OK. Oh great, here's the food. About bloody time."

The waiter arrived with a tray of steaming food in stainless steel bowls and placed them on the table. The aromas blended into a rich tapestry of scents that made John's stomach grumble in anticipation. He piled his plate high and took a large mouthful of the chicken madras.

"Mmm, this is really good. I've never tasted anything quite like it."

Sweat beaded on John's forehead, and he reached for a glass of water.

Marie sniggered. "Everything alright, John?"

"Yeah, great. It's just..." He took another mouthful of water and then another mouthful of the curry. "...a bit hotter than I expected it to be."

"If you're going to experience a good curry for the first time, there's no point in starting off with the wimpy stuff. Might as well have a baptism by fire."

John wiped the sweat from his brow again and took his jacket off. "So you started me off with the hottest one?"

Marie grinned and shook her head. "No, that would have been cruel. What you've got there is a six, maybe a six and a half. We'll have to work you up to the really hot ones."

"I suppose I should be grateful that you didn't give me a ten. I think my mouth's melting as it is."

"You'll be fine. By the time you finish you won't even notice the heat."

"Yeah, because it'll have burned all of the nerve endings out of my mouth."

"You think it's bad now, just wait till tomorrow."

"Why? What happens tomorrow?"

Marie put on an innocent expression. "I wouldn't want to spoil the surprise."

The rest of the evening flashed past. They talked about things that John had half forgotten. Old memories that filled him with warmth and a faint sense of nostalgia, tinged with regret. Marie talked about her job and some of the places that she'd been. John responded with amusing stories about his customers. All too soon the restaurant staff turned the lights down and stood around the bar with impatient expressions.

John nodded towards the waiters. "I think they're trying to tell us something. Not sure what, though."

Marie laughed. "Yeah, their problem is that they're being too subtle instead of just telling us to fuck off so they can go home."

"I suppose it is quite late. I've really enjoyed tonight, Marie. I can't remember the last time I had this much fun."

Marie reached across the table and took his hand. "Well, you know, we might not be so young anymore, but the night still is. I've got a bottle of wine back at the flat I'm renting. You could come back and we could carry on talking...or something."

John felt panic surge in his stomach. He snatched his hand back and got to his feet. "Erm, I'm sorry, but I can't. I've got an early start in the morning. I'll give you a call later." He put on his jacket and walked to the door, then paused and turned back to face her. "I really will call, Marie. I had a great time tonight, and it's been amazing to see you again. I'll talk to you soon." Then he turned and walked out into the night.

***

Marie slapped herself on the head with the palm of her hand. "Way to go, Marie. Real subtle. Nice one." She upended the wine bottle and drained the last dregs into her glass, then downed it in a single gulp. She put her head in her hands and exhaled a long, slow breath, then looked at the empty doorway. "Bollocks."

***

1st November 2008. High Moor Town Centre. 01.25.

From a van parked across the street, Steven watched John leave the restaurant. John appeared to be flustered. His body temperature was elevated by several degrees, according to Steven's infrared goggles, and he appeared to be cursing as he strode down the street towards the taxi rank.

He stopped after a few yards and looked back, uncertain of himself. Then he punched a wooden billboard with a force that made Steven wince and joined the back of the taxi queue. The readings on John's body temperature returned to normal, helped by the cold night air. Steven relaxed and removed the goggles, then ejected the silver bullet from the high-powered rifle at his side.

High Moor

Things had been on the verge of going bad earlier. John's altercation with the local meatheads had driven him to the very edge of changing. His body temperature soared, and Steven had been seconds away from putting a heavy calibre round into his skull when the woman intervened.

The woman. Who the hell was she? John clearly knew her, but as far as Steven was aware, he'd been isolated from the rest of the world since he was a child. He thought back, trying to focus his mind through the haze of his pain medication. There had been a girl, once. Of course. He couldn't believe he'd forgotten. The Williams girl. The one that had lived next door to him. The one whose brothers had died. If John suspected that Michael was still alive, it made sense that he'd contact the sister. Satisfied that the evening's loose ends made sense, Steven stowed his equipment and drove out of town towards his home.

After fifteen minutes, he turned off the main road and drove through a maze of narrow lanes until he came to a pair of imposing metal gates, flanked by ten-foot-high granite pillars and high stone walls. Steven pushed a button on his key-fob.

The gates slid open to allow the van access and then closed when the vehicle had passed. Floodlights clicked on across the front of the property as the infrared sensors registered the car. He pulled up to the front of the house, a former Georgian farm constructed of red brick with steel bars across all of the windows, removed the holdall that contained his weapons from the passenger seat, and walked up the steps to the front door. He punched a code into the silver numeric keypad and stepped inside.

A high-pitched electronic whine, just above the human auditory range, made his fillings vibrate. He walked to a control panel on the wall, disabled the ultrasonic siren and the sprinkler system that would have dumped five-hundred litres of silver nitrate over every inch of the house in another ten seconds, then checked the alert logs on the motion-sensitive cameras. When he was satisfied that nothing bigger than a badger had breached the property's perimeter in his absence, he hung up his coat and walked into his sitting room with a 9mm pistol in his hand. He poured himself a brandy and went to a large corkboard that he'd installed on the rear wall.

Post-it notes and photographs covered the board. Long-range pictures of John. Satellite photographs of the area with a red pin in the centre of Coronation Park where the attack had occurred. Coloured yarn stretched between the pictures on drawing pins.

Steven picked up the yellow pad of paper and a marker pen, then wrote Marie Williams on it. He stuck the paper onto the board with pins and linked her name with John's photograph with a length of green wool.

He looked at the board and shook his head. "I'll be damned if I know what to make of it all. You'd probably put it together in a second, you cantankerous old bastard."

He walked across to a bookcase and took down a photo album. He opened it and looked at a faded Polaroid picture of Carl Schneider. "All these bloody years and you can't let me retire in peace. Yeah, I took the money you left me, and I agreed to the conditions in the will, but for fuck's sake, Carl, I'm an old man now. I'm dying.

"I've hunted the things wherever I found them, like you wanted. I should have called it quits after '94 when the bastards were showing up everywhere, but I didn't. All I wanted to do was come home to die in peace, and you bring it right to my bloody doorstep."

He tossed the photo album into the fireplace and watched as the glowing embers melted the plastic, and flames danced around the book. Carl Schneider's photograph turned up at the edges and browned as the flames grew higher. He downed the brandy in a single gulp, enjoying the warmth as it spread through him.

"Fuck you, Carl," he said, then turned and walked out of the room while the photographs burned.

Chapter 26

13th November 2008. Coronation Estate. 14.25.

Simon Dobbs hurried through the rows of terraced houses towards Malcolm's home. He reached the low metal gate and paused to catch his breath before he walked up the concrete path and pushed the doorbell.

He heard a woman's voice inside, shouting at the children. Simon couldn't make out the exact words, but he didn't need to. The acidic tone left anyone listening under no illusions as to the intent of the speaker. He remembered his father referring to that particular sound as "The Mother's voice" and that it would strike fear into the heart of any man. This was, of course, before the old man was electrocuted trying to steal live copper wire from an electrical substation. Simon was about to push the bell again, but then thought better of it and waited until the shouting subsided before he pressed the plastic button. A shadow darkened the frosted glass in the front door, and he could hear thunderous steps approaching. Then the door opened. Karen Harrison stood in the open doorway, her hands on her hips and a cigarette hanging from the corner of her mouth.

Karen had been a beauty once, when she was a teenager. A dark-haired bad girl who could drink most men under the table and was brought home by the police most Saturday nights.

Time, alcohol, and the stress of raising three children had robbed her of her looks by the age of thirty. Her dark hair had turned grey, and the constant application of dye had given it the texture of straw.

The hour-glass figure she'd maintained into her early twenties had slowly morphed into the shape of a pear, her skin was prematurely aged from twenty years of weekly sun-bed sessions, and dark rings circled her eyes. The faint purpling of an old bruise was just visible on her jaw line, despite the layers of foundation applied over it.

"What the hell do you want, Simon?"

"Is Mal here? I need to talk to him."

Karen snorted. "You'll not get any sense out of him. He's laid up in bed, sick. Bloody man flu if you ask me."

"It's important. Can I go up?"

She shrugged. "Suit yourself. Just don't blame me if you come down with it as well."

A crash came from the kitchen. Karen turned and stormed away from the front door to investigate the noise, leaving it open behind her. Simon stepped inside and closed the door, then went upstairs as quietly as he could so not to incur Karen's wrath.

He knocked on the bedroom door and waited. When there was no reply, he opened the door a crack and eased his way inside.

"Mal? You alright, mate?"

Malcolm lay in the bed, covered in sweat. The duvet was drenched and thrown to the side. "Course I'm not alright. I'm fucking dying here. Told that bitch to call an ambulance, but do you know what she said?"

Simon shrugged. "No idea?"

"She said it was nothing but a cold from one of the kids and told me to take two bloody aspirins."

"Well, I've got some news that might make you feel a bit better. We found him."

"Found who?"

"John sodding Simpson. Who do you think? Billy's brother-in-law works at the builders' merchants, and he said that he'd been in and out of there for the last few weeks. His address was on the invoices."

Malcolm managed a smile. "Nice one. Any sign of the bitch?"

"Na, no idea where she's at. We'll have to make do with putting him in hospital for now."

"Well, as soon as I get over this flu, we'll go over there and have a nice little chat with our friend John. That'll give me something to look forward to."

"I don't know if we can wait that long. Lawrence was out there earlier and he saw him putting suitcases in his car. It looks like he's packing up and leaving. We're gonna go over there tonight, just after it gets dark."

"Not without me, you're not. Hold on and I'll get ready." Malcolm tried to stand up, but collapsed back onto the bed. He reached for the bucket by his side, and added to its already considerable contents.

"Mal, you're in no fit state to be anywhere but bed. We'll sort it out. Me, Lawrence, and Billy all owe that bastard at least one broken bone each. I'll record it on my phone and send the video over to you. Might make you feel a bit better."

"Simon, I'm telling you. Don't do this without me. Just hang on a couple more days."

"Sorry, mate, but we can't risk him fucking off to God-knows-where again. This might be the only chance we get. Don't worry, we'll take care of it. You just concentrate on getting better," he said, then turned and left the room without another word.

***

Malcolm lay on his bed for a while and scratched at the infected scab on his knuckles. "Bastards. The lot of them are a bunch of bastards. Just wait till I'm better. I'll sort them all out. I'll..." Then the nausea bubbled up from inside again, and he returned his attention to the bucket at his bedside.

***

13th November 2008. Mill Woods, High Moor. 15.02.

Steven checked his harness and hoisted himself off the ground, up to the platform that nestled in the bare arms of an oak tree. The tree trunk was over eight feet across and had fabric strips wrapped around its entire surface.

Rows of silver-tipped spikes protruded from the material. Steven remembered his first ever encounter with a werewolf, less than a hundred yards from the tree that he ascended. He did not want a repeat of that experience.

The platform was a solid piece of engineering, secured to the branches and trunk of the old oak with half-inch-thick steel bolts. Branches had been removed at strategic points to allow Steven a three-hundred-and-sixty-degree view of the woods around him.

A high-powered rifle with a night vision sight rested in a weapons rack bolted to the platform's base. A small goat, chained to an iron spike in the ground, waited in a clearing to the west of Steven's hide.

He had thought about the best way to handle High Moor's latest werewolf. There were two options. If The Pack were trying to flush John out of hiding, then the effort and expense of setting this trap would have been wasted. They would ignore the goat and go for John. If John managed to survive the attack, then the problem was solved. If John fell to the other werewolves, then they would, in all likelihood, leave the area afterwards, in which case the problem was also solved.

If, however, this had nothing to do with The Pack, and he was dealing with a lone lycanthrope, then the trap should bring it right to him, like it had done so many times before. Again, the problem would be solved and he could go back to what remained of his life.

The sky had cleared earlier that day, and the last of the afternoon sun shone through the trees from a clear blue sky, although the air remained cold with a chill wind gusting from the northwest. Without cloud cover, the night temperature would drop like a stone. Steven imagined the uncomfortable night ahead and did not relish the thought.

"This is the last bloody time. I'm too old to be climbing trees in the middle of the night, waiting for monsters. You hear me, Carl? After tonight, I'm done. You've had your money's worth."

The only answer was the rustle of wind in the bare branches of the trees and the roosting calls of the birds. Steven settled into the padded seat bolted to the centre of the platform, poured himself a coffee from the thermos flask by his side, and waited for his prey to take the bait.

**

13th November 2008. Treworgan Farm. 16.14.

The last twinkling rays of sunlight glimmered on the horizon and then vanished. It would be dark within the next hour. The moon was due to rise an hour after that. John put the last of his clothes into a suitcase and looked around the room. Everything he needed was packed, along with a few precious mementos that he'd come across. The rest could rot as far as he was concerned.

He lugged the case downstairs and placed it in the hall, next to several other bags, then looked at the closed basement door. He'd failed here. He wasn't even sure what he thought he could achieve. Steven was right. His presence in his hometown was risky at best. He'd sensed nothing of another werewolf, and Marie hadn't returned any of his calls after their last disastrous encounter. There was nothing left for him here. He'd lock himself up for the night and leave first thing in the morning.

He jumped at the sound of his mobile telephone and dashed across the room to where it rested on the windowsill. The phone's display showed the name of the caller. Marie.

He picked it up and placed it to his ear, trying to control the butterflies in his stomach and the sudden lack of strength in his arms.

"Hello? Marie?"

"John? Hi. Listen, I'm sorry for not calling you sooner. I've been a bit busy, and to be honest, I wasn't sure how I felt about the way we left things."

"Marie, I'm so sorry for that. I panicked. I'd had a few drinks and I thought we might end up...well."

"I thought we might as well. Was the thought of that so bad?"

"Oh God, no. Nothing like that. It's just that...well...I've got something wrong with me. A kind of contagious blood infection. I didn't want to risk you getting sick."

"An infection? You mean like Hep C or something?"

"Yeah, something like that. It's pretty rare. I don't even think the doctors have a proper name for it. It's spread through body fluids, and I couldn't risk kissing you, no matter how much I wanted to."

"You can catch it through kissing? Is that how you got it?"

"No, I've had it since I was a little kid. It's manageable, but not something I would be prepared to inflict on someone else. I admit, I handled it badly."

The line was silent for a moment. "So, if you've had this since you were a kid, does that mean you've never kissed anyone? Ever?"

John's face flushed. "No. Never. It's not worth the risk."

"So...if you've never been kissed, does that mean...oh my God, are you still a virgin?"

Now it was John's turn to be silent. He had no idea how to have this sort of conversation. He'd never needed to before. He tried to sort out the jumble of words and emotions that flooded his skull before he answered. "Erm...technically...yes."

"Oh, John, you silly bugger. We need to talk. Now. Can I come over?"

John felt the tug of the rising moon in his blood. Somewhere deep inside, the beast stirred from its dreams. "I really can't tonight, Marie. I know this looks like I'm giving you the brush-off again, but I'm not. Can we meet up tomorrow morning? Maybe grab a coffee or something?"

"John, this can't wait. There are some things I need to tell you. Things you need to know. I'm coming over."

"No, please. I have to go away tonight. Business meeting in Bradford. I'll be back in the morning. We can talk then."

"John, I'm coming over now. See you in a bit."

"No, Marie, wait!" he said, but the only response was the dial tone. He tried to redial Marie's number, but the phone went straight to voicemail. "Listen, Marie. Don't come over here tonight. I'm begging you. Please. Call me in the morning and I'll explain everything. Just promise me that you'll stay away from here tonight."

John put his phone down and massaged his temples. "Great. Now what the hell am I supposed to do?"

***

13th November 2008. Shafto Road, High Moor. 16.43.

Marie disconnected the call and turned her mobile off. John was proving to be a neurotic mess, no wonder, considering his upbringing and lack of human contact. She'd caught glimpses of the real John Simpson at the restaurant, once he relaxed and let his guard down. She wanted to see that man again, to rescue her childhood friend from the prison that he'd built himself. It wasn't going to be easy though, especially given his reluctance to talk to her tonight.

She realised that she didn't care. There were a whole lot of things that had been left unsaid, and it was time to get it all out in the open. Time to stop playing games. Leaving it until tomorrow would give John time to build his defences to the point where she might not be able to break through.

It had to be tonight. She pulled on her coat, put her car keys in the pocket of her jeans, then opened the front door and stepped out into the night.

The cold air stung her cheeks, and she wrapped her arms around herself to ward off the chill as she took the concrete stairs down to the street. The tarmac arteries of the town were clogged with traffic, commuters heading home after the day's work, or parents taking their children home from school. She crossed the street to the car that she'd been renting.

Something seemed odd about the vehicle that she could not put her finger on until she got closer. Someone had let the front driver's side tire down.

A wooden matchstick protruded from the valve, and she could just hear the last of the air hiss out.

"Oh, that's just perfect." She looked up the street and saw a small child's head vanish behind a wall. "Thanks a lot, you little shit. Shouldn't you be out playing in traffic?"

Despite her annoyance, she couldn't help but be amused. She'd done much worse as a child. She opened the boot and pulled back the carpet to retrieve the spare tire only to discover that it was missing.

"Oh, for fuck's sake."

Marie retrieved the mobile phone from her coat pocket and turned it back on. The display showed six missed calls, all from John, plus three text messages and two voicemails. She ignored them and scrolled through her contacts until she found the number she wanted, then hit dial.

"Hi, when's the soonest I can get a taxi from Shafto Road in High Moor? Going to Treworgan farm. Yes please, I'll be waiting in the bus shelter."

***

13th November 2008. Treworgan Farm. 17.48.

The white van drove along the country lane and passed the turning for the old farm. It stopped, reversed back, and turned onto the track. The lights flicked off and the engine stopped. Billy, Lawrence, and Simon clambered out of the vehicle.

Simon pulled on a black balaclava and rubbed his arms. "Why do we have to walk all the way? It's miles, and it's fucking freezing."

Billy punched him on the arm. "Don't be a tit. We don't want him to know we're coming. He might notice us driving a bloody transit van up to his front door. And why are you putting that on now?"

Simon adjusted the balaclava until the holes lined up with his eyes and mouth. "I don't want anyone to know it's me. Besides, it's nice and warm."

Billy rolled his eyes and turned to Lawrence. "You got all the gear?"

Lawrence opened the van's side door and removed a large canvas holdall. "Yeah. Got it all. Cable ties, duct tape, hammer, blow torch, hacksaw. Once we've used that lot up, we might have to improvise a bit."

Simon shuffled from one foot to the other. "Are you sure about this, lads? I mean, we could get in a lot of trouble for this. I don't want to go back inside."

Lawrence hefted the bag onto his shoulder and looked at the other man with disdain. "Stop being such a big bairn, Simon. We'll go there, have our fun, and make sure he knows that if he goes to the cops then there'll be worse on the way. I'll break a couple of fingers when I'm telling him, to make sure he gets the message."

"What if something goes wrong?"

Billy slapped Simon on the shoulder. "You worry too much. There's three of us and one of him. What could go wrong?"

***

High Moor

John had been a nervous wreck since Marie's call. He'd tried to call, but her phone was still turned off, and he'd been expecting her to turn up on the doorstep at any moment. Now the moon was rising. He could feel the beast stir inside, testing his defences. In another ten, maybe fifteen, minutes, he wouldn't be able to keep it in. He had to be locked away before that happened. He couldn't wait for Marie any longer.

He opened the door to the basement and was about to descend into the darkness when he heard two sharp knocks on the front door.

"Oh, Christ. Not now, Marie."

He had to get rid of her. There was no time to be pleasant about it. Better that Marie spend the rest of her life hating him than any harm come to her. He almost sprinted across the living room and pulled the front door open.

"Listen, Marie, I..."

The person at the door was not Marie. Three masked men surged forward as soon as the door opened, grabbed John's arms, and dragged him into the living room.

He lashed out with his feet and tried in vain to free his arms. "God, don't. You don't understand. You have to get out of here."

One of the men took a claw hammer from his pocket and brought it down onto John's right knee with a sickening crack. "If it's all the same to you, John, I think we'll stick around for now. We've got one or two things to chat about."

13th November 2008. Treworgan Farm. 18.05.

The taxi stopped at the bottom of the lane. "Sorry, luv. That van's blocking the track up to the farm. I can't get you any closer than this."

Marie took a ten-pound note out of her jeans and handed it to the driver. "That's alright, mate. It's a nice night. I can walk from here. Keep the change."

"You sure you're going to be alright? It's a good half-mile up to the farm from here."

She unlocked the door and stepped out into the cold night air. "Thanks, but I'll be fine. I've got your number in case I need to get picked up."

"You want me to wait here for a while?"

"No, seriously, I'll be OK. I think this might take a while."

The driver shrugged. "OK, have a good night, miss."

Marie watched the taxi turn around and head back to town. When the tail lights disappeared around the corner, she stuffed her hands into her pockets and started the long walk up to the farm.

Chapter 27

13th November 2008. Treworgan Farm. 18.11.

The hammer came down again, splintering John's other knee cap. A wave of pain and nausea washed over him and he screamed in agony. Lawrence grabbed his arms and tied them behind his back with vinyl cable ties. Simon removed a roll of duct tape from the holdall. Billy swung the hammer again, this time connecting with John's ribs. Two shattered, driving bone shards through his skin.

John could hardly breathe, let alone speak. He felt the damage repairing itself already, the bones in his kneecaps crunched back into place, and the bone shards from his ribs sank back into his body. He spat blood onto the floor and gasped. "Stop, you have to stop. Oh God, you don't know what you're doing."

Billy laughed. "You hear this, lads? We don't know what we're doing." He leaned in close. "I think you'll find we know exactly what we're doing, John. This won't be the first time we had to teach someone to mind their manners."

John raised his head and looked into Billy's eyes. "I'm going to kill you all."

Billy turned to Simon. "I've heard enough from this prick. Tape his mouth up."

John thrashed his head when Simon pulled a strip of tape from the roll. Lawrence grabbed a fistful of his hair and held him steady while Simon applied the tape.

Billy put down the hammer and removed a Stanley knife from the holdall. "Peace at last. Any more clever comments, John? No? Didn't think so. Lawrence, you go and check the house. See if there's anything here worth nicking. Simon, get your phone out and record this. Mal will want to watch it later."

The beast hurled itself at the walls in John's mind. It flooded his consciousness with a stream of emotions and images.

Let me out. Kill them. Eat their faces. Feast on their hearts. LET ME OUT.

Billy brought the blade up to John's face. "I'm going to take one of your eyes now, John. Just the one. I want you to be able to see what we've done to the rest of you." The blade sank into the skin of John's left cheek, and Billy sliced through the flesh in a slow, deliberate journey to John's eyeball. He felt the warm blood trickle down his face.

The beast redoubled its efforts; pain and fury combined in a furious assault. John felt his defences crumbling. The moon was moments away from rising, but it wouldn't happen fast enough to save his eye. John had no idea whether he'd heal from an injury like that, and he didn't feel like finding out.

LET ME OUT.

Left with no alternative, he tore down the barriers in his mind and set the beast free.

The change began at once, hitting John like a jolt of electricity. His muscles went into violent spasms, and he fell back onto the floor.

High Moor

Simon's hand wavered as he held the mobile phone in front of him. "Billy? What's happening to him? Is he having a fit or something?"

Billy shook his head. "I don't know. I've hardly touched him yet. Get the tape off his mouth. He might be having trouble breathing."

Simon inched forward to where John thrashed on the floor and tore the strip of tape from his mouth. "There you go, mate. No harm done, eh?" Then he saw John's eyes and backed away. "Oh Jesus...he's...it's..."

John turned his head to look at Billy. The cut on his cheek was gone, and his eyes had turned from blue to yellow. John's jaw dislocated with a loud snap, and the front of his skull warped as the bones shattered and reformed. Hair burst from John's pores, covering his pale skin in a thick brown carpet. His arms swelled with new muscle tissue, and tendons like steel cables stood out on his neck and forearms. The vinyl ties around his wrists burst open as the transformation completed, and the creature that had once been John Simpson got to its feet.

Simon and Billy bolted for the front door. The werewolf snarled and was about to pursue them when Lawrence walked back into the room.

"What the bloody hell is going on in..."

The creature turned to face him and peeled back its black lips to show twin rows of razor-sharp fangs. Blood-flecked saliva ran in rivulets from the werewolf's mouth. It bunched its muscles, ready to pounce.

***

Lawrence turned and ran through the nearest door, into the basement. He leaped down the stairs and twisted his ankle when he hit the concrete floor. The werewolf filled the doorframe. He hobbled into the open cell, pulled the door closed behind him, and locked it.

The werewolf was at the door a second later. It's terrible face filled the small hatch, and it slammed against the metal door.

Lawrence was sick with fear, but the relief he felt at his narrow escape elated him, and some of his bravado returned. "Ha, you can't get me in here, can you? What you gonna do now, you ugly bastard?"

The werewolf cocked its head, as if studying its prey. Then it reached down and the deadbolt began to move, and then slide back. The click as it unlocked the door had a terrible finality to it. Lawrence whimpered and watched the door swing open. "John, I'm sorry. I didn't mean to..."

The werewolf filled the open doorway and sniffed the air, then walked into the cell. Lawrence's whimpering became a high-pitched, thin squeal of horror as the creature brought its face to within inches of his and sniffed him. He felt his bladder loosen, and hot urine streamed down his leg. "Don't...please...I'm sorry...I'm..."

The werewolf darted forward and bit down. Fangs tore through muscle and ligaments and shredded flesh. Blood ran from the creature's mouth and mingled with steaming pool of urine at its feet. The werewolf pulled its head back and ripped Lawrence's face off, leaving a screaming bloody skull with staring eyes.

It swallowed its meal and howled in triumph, then shoved its claws into Lawrence's chest and cracked his rib cage open like a lobster. Lawrence was still screaming when the monster pushed its snout into his open chest and sank its fangs into his heart.

***

Marie shoved her hands deep into her pockets and made her way along the dark trail to John's house. The stars were visible, but shed little light, just enough to cast faint shadows against the darkness that gave it the appearance of a living, moving thing. A silver halo appeared on the eastern horizon, and Marie was thankful for the extra visibility. She saw the lights of John's house through the trees and hurried onward, keen to get out of the cold.

The moon was completely above the horizon when she came to the end of the long track. She was about to cross the yard when the front door burst open, and two men dressed in black combat gear and balaclavas ran from the house. She stepped back into the shadows and took cover behind an overgrown laurel bush.

The two men looked as if they would run straight at her, but then they changed direction, sprinted into the disused barn by the side of the house, and pulled the heavy wooden door closed behind them.

A long, savage howl sliced through the silence. After a second, a desperate scream followed, increased in pitch, then cut off.

Marie felt her heart race. She looked up at the full moon, now clear of the treetops, then back to the house. A dark shape emerged from the front door and sniffed the air.

"Oh no."

***

Billy and Simon crouched in the barn between a pile of mouldering hay bales and the wooden walls of the building. Simon pulled his balaclava off and looked at Billy with wide eyes.

"What the fuck was that, Billy? What just happened?"

Billy shook his head and struggled to catch his breath. "Christ only knows. Either someone slipped us a shitload of acid, or our old mate John just turned into a bloody werewolf."

Simon's voice stammered as he spoke. "Do you think it got Lawrence?"

"What the hell do you think? You heard the screams same as me."

Simon grabbed Billy's arm. "It's going to come after us, isn't it? What're we gonna do?"

Billy shook his arm free and hissed at his friend. "If you don't keep your fucking voice down, then yes, it's going to come right at us. Now shut the hell up and let me think."

A howl reverberated around the courtyard. Simon turned white and backed against the wooden wall. "Billy?" he whispered.

Billy's eyes were wide open in abject terror. He crouched behind a pile of hay bales and tried to control his breathing. He hissed at Simon through his teeth. "Quiet. See if you can see anything through that window."

Simon edged his way along the wall to the single windowpane and peered through. The moon highlighted the trees in silver and cast soft, wavering shadows across the open ground between the forest and the barn. An owl hooted nearby. Then all was quiet. Simon withdrew from the window and stood with his back to the wall once more.

"I can't see anything. Do you think it's gone?"

Billy's eyes widened even more. He tried to speak, but his voice had deserted him. He raised his trembling arm and pointed to the window.

Simon's heart lurched in his chest. He looked across to the window, but saw nothing except a large patch of condensation on the outside of the glass. "What? What did you see?"

Two clawed hands burst through the rotting wood to either side of Simon's head. Talons sliced through his face and dug into his skull.

"Oh God, Billy. Help me. Do something. Do..."

The arms yanked Simon back through the splintered wood. A two-foot-long shard tore into his back and burst out from his stomach, bringing a section of his intestine with it. The werewolf pulled again, and the massive splinter sliced through the man's torso with a ripping sound that made Billy want to throw up.

Billy shook off his terror and grabbed his friend's feet in a vain attempt to pull him back inside. Simon's scream turned into a gurgling wail, and his legs thrashed about in Billy's hands.

The splinter creaked and then snapped, separating itself from the main barn wall. Billy braced himself against the base of the wall and pulled with every ounce of strength. He felt Simon slip towards him and, heartened by this, he redoubled his efforts, despite the fact that his friend had stopped kicking.

A wet, tearing sound filled the air, and the lower part of Simon's body separated from the top half. Billy fell back onto the floor, still holding Simon's legs. The upper half vanished through the hole and into the night. The blue-black loop of his intestines caught on another jagged piece of wood and then unravelled after the werewolf and its victim like a wet, meaty streamer until it pulled taut and snapped.

Billy stood shivering for a moment and looked at the gaping, blood-smeared hole in the barn wall. "Oh fuck this," he said, and sprinted out of the barn, onto the long dark lane that led to Lawrence's transit van.

***

The beast rammed its snout into the man's chest, relishing the crunch of bones under its teeth and the sweet taste of the marrow on its tongue. It raised its head and howled in elation. After years of confinement, it knew the taste of freedom once again. The moon shone down on the creature and made its blood sing, and it let out small yaps of pleasure as it consumed its prey.

High Moor

The beast could smell the fear on the other human and listened to the sound of its heart as it threatened to burst in the man's chest. The prey was running. Millennia-old instincts awoke within it. The chase, the anticipation, and the kill. It turned away from the eviscerated corpse and bounded off in pursuit of its next victim.

***

Billy ran faster than he'd ever done before. Terror gave strength to his trembling legs, and the cold night air burned his throat as he fled for his life. He tried not to think about his heart pounding in his chest, or the pain in his lungs. His only thought was to get away, to put as much distance as he could between himself and the monster that had killed two of his friends.

He emerged from the shadows of the tree-lined driveway, and into the open countryside. He saw the van at the end of the track, its white paint turned orange by the street lights that flanked the main road.

I'm going to make it. I'm almost there.

He fished the keys out of his pocket without breaking stride, gripped them in his fist, and urged his tired legs to greater speed. Then he glanced over his shoulder.

Two green eyes bobbed in the shadow of the woods, getting closer at an alarming rate. The werewolf dropped down onto all fours and emerged from the darkness at a full gallop. Its ears flattened against its head, and its tongue trailed from the side of its open mouth as it ran. Muscles moved beneath fur with a sinuous grace that would have been mesmerising if it had not been so terrible.

Billy squealed in horror and tried to go faster. Then his foot caught in a pothole. The bones in his ankle broke with a wet snap, and he collapsed onto the track. White-hot pain coursed through his leg, and he cried out in misery and desperation. He looked behind him and whimpered.

The werewolf stopped running and stood on two legs once more. It advanced in slow, measured paces with clawed hands outstretched and its face contorted into a snarl. Billy picked up an egg-sized rock and threw it at the beast with what little strength he had left. It bounced off the werewolf's chest. The creature did not even flinch. It stood over the man and howled in triumph. Then Billy punched it in the testicles.

The howl went up an octave, and for a moment, the creature stood frozen, stunned by the unexpected pain. Billy crawled away from it and tried to get to his feet. The bones in his ankle ground together in a flash of blinding agony, causing him to collapse to the ground again.

He tried to crawl away, but he had no more strength. The adrenaline that fuelled his flight had long since been expended. He felt cold, despite his layers of clothing. Then four-inch-long talons embedded themselves in his calf and ripped away muscle and sinew in a single swipe.

The bomb-burst of pain was almost too much for him; he wavered on the edge of consciousness. Only the agony that coursed through his body kept him from slipping into the mercy of oblivion as the werewolf started to eat him.

***

High Moor

The beast tore into the carcass with its claws, eviscerating the body. The liver and heart were diseased, and the creature discarded them along with the intestines and stomach. It gulped down the kidneys, and when the torso had been emptied, it pushed its talons into the corpse's eye sockets and cracked open the skull to feast on the succulent brains within.

When it had finished, little more than a pile of partially eaten organs and gnawed bones remained.

It sniffed the air and sorted through the myriad of scents that filled the night. The family of deer trembling amid the bracken to the north. The pungent aroma of a fox carrying a dead chicken back to her cubs deep in the woods. The scent of a human female, back along the trail near the house.

It left the shredded corpse behind it and ran back along the track, eager for the hunt to begin once more.

***

14th November 2008. Mill Woods, High Moor. 03.02.

Steven shuffled in his seat and picked up the infrared goggles from the floor. The woods were silent except for the occasional displeased bleat from the goat in the clearing and sporadic calls from a barn owl as it searched the woods for its next meal. He scanned the trees for what seemed like the hundredth time and saw nothing in the grey haze to indicate any sort of life. Frustrated, he put the goggles back into their box.

The cold night air hurt his lungs with each breath that he took. It seeped through his layers of warm clothing and into his aching bones. He was grateful at least that the skies remained clear and the forecast rain had not materialised.

Something was wrong. The werewolf should have taken the bait by now. In his experience, a wounded goat was too tempting a meal for any lycanthrope to pass up, or at least, too tempting for the bi-pedal moonstruck variety. The other kind, like those in The Pack, were another story. They were smart and acted, for the most part, with a specific purpose in mind. It dawned on him that he might have made the wrong choice. His suspicion that The Pack was involved was looking more likely with every second that passed. If the werewolf was not in the woods, then the chances were that it was at John's farm on the other side of town.

He felt something come loose in his lungs, and his breath turned into a rasping wheeze, then into a full-blown coughing fit that lasted for almost a minute. When he regained control of himself, he looked at the black fluid that was pooled in his hand and wiped it against his trouser leg. If there was a lycanthrope within a mile of the platform, it would know exactly where he was. The thought made him uneasy, and he reached for his hunting rifle.

Then he looked down into the clearing. The goat was still chained up. Most of it at least. The animal's head lay four feet away from the body. Steven grabbed his goggles and scanned the trees, but there was no movement. The only heat sources were the cooling body of the dead goat and some droplets of blood that led back into the trees.

The damn thing was playing with him. Making a point. This wasn't the mindless violence of a moonstruck werewolf. This was calculated. The work of an intelligent monster. One that could change at will. He was caught in his own trap. It would not be safe to come down, even in daylight.

Steven gripped the stock of his rifle harder and prayed for the dawn to come.

**

14th November 2008. Mill Woods, High Moor. 07.18.

Marie stood over John's naked, blood-stained body and removed the silver knife from her belt. It would be so easy. She could reach over and slice his throat open while he slept, let his blood seep out into the carpet of dead leaves on the forest floor, and end his nightmarish existence.

The thought made her sick to her stomach. She couldn't do it. Not to John. She put the blade away and threw a duffle bag at him.

John groaned and opened his eyes. "What? Where am I?"

Marie's face was a stone mask, with only her eyes showing any hint of her conflicting emotions. "There are some wet wipes and clothes in the bag. Clean yourself up, get dressed, and then come with me. It's time we had a talk."

Chapter 28

14th November 2008. Treworgan Farm. 07.45.

Despite her earlier insistence that they talk, Marie stayed silent on the journey through the woods. She brushed off John's attempts to engage her in conversation with curt monosyllabic responses, and after several failed attempts, he lapsed into a nervous silence.

After twenty minutes, they emerged from the woods, into the back garden of the old farm. John reached out and grabbed Marie's arm, then turned her around to face him.

"So, come on. You wanted to talk. Let's talk. Enough with this silent treatment bollocks. At least tell me that you're alright."

Marie sagged. "Yes. I'm fine."

"But you were here? Last night?"

"Yes, John. I was here."

John looked at his feet. "So, now you know. I'm a werewolf."

"Don't be a tit, John. I've known you were a werewolf since we were kids. Remember?"

"I do, but I'm surprised that you still believe what I said, after all these years."

"Well, you could say that I had some first-hand experience to back up your story."

John's brow furrowed. "What do you mean, first-hand?"

Marie pulled back the sleeve of her jacket and showed John her right forearm. Four, thin silver scars encircled the wrist. "I mean this kind of first-hand. When Michael changed, I was with him in the hospital. He grabbed my arm when he started to transform. Broke the skin, as you can see. Left me with some nice scars and...something else."

John's eyes widened. "So, you're telling me that you're a werewolf, like me?"

Marie turned away. "No. I'm not like you. You're a fucking moonstruck, John. You're at war with your wolf, and because of that, you turn into a bloodthirsty monster every full moon."

"So, you can change whenever you want? Like the ones in The Pack."

Marie's shoulders dropped, and she turned around to face John. "Exactly like the ones in The Pack." She paused and looked straight into his eyes. "Exactly."

John's head span as Marie's meaning sank in. "I think you'd better tell me exactly what's going on. Why the fuck didn't you tell me this before now?"

Marie exhaled. "OK, John. I'm sorry that I didn't come clean that night. You were being a bit pathetic if I'm honest, and I wanted to mess with your head a little. I told you the truth about coming back here for my mother. She really was sick. She really did die."

"But the rest was a pile of horseshit?"

"The rest of it was true, sort of. I do work in recruitment, but I do it for The Pack. I track down other werewolves and offer them a chance to join us."

"And if they say no? Or if they're like me? Then what?"

"Then I kill them. No, for fucks sake, John, don't look at me like that. If I'd wanted you dead then I could have done it in the woods."

"So, it was you? The one that ate Malcolm Harrison's dog?"

"Yeah. I saw the fat prick out in the town one night, and it occurred to me that a close encounter might be enough to bring you out of hiding. So, I stalked him and put the fear of God into the tosser. You have to understand, John. I had no idea you were moonstruck, although to be honest, the clues were there. Maybe I just didn't want to see them."

"So, now what? If you're not going to kill me, and you're not going to recruit me, then what are you going to do?"

She reached down and took John's hand. "I'm going to try and help you, if you'll let me."

John pulled his hand away. "How the fuck can you help me, Marie? Nothing short of a silver bullet in the skull can make this go away."

"You need to accept your other self. Your wolf is like a scrap yard guard dog that's been kept on a very short leash for its entire life. It's angry, and it's hurt. You fight against it, but when it's a full moon, it gets too strong for you to contain. You end up caught halfway between the two states instead of completing the change."

"You just want me to let it out? Are you out of your mind? You've seen what it can do."

"When the two of you work in harmony, then you're still in control of your actions. You have some pretty strong instinctual drives, but you retain your intelligence and personality. Can you honestly say that you prefer being how you are now?"

John looked at the floor. "No, it's hell being the way I am now. Do you really think I can do this? I've been fighting it for my entire life."

She shrugged. "Fuck knows. I'd say you need a shitload of therapy, but I can't think of any werewolf-friendly shrinks off the top of my head. We're going to have to manage this ourselves. Oh, and I think you should know something. Lycanthropy isn't sexually transmitted." Marie took John's hand again. This time he let her. "Come on. We've got a load of cleaning up to do. Your wolf's a bloody messy eater."

"Oh shit, I'd forgotten about that. Is it that bad?"

"Oh yeah, it's not good. What's left of Lawrence is in the basement. Simon's stretched over about two hundred meters of your garden, and there's not enough left of Billy to fill a bin bag. I know this because I shovelled him into one while you were asleep. He was too close to the main road, and I didn't want to risk anyone coming across the body."

"Jesus. I swore that I'd never let this happen again. Maybe you should just kill me now. They were a bunch of sociopathic idiots, but they didn't deserve to die like that."

"Don't talk shite. If they hadn't broken in and tried to maim you, then they'd all still be living their scummy little lives. The world is better off without people like that in it. I wouldn't lose a second's sleep over it."

John picked his way towards the house through the tangle of overgrown vegetation. "So, what happened last night? I mean, apart from the obvious. Did I hurt anyone else?"

She shook her head. "No. When I saw you come through that door, I hid and waited for you to finish with Simon and Billy. Then, when Billy's screaming stopped, I changed and let you spend the night chasing me through the woods. I was knackered by the time the sun came up. Once you fell asleep and changed back, I went to the house, cleaned up some of your mess and got you some clothes. You know the rest."

John opened the back door and walked through the kitchen into the hallway. The basement door stood open, and he looked down the stairs with dread. "I think I remember this. Parts of it, anyway. That's never happened before."

"You remember it? That's good. Was anything different? Apart from being tied up in a chair and being beaten to a pulp?"

John replayed his last memories of the previous night. Something had been different, but he could not quite remember. Then it came to him. "I changed before the moon was up. Billy was going to blind me, so I let it out, or at least, tried to."

Marie smiled. "Then there might be hope for you yet."

They were about to descend into the basement when John's home telephone rang. She looked at him with a raised eyebrow. "Expecting any calls?"

"No, I wasn't." He crossed the hallway and picked up the receiver. "Hello?"

Steven's voice crackled through the speaker. "John, I'm sorry to call you so early, but I didn't have anyone else to go to. I'm in a bit of trouble."

"Trouble? Why? What happened?"

"I'm stuck up a bloody tree, and I think there's a werewolf out there, waiting for me to get down."

"There's no other werewolf, Steven. I found out who was responsible for last month's attack. It's all sorted."

"Yeah? Well, you better tell that to the werewolf that took the head off my goat. Damn thing's been stalking me all night. It shows up for a couple of seconds, and then pisses off again for an hour or more, before I can get a shot."

John put his hand over the receiver. "Did we go anywhere near a goat tied up in the woods last night? Or a man up a tree with a gun?"

Marie shook her head. "No, nothing like that. Why?"

"I think we might have a problem."

***

14th November 2008. Town Centre, High Moor. 08.17.

John and Marie drove through the centre of the town, towards where Steven had parked his car. The roads were busier than usual. They progressed at a crawl through the slow-moving traffic that clogged most of the roads.

As they passed the shopping precinct, the reasons for the delay became clear.

The Sandpiper car park and several surrounding streets were sealed off by police forensics teams. Traffic officers ushered vehicles around the cordoned off areas. John wound down the window as they passed one of them, "Hey, mate. What's going on?"

"I'm afraid I can't discuss that with you, sir. Please move along."

John wound up the window and followed the lines of traffic away from the town centre. Marie turned the radio on just in time to catch the end of the local news.

"So far, police have no leads with regards to the three deaths, nor would they confirm any link to an incident last month. As a result of the attacks, all schools in the town have been closed until further notice. Police are advising people to stay in their homes and to avoid rural or wooded areas if possible."

Marie turned down the radio. "I don't understand it. There shouldn't be any other werewolves around here."

"Could it be one of your little Pack friends checking up on you?"

"No. The Pack doesn't kill unless it's necessary. This sort of wanton slaughter looks like the work of a moonstruck. But if your friend is telling the truth, then it can't be one of those, or it would have changed back when the sun came up. Is he sure that it's still there?"

"He seemed pretty sure. So, if it's not Pack and it's not a moonstruck, then what the hell is it?"

316

She sighed. "There's only one thing it can be. A werewolf that can change shape at will, but with no regard for life and no restraint. A man that's surrendered himself to his beast. In a lot of ways, that's worse than a moonstruck. Instead of being something that's all rage and instinct, it's something that can think like a man. John, please don't take this the wrong way, but you haven't...bitten anyone since you got here, have you?"

John looked aghast. "No, of course not. I would never...oh shit."

"What?"

"That fight. Malcolm punched me in the mouth. If he caught his knuckles on my teeth..."

Marie groaned and put her head in her hands. "Then you would have basically bitten him. Nice work, John. You've turned Malcolm Harrison into a bloody werewolf."

"Which would explain why he wasn't with the rest of his mates last night. What the hell do we do now?"

"We go get your friend, and if Malcolm shows up, I'll tear the bastard's throat out. How's that for a plan?"

John reached into the glove compartment and removed his pistol, then put it on his lap. "Not if I see him first."

They turned off onto a side street and wound their way through a housing estate until they came to the edge of the woods. Steven's 4x4 was parked on the side of the street, near to the trees. John pulled up behind and got out of the car.

Marie removed her coat and undid her top. "Wait here for a second while I change."

"What? Are you sure that's such a good idea?"

She looked at him with exasperation in her eyes. "Well, it's not like I can just change at short notice. It takes a little while. If I wait until Malcolm turns up, it'll be too late. He'll rip my head off before I can get out of my clothes." She winked at John. "It's alright for you wolf-man types. Your clothes still sorta fit afterwards. It's a bit different for us quadrupeds."

"Well, you'll have to stay out of sight. If Steven spots you, he'll shoot first and ask questions later."

Marie frowned. "Steven? Your friend's name is Steven? Steven what?"

"Wilkinson. Steven Wilkinson. He was the one that saved me the night I was attacked, and a couple of times since. Why?"

Marie's face turned scarlet. "Because he's a fucking murderer. For years he's slaughtered people like us, all over the world. He's killed dozens, including some that were...important to me. Why do we want to help that bastard? We should be helping Malcolm tear his throat out."

John stepped back in shock. "Jesus, Marie. I don't know what he's done to you, but he's saved my life at least three times now. He called me for help, and I'm not leaving him here. Leave if you want to. I'll do it myself."

"You don't understand what it was like, John. Not long after I was recruited, something happened. The Pack was scattered. Fragmented. Every time we found a safe place, your friend would turn up and slaughter any werewolves he could find. He killed...he..."

John put his hand on her shoulder, but his voice was firm. "Look, I'm sorry for what's happened in the past, but I owe Steven my life, and we're going to need him if we want to stop Malcolm. Whatever problem you have with him can wait until after this is over. I mean it, Marie. If you're not here to help, then fuck off home and let me handle it."

Marie looked like she was about to say something, but bit back the words and took a deep breath. When she spoke, her voice was level. "Alright, John. I'll come along. I'll keep myself under control, but you better keep the bastard away from me, or I won't be responsible for what I do."

John nodded. "You go and change, and then guard the perimeter. I'll meet you back at the car once I get him. And, Marie? Make sure you stay out of sight. If I see anything that looks like a werewolf, I'm putting a bullet in it. There's no way I will be able to tell if it's you or Malcolm, so stay away unless we get into trouble. OK?"

John did not have to be psychic to tell that Marie was unhappy with the arrangement. Her bottom lip puffed out, just as it had when they were children. "Marie? OK?"

She nodded. "Alright, dammit. I'll stay out of the way. You go and get your butcher friend, and I'll watch your back. Now, look away while I change. And put my clothes in the car after, OK? Those jeans were expensive."

Marie walked into the woods and removed her clothes. John couldn't help himself. He angled his head, looking out of the corner of his eye. He caught a glimpse of her creamy white flesh through the undergrowth and felt himself become aroused, despite the circumstances.

Then he heard the sounds of bones breaking and saw the white skin vanish beneath rippling waves of light brown fur. He shuddered, and his ardour died as if someone had thrown him into an ice-cold river. He waited for a few minutes, to make sure that Marie had moved away, then retrieved her discarded clothes and locked them in the car.

He removed the pistol from his pocket and chambered a round. "Here goes nothing," he said to himself, then moved off into the woods to find his friend.

***

The woods were silent as John picked his way through the bracken. No birds sang in the skeletal arms of the trees. It was as if the entire area were holding its breath in anticipation. He held his pistol out before him in his right hand while he followed the GPS on his telephone to the co-ordinates that Steven had given him.

It took almost twenty minutes to make his way to Steven's location. Twenty agonising minutes where he jumped at every shadow, and swung the pistol around at every whisper of wind in the bare branches overhead. There was no sign of Malcolm, or Marie. This did little to calm his nerves. He emerged from the trees, into a clearing, and gagged. The coppery stink of blood combined with the sickly sweet smell of rotting leaves, and the result was not pleasant. The body of a goat lay chained to a metal spike, with the head lying several feet away. He looked up.

"Aren't you a bit old to be climbing trees, Steven?"

Steven peered over the edge of the platform. "Fuck you, and the horse you rode in on. Did you see anything on your way here?"

John shook his head. "No, nothing. I've got someone watching our backs, but I don't feel like hanging around here longer than I have to. Get your arse down from that tree, and let's get the hell out of here."

Steven connected a rope to his harness and lowered himself onto the ground. "Someone's watching our backs? Who?"

"It's a long story. Grab your stuff and let's go. I'll fill you in when we get back to the car."

Their progress through the woods was slow and torturous. Brambles tore at their legs, and they met every noise with raised weapons and nervous expressions. Neither man spoke. John thought he saw movement through the trees once or twice, but by the time he brought his pistol to bear, the woods were silent and still once more.

They'd been walking for almost ten minutes when a long howl echoed through the forest. John's eyes widened, and Steven disengaged the safety catch on his rifle. Both men stood still and held their breaths for what seemed like forever, but was, in reality, a little under ten seconds.

A roar of rage and pain erupted from the woods somewhere to the north of their location. The roar became a series of snarls and short aggressive barks intermingled with the sounds of breaking wood. After a few seconds, a pitiful howl of pain resounded through the forest, followed by another, deeper howl of triumph.

John turned to Steven. "Oh my God. Marie. It's gone after Marie."

"Marie? That woman you were with? What the hell is she doing out here?"

"She's not a woman. She's a werewolf, and she's out here watching our backs." He clicked the safety catch off and plunged through the woods towards the source of the howling. After a seconds consideration, Steven shouldered his rifle and followed the younger man.

John burst into a small clearing, bordered by a stream, and put his hand over his mouth. Blood was splashed across the tree trunks and grass, and several saplings had been snapped in half by the battle. The air was thick with the stench of blood and a sharper, musky odour that John didn't recognise at first.

Steven put his hand on John's shoulder. "Come on, John. There's nothing we can do here."

"There's no bodies. Maybe she got away."

Steven shook his head. "You smell that? It's wolf piss. The fucker's marking his territory."

"What do you mean?"

"It's challenging you. It's taken your hairy little girlfriend and it's calling you out."

John's lip curled up in a snarl. When he spoke, his voice was low, almost a growl. "Then I'd hate to disappoint the bastard."

Chapter 29

13th November 2008. Coronation Estate. 17.56.

Malcolm Harrison had never been so ill in his entire life. Even a bout of scarlet fever in his teens paled in comparison to the way he felt now. Every muscle and joint pulsated with pain, and his entire body was sticky with sweat. He felt like he was on fire. The air inside the bedroom was hot and thick. He drew large gasping breaths that did little to satisfy.

He propped himself onto one elbow and yelled out to his wife downstairs. "Karen, for Christ's sake, will you turn the bloody heating down?"

A muffled reply came from the kitchen. Irritation picked at his nerves and he shouted back, "What?"

Thunderous footsteps pounded their way up the stairs, and Karen stood in the doorway with her eyes ablaze. "I said, you can get off your fat arse and turn the fucking radiator down yourself if you're too hot. You got shit in your ears or something?"

"In case you hadn't noticed, I'm NOT FUCKING WELL. I work my arse off to provide for this bloody family, and the one time I need someone to do something for me, you go on like that. You're an evil bitch, Karen."

Karen laughed. "You? Work your arse off? Don't make me laugh. You wander around that school all day, mopping up piss and puke, then hide out in the basement, smoking spliffs with Billy. You've never done a proper day's work in your life."

Malcolm felt a familiar rage building inside. Starting off from a kernel of irritation, it fed on itself and became a living thing that made his hands tingle and his mind go dumb, so that only a single thought remained. He got to his feet and clenched his fists. "How many times do I need to tell you to talk to me with some respect? Do I need to teach you your manners again?"

Karen flinched, then her face switched from fear to blazing anger in a second. "Go ahead, fat boy. Fucking try it. Our Darren said he'd break your legs if you laid another finger on me. Do you think he won't?"

Darren was Karen's younger brother. He worked as a bouncer in the local nightclub and had won several cage fighting tournaments. The guy was six-foot-four of muscle and attitude. Malcolm knew that Darren would snap him in half given an excuse. The red mist behind his eyes subsided and was replaced by an empty feeling of impotence and frustration. He opened his mouth to speak, but instead fell to his knees and dry heaved.

Karen's face was a mask of contempt. "For God's sake, you useless prick. Don't puke on the carpet. Use the bloody bucket."

Sweat poured from Malcolm, sticking his nylon pyjamas to his skin. Waves of claustrophobia washed over him. He couldn't breathe. Too hot. No air. He got to his feet and stumbled past his wife and down the stairs.

"Where do you think you're going?" she called after him, but he ignored her and threw open the front door.

High Moor

The cold air was heaven. Clouds of steam billowed from his body, and he walked barefoot down the concrete garden path into the street.

Karen ran after him. "Malcolm, get back in the bloody house before the neighbours see you."

The moon rose above the roofline of the council estate, casting a silver sheen across the rooftops before becoming lost in the sodium glare of the streetlights. Malcolm felt something shift inside him, and he fell to his knees as pain shot through his body. Pain and something else. A pure, primal power that made his limbs tingle even as the pain drove bright daggers into his bones. It was within his grasp. All he had to do was reach out and claim it for his own. So he did.

He felt Karen's tentative touch on his shoulder. *Fucking bitch. Always going on, always interfering and making me look stupid. Why won't she just PISS OFF.*

He lashed out at her, with what he intended to be a heavy slap. Talons burst from his fingertips mid-swipe, tearing away the lower part of Karen's face and throat. She staggered back, eyes wide in shock. Blood bubbled from the ragged wound, and she fell to the floor, grasping at the torn remains of her neck.

The scent of blood filled Malcolm's sensitive nostrils and hastened the change. He welcomed the pain and the power it brought him. He shed the remains of his flabby, old body and marvelled at the strength and boundless energy of the new, improved one.

Karen dragged herself back towards the house, a trail of dark blood staining the concrete behind her. Malcolm tried to say, *"Where's your fucking brother now?"* but all that came out of his mouth was a vicious snarl. He put both paws on the dying woman's back and pinned her in place. She tried to plead for her life, but her words were lost in a bloody gurgle. Malcolm reached down and placed his jaws around the back of his wife's neck, then bit her head off.

The sounds of shouting and breaking glass came from inside the house. Malcolm drew back his lips in a snarl. *Fucking kids. Can't leave the little bastards alone for five minutes.*

He bit down into the shoulder of his dead wife and dragged the corpse back inside the house. A moment later, he retrieved her head and dropped it in the cat's litter tray. Then he went to the living room to discipline his children.

***

13th November 2008. Sandpiper Pub. 22.43.

Malcolm moved from shadow to shadow as he made his way around the outskirts of the car park. The taste of blood was still fresh on his tongue.

If I'd known Karen and the kids tasted so good, I'd have eaten them years ago.

After he left the house, the sensations almost overwhelmed him. He'd lain under a bush in Coronation Park and let the sounds, smells, and tastes of the town wash over him. After a couple of hours, he'd learned to process the information. It was as if a light had gone on in his head.

High Moor

He could smell the people in their homes. The myriad cooking scents from each household's evening meal. The subtle undertone of fear in the household pets that cowered under beds and waited for the predator to pass. The sounds of passing traffic and the footsteps of the people walking the streets. The taste of pollution in the air from the exhaust fumes. It was like a man, blind from birth, seeing for the first time. Malcolm could hear, smell, and taste everything around him for a mile in every direction. He felt like a god.

He moved back into the estate and wound his way through back alleys and gardens, leaving a chorus of panicked, barking dogs in his wake, until he came to Karen's brother's house. Darren walked their stupid little terrier at nine-thirty every night, so Malcolm waited behind a hedge for him.

When his brother-in-law passed, he leaped from his hiding place and tore him into chunks of shredded meat before he even had a chance to scream. The terrier ran yelping down the street with Darren's severed forearm still clutching the lead. His task complete, Malcolm sniffed the air and then headed towards the town centre on a compulsion.

***

Malcolm crouched beside a parked car and looked through the windows of the pub. It was quiet for a Thursday night. He saw only a few bored people standing at the bar and a group of drunken girls doing a terrible karaoke version of "I will survive" on a makeshift wooden stage.

The sound hurt his ears, and he crept behind a line of green refuse containers to the other side of the pub. The walls reduced the grating cacophony to a dull shriek that bored into his nerves like a dentist's drill. He considered going inside the bar and putting an end to the noise once and for all.

I will survive? Not if I have anything to do with it, you won't, you tuneless cows.

Then the door opened and two people stepped out into the car park. Malcolm recognised one as Lizzie Fletcher, Karen's mate. The other one was some bloke...Brian or something. Brian had his arm around Lizzie's shoulder. Malcolm lay flat on the ground and waited.

"It's crap in there tonight," he said. "Where's your mate, Karen? She's usually a good laugh. Nice arse as well."

Lizzie pulled away and punched him on the shoulder. "Watch it, you. Don't talk about my mates like that."

Brian shrugged. "All I'm saying is that I would."

Lizzie rolled her eyes. "That's not saying much. You'd shag anything with a pulse."

"Well, I'm shagging you aren't I?"

"Not if you keep up with the gob, matey. Anyway, Karen had to stay in. That useless dickhead she married has 'man flu' and she has to look after the kids."

"Is she married to that sweaty, fat bloke that hangs around with Billy Phillips?"

"Yeah, the sad bastard's a janitor at King's Close School. Anyway, enough talking about that loser. I want to hear about what you're gonna do to me when we get back to yours."

Brian grabbed a fist full of Lizzie's backside and pulled her close. "Wouldn't you like to know...hang on, did you hear something?"

Malcolm let out a deep, bass growl and stepped out from behind the bins.

Brian backed away and put his hands out in front of him. "There. Nice doggy. Good boy."

Malcolm snarled. *Patronising prick!*. He leaped forward and collided with the man, knocking him onto his back. His head dove forward, and he chewed a hole in Brian's abdomen. Brian beat at the creature and screamed for someone to help as tides of blood flowed from his ruined mid-section.

Lizzie Fletcher stood motionless for a moment and then rushed forward, wielding her handbag like a mace. "Get off my boyfriend, you hairy piece of shit."

The handbag struck the side of Malcolm's head with a savage crack, knocking him a step to the side. He snarled at her and the handbag came down again. This time it struck him between the eyes, setting off a bomb burst of light and pain inside his skull. He remembered something Karen had told him. Lizzie Fletcher kept a half brick in her handbag, for self-defence.

He backed away and shook his head to clear his senses. Lizzie appeared to be in no mood to accept a surrender. She stepped over Brian's motionless body and advanced on the blood-soaked werewolf with murder in her eyes. She raised the bag. Malcolm flinched and retreated into himself. Then the beast took over.

Jaws flashed out at impossible speed and severed Lizzie's arm just below the elbow. The rest of the arm was carried by the handbag's momentum and sailed through the plate glass window of the pub. Shouts came from inside. Movement.

The beast leaped forward and tore out Lizzie Fletcher's throat in one swift movement and then ran off, away from the strange noises and offensive scents, out of the town and into the woods beyond the housing estate.

***

14th November 2008. Mill Woods, High Moor. 02.48.

The werewolf moved through the forest, as silent as a shadow. The taste of deer meat was still fresh on its tongue, but already the hunger was starting again. An irresistible urge to hunt, kill, and eat dominated its mind.

The wind changed and it caught a musky animal odour, spiced with subtle tones of pain and fear. *More Prey.* The great beast howled and ran off through the trees toward its next victim.

High Moor

The dark shapes of the trees passed in a blur of movement, and after a few minutes, the creature drew close to its prey. The smell of blood and fear overwhelmed its senses, and every instinct screamed at it to attack, tear, and eat the tender flesh of the goat. It crouched low to the ground and began to circle the animal.

Wait. Not yet. Don't you smell it?

The beast tried to ignore the small human voice, but it was insistent. Irritated, it lay still and filtered the scents. There. Metal and oil. The scent of human sweat, muted but still close by, with a sickly undertone of illness.

It's a trap. He's in a tree on the edge of that clearing, just waiting for us to take the bait.

The beast was outraged. It could see the platform in the tree now, and in the moonlight it could make out rows of silver spikes wrapped around the trunk. Something about those spikes made it uneasy, and it shuffled back, unsure as to how it could get to the insolent human that dared to hunt it.

The voice persisted, like an irritating gnat that buzzed just out of reach. *Just lay low. Keep out of sight. He has to come down from there eventually. When he does, we'll tear him apart.*

The man in the tree coughed. A wet rattle that grew in intensity until it seemed that he would not survive the experience.

Now, while he's distracted. We'll send him a little message.

The beast moved like liquid through the undergrowth. Swift and silent, it closed on the goat. Before the animal could so much as bleat in terror, a massive clawed paw lashed out and tore the goat's head off with a single swipe.

The urge to feed on the carcass was overpowering. The gushing blood enflamed its senses, and it bowed its head to feast.

No. Move away. Back, into the woods. Quick, before he stops coughing his guts up.

The beast was struck with indecision. The human voice was right, but the instinctive urges were powerful and difficult to resist. The human forced his way into the beast's mind and added his will to its own. With reluctance, the werewolf bounded away from the bleeding carcass and back into the woods.

After a few seconds, the man in the tree stopped coughing and looked down into the clearing. The heady scent of fear blossomed from him, and he scanned the undergrowth with his rifle in panicked, darting movements. Satisfied, the beast settled in and waited for the prey to come to it.

***

14th November 2008. Mill Woods, High Moor. 09.06.

The creature that had once been Malcolm Harrison sniffed the air and let out a small growl of frustration. The old man in the tree had not yet come down from his hiding place and had even called for help.

High Moor

The beast's sensitive ears had listened to both sides of the telephone conversation while the human half of the creature's mind recognised the voice on the other end of the line. John Simpson. The anticipation was almost too much. Once John arrived, the old man would leave the security of his platform, and then they would both be prey.

A scent drifted through the woodland. Faint and strange, yet familiar somehow. The beast moved away from the clearing, picking a wide circle through the bracken as it homed in on the smell. Growing closer, it could identify two such odours. One was muted, masked against the stink of man-sweat, dirt, and dried human blood. The other was stronger. A heavy, animal musk, laden with pheromones. Female. Both scents moved into the woods, with the female circling the male in long arcs that never came closer than a hundred yards. The male was heading straight for the clearing where the old man cowered. *Simpson. It has to be John Simpson.*

The Malcolm part of the creature understood in that moment what had happened. Simpson and the female, most likely the Williams bitch, were like him. He remembered his split knuckle from the fight and the subsequent infection. The stink of dried blood emanated from the male, but lacked the raw animal reek of his flesh. It wasn't his blood. Malcolm had a good idea who it belonged to, though. He felt a pang of regret for his dead friends that turned into righteous anger in a heartbeat. Taking care to stay downwind of the female, he circled around and moved in to engage his enemies.

333

He got to within two hundred yards before the female picked up his scent. She came crashing through the undergrowth towards him at an alarming rate. He sprayed hot dark-yellow urine against a pine tree to mark his territory, then submerged himself in a black stagnant pool and waited.

The female, a large beast with green eyes and light brown fur, burst into the clearing and snarled. She sniffed the air and followed the scent to the tree that he'd sprayed moments before. The female bent to sniff the mark. That was when Malcolm pounced.

He burst from the water in a flurry of teeth and claws and barrelled into the surprised werewolf. She struggled to regain her footing, but Malcolm was on her before she could recover. His jaws grasped the back of her neck and squeezed. Marie thrashed about, but was unable to break his grip. He applied more pressure. Vertebrae popped and Marie whined in pain and frustration.

Malcolm felt the beast inside his thoughts as a series of mental images and emotions. *No. Don't kill female. Mate with female. Kill other male. Be strong. Be Alpha.* He tightened his jaws a little more and felt the female go limp. He dropped the unconscious body to the ground and watched with disgust as the wolf retreated back into the woman.

He heard the male stumbling through the undergrowth towards him, shouting the woman's name, and knew he would have to get away from this place and take the female with him. Somewhere dark and safe.

With great reluctance, he transformed from the powerful wolf to his human form, now devoid of all excess body fat, picked up the unconscious woman in a fireman's lift, and walked off into the woods.

Chapter 30

14th November 2008. Mill Woods, High Moor. 09.34.

John and Steven trudged back to their parked cars. The mood was tense, and although Steven insisted that Malcolm was long gone, both men scanned the trees with nervous eyes as they left the deep woods and stepped onto the maintained footpaths near the housing estate.

When they arrived at the cars, Steven let out an audible sigh of relief and unlocked his 4x4. John grabbed the older man's arm. "Where are you going? We need to get after them."

Steven's pale face had the texture of parchment. "John, stop and think for a second. We don't know where they've gone, and even if we did, neither of us is in any shape to go after them."

"I couldn't give a shit. I'm fine. Marie might not be. God knows what that sick fuck's doing to her right now."

"You've not slept for more than twenty-four hours, John. You look ready to drop, and I know that I'm running on empty as well. Like I said, we don't know where they are, and we have no plan. Charging in like idiots will just get us both killed."

John looked back to the woods and sighed. Steven was right, no matter how much he hated to admit it. There would be no full moon tonight. When he went up against Malcolm, he would be doing it as a man, not a werewolf. "OK, so what are you suggesting?"

"Follow me back to my place. We can get cleaned up, grab some breakfast and coffee, then try to outthink the son-of-a-bitch instead of running headlong into a trap. Sound like a plan?"

John's shoulders sagged. "I'm not happy about it, but it'll have to do for now. It's not like we have much choice."

John got into his car and followed Steven through the town. The national press had picked up the story of the deaths last night, and the news reports on the radio talked about nothing else. Even the DJs on the music station were talking about Malcolm's handiwork. Six people dead, including his wife, their two children, and his brother-in-law. Malcolm was listed as missing, but was not yet a suspect.

John knew that he was responsible for this. All of it. If he'd stayed away, then nine people would still be alive. The guilt gnawed at his already frayed nerves. More people were going to die today, and those lives would be on his conscience as well. He cursed himself.

They left the town and drove along a series of winding country lanes until they arrived at two huge metal gates that slid open to allow them inside. They pulled up to the farmhouse and Steven got out of the car. John was about to follow when Steven shook his head.

"You probably want to stay here for a minute, until I turn the security systems off."

"Why? You worried I might sneak a look at your alarm code?"

Steven chuckled and then fought to suppress a cough. "No, the security system has a few special features. Just knowing the code won't really help. Wait here and you'll see what I mean."

Steven opened the front door and stepped inside. A penetrating, high-pitched shriek rang out from the house. John gasped in pain and clamped his hands over his ears as the sound reverberated inside his skull. Three seconds later, the ultrasonic alarm cut out and Steven stepped out of the front door.

"OK, now you can come in."

John got out of the car and followed Steven inside the house. His ears were still ringing, and he felt nauseated. "Can't say I'm loving your anti-werewolf alarm. How the hell did you afford this lot on an ex-copper's pension?"

"Carl. The old bastard left me everything in his will, on the condition that I carry on with his work. Ten million quid. And that was back when ten million was considered a lot of money. He knew I was screwed, financially. Laura had just left, and I was suspended without pay. Son of a bitch knew I wouldn't be able to say no." Steven pointed to a door, further down the hall. "There's a shower in there. Get yourself cleaned up. No offence, but you smell like an abattoir. I'll get some coffee on, and then we can try to figure out our next move."

***

John emerged from the shower to the smell of frying bacon. He got dressed in a clean T-shirt and baggy sweat pants that Steven had put outside of the bathroom door, and followed his nose to the living room.

Steven looked up from his desk as John entered the room. "You took your time. My ex-wife was faster in the shower."

John shrugged. "You know how it is. After last night, I needed to do a lot of scrubbing. Even then, the stain never really goes away."

Steven turned back to the desk. "Well, there's some bacon sarnies and coffee on the table. Help yourself and then come take a look at this."

John took two bacon rolls from a serving dish and poured himself a large black coffee, then joined Steven at the desk.

Steven had spread out an ordinance survey land-ranger map of the area in front of him. Coloured pins with yellow Post-it notes beside each one adorned the map. He pointed to a red pin. "It looks like your friend changed while he was still at home, around six o clock last night. The next attack took place roughly four hours later, here," he said, and pointed to a yellow pin in the centre of the Coronation Estate. "And then the last two happened here, in the town centre, just before eleven. After that, there's no sign of him until he shows up at three a.m. in the woods. The purple pin is where my hide was located. The orange one is where he attacked your friend."

"So, where did he go after that? Back into the woods?"

"I hope not, for our sake. I'm just not sure where else he could go. He can't have gone home. The place will be crawling with police and reporters by now. He can't have walked naked through a housing estate carrying an unconscious naked woman either. If he's found a lair in the woods, then we're screwed. Tracking him will be nigh on impossible, and he'd know we were coming long before we spotted him. You knew him. Can you think of anywhere that he might have taken Marie?"

John shook his head. "I knew him when we were kids, but I've only been in contact with him once since then, and it's not like we talked about much. He was too busy kicking the crap out of me. I've got no idea where he might have gone."

Steven pulled out a chair for John and took a sip from his coffee. "Well, grab a pew and let's see if we can work it out."

***

14th November 2008. King's Close School. 11.14.

Marie awoke to find herself lying on a cold, concrete floor. The back of her neck still ached, and she felt the sting of several open wounds across her naked body. Her arms and legs were bound so tight that her fingers and toes were numb. She ran a mental inventory of her wounds, and, when she was satisfied that nothing important was missing, opened her eyes.

High Moor

The room was large, windowless, and constructed from rough concrete blocks. Metal pipes ran along the ceiling, and rows of steel shelves stacked with cleaning equipment and tools ran in parallel lines along the entire length of the room. An industrial gas boiler growled in the far corner. Opposite the boiler was a concrete staircase that led up to a single wooden door. The stink of bleach hung in the air.

She rolled over onto her side and then sat up, wincing as the electrical cable bit into her wrists and ankles. She ignored the pain and wriggled in an attempt to slacken her bonds.

"I wouldn't do that if I were you."

Marie jumped at the voice and craned her head to find the source.

Malcolm Harrison squatted in the corner of the basement, behind the boiler. He was naked and covered in dried blood. His face was hidden in the deep shadows, but his eyes gleamed out from the darkness.

"Malcolm. You need to listen to me."

Malcolm shuffled forward on all fours and grinned at her. "I don't need to do anything, bitch. I'm the fucking alpha here, and you do what I say, or else. Got it?"

"I know what's happened to you is confusing, Malcolm, but I can help, if you'll let me. I work for some people. People like us. I find others and bring them into the family. Teach them about what's happened. How to live with it. How to control it."

Malcolm snorted and the bones of his right hand began to contort and stretch. "I can control it just fine. I don't need your help or anyone else's."

"Do you have any idea what you did last night? The number of people you killed? The police will be looking for you. Everyone will be looking. Eventually they'll find you, and then they'll either kill you or dissect you in a lab. I can get you out of the country. Get you somewhere safe. But first, you need to untie me."

Malcolm shuffled closer and brought a single talon up under her chin, pushing her head back. "This is my place. My lair. Let them come. I'll kill them all."

"You can't kill everyone. I know you feel invincible now, but that's just your beast talking. You're letting it take over, and soon you'll just be a little voice in the back of its mind. You say that you're an alpha? You're not even in charge of yourself at the moment, let alone anyone else. If you don't take control of the situation, then you're going to spend the rest of your life pissing against trees in the woods. This is your last chance, Malcolm. Let me go and let me help."

Malcolm pushed his face forward so that he was almost nose to nose with Marie. His lip was curled up in a snarl as he spoke. "You're going nowhere. You'll see. I'll kill your friend John, and then you'll know that I'm the strongest."

Marie shook her head. "Don't say I didn't warn you."

***

14th November 2008. Steven's House. 14.26.

John slammed his fist against the wall. "This is useless. We're getting nowhere."

Steven sat back and cricked his neck. "Maybe we should take a break and look at it with fresh eyes. I need a smoke."

John walked back across to the table and looked at the map again. The woods were bounded by the river to the north and a mixture of housing estates and open farmland to the south, east, and west. There were no obvious places where he could exit the woods without being seen. Nowhere that indicated where he might go. Perhaps Steven was right. He needed a break. He walked across to the table, poured himself a glass of water, turned on the television, and selected the BBC news channel.

The same woman that John had seen reporting on the initial attack was back in town and didn't look happy about it. She read her report with the expression of someone that had just been served uncooked road-kill in a five-star restaurant. "So far, no further bodies have been discovered. Mr Malcolm Harrison, a janitor at the local school, is still missing, and further missing persons' reports have been filed for several of his acquaintances. Police are, at this time, refusing to comment on any connection between the disappearances and the deaths that occurred last night."

John turned off the television and checked the map again. King's Close School, the place that Malcolm had burned to the ground as a child, lay nestled within a housing estate, but one side of the school field bordered Mill Woods. The school was less than half a mile from where Marie had been attacked. And all of the schools were closed. John ran from the room, out to the garden where Steven was smoking a cigarette.

"What? Can't a bloke finish his ciggie in peace?"

John grinned. "You can finish that later. Come on. I think I know where they are."

***

14th November 2008. King's Close School. 17.44.

John and Steven sat in the back of a white transit van, parked in a residential street close to the school. Steven had helped John prepare. He'd scrubbed himself raw with unscented soap, brushed his teeth with baking soda, and had been doused in a nasty chemical spray that burned his skin. He'd then been ushered into the back of the van wearing nothing but a towel, and Steven had driven to their destination.

John shuffled on the wooden seat. "Did I mention that this is a stupid plan?"

"You did. Several times. Unfortunately you didn't come up with any better suggestions, so this is the one we're going with. You know what you have to do?"

"Yeah. It's not me that I'm worried about. Are you sure you want to do this?"

Steven laughed. "Like hell. Again, not really seeing an alternative. Come on, it's almost time. Get your gear on."

John removed an airtight container that held a full set of clothing, including boots. All the items had been sprayed with the scent eliminator after they'd been washed. John broke the seal and dressed as quickly as he could. Steven handed him a pistol.

"You sure that pop gun's going to be enough? I've got plenty of guns with more punch."

"It's fine. I'll stick with what I know."

"OK. You ready?"

John fought down the butterflies in his stomach and managed a weak smile. "As I'll ever be." He opened the rear door of the van and stepped outside. "Good luck."

Steven nodded. "You too, John, you too."

***

14th November 2008. King's Close School. 17.57.

Marie wriggled and tried to get comfortable. She couldn't feel her hands and feet anymore, and she worried that if she didn't get out of her bonds soon, she'd be damaged beyond her ability to heal. Dead flesh didn't get better. It stayed dead.

Malcolm paced the basement. He'd been doing it for over an hour now, and it was getting on Marie's nerves. She supposed that it was an improvement on the hours before that, when Malcolm had just crouched in the corner and stared at her.

"Malcolm, you need to undo these cables or I'm going to lose my hands and feet. Come on, please. What am I going to do? We both know that you're stronger than I am."

Malcolm stopped his pacing and looked at her with a feral gleam in his eye. "Do you think that I'm stupid, bitch? There's no way I'm letting you go. Not until I've dealt with your little friend."

Marie's temper flared. She'd been trying to play nice and it was getting her nowhere.

"Do I think that you're stupid? Fuck yes. You're given an incredible gift and you waste it by hiding out in a bloody basement, holding prisoner the one person on the face of this earth that has a chance of helping you survive this. Stupid? Stupid doesn't even come close. You're a fuckwit, Malcolm. A pathetic excuse for a man and an even worse excuse for a wolf."

Malcolm snarled and ran across the room. He towered over Marie and, for a moment, looked as if he were about to strike her. Instead, he reached down and grabbed her by the throat. "You know what your problem is? You've got no respect for me. Maybe it's time I made you learn."

Marie felt something brush against her leg, then realised in horror that it was Malcolm's erect penis. She thrashed in his grip and tried to lash out, but Malcolm pinned her to the floor. "You touch me with that and I'll tear it off. Get off me, you bastard. I'll fucking kill you. I'll..."

Malcolm relaxed his grip and stood up. For a moment, Marie thought that she'd gotten through to him. However, the look on his face told her otherwise."

Malcolm sniffed the air and growled, then stepped away from her towards the stairs. Hair bristled from his pores, and his bones were already starting to shift and reform. He climbed the stairs and opened the door.

"Don't think you're getting off, bitch. I'm gonna take care of our visitor, then I'm coming back to finish what we started."

He dropped onto all fours and let the transformation sweep through him. In less than thirty seconds, a huge grey werewolf stood at the top of the stairs. It snarled at her and then walked out into the corridor. The door slammed behind it.

"Visitor? What bloody visitor?" She sniffed the air and caught the scent as it wafted down the stairs.

"Old Spice? What the fuck?"

Chapter 31

14th November 2008. King's Close School. 18.06.

Steven climbed the spiked railings and then walked down the dark driveway, towards the main school building. He had to suppress a cough, a result of the fumes that emanated from his clothing. He'd emptied an entire bottle of aftershave over himself when he'd gotten out of the van.

He walked with what appeared to be casual arrogance. Only the nervous twitch of his eyes betrayed the mortal fear he felt. He tightened his grip on the silenced Ingram Mac-10 and disengaged the safety catch with his thumb. The weapon felt reassuring in his hands. The gun contained special ammunition: lead rounds drilled out into hollow points filled with mercury and silver filings, then sealed with wax. The rounds would explode on impact, devastating whatever they hit, and delivering a double dose of silver and mercury poisoning on top. The weapon could empty a thirty-round magazine in less than two seconds. In truth, Steven disliked the Ingram. The suppressor gave it balance, but it was still very much a "spray and pray" side arm. Steven had spent his life believing in the philosophy of "one shot, one kill." The Mac-10 seemed crude, almost vulgar in comparison to a decent rifle. Nevertheless, there was no denying the thing's lethal efficiency. Steven had only to point, pull the trigger, and whatever stood before him would be obliterated.

High Moor

The orange haze of the streetlights on the main road seemed very far away now, and rows of conifers that encircled the perimeter of the school field muted the hum of passing traffic. He steadied his breathing and listened for any sounds that might indicate he was not alone.

Nothing.

He passed the main entrance to the school and crossed through a square courtyard surrounded on three sides by two floors of glass windows. The sound of his footsteps echoed off the glass, making it seem like there were three people walking across the concrete paving slabs instead of one, terrified old man.

Steven stood in the centre of the yard and shouldered the machine pistol. *Here goes nothing.* "Come on, you mangy, flea-bitten piece of shit," he shouted. "I know you're here, you fucking chav. You think you're the big man? Prove it. Or hide in your kennel like a whining puppy. Your choice."

His voice echoed around the yard, changing in pitch as the sound waves reflected off the glass sheets. The noise faded, and the only sounds Steven could hear was the distant hum of traffic and the rustling of the wind in bare tree branches.

A howl shredded the silence. Long. Furious. Close.

Steven tightened his grip on the Ingram. *Here we bloody well go.*

***

John waited until he heard the howl and then crept around to the basement door. It looked like Malcolm had taken the bait. Now, he just had to find Marie and hope that Steven could hold the werewolf off. He put his hand out and felt a wall of fear rise up inside.

What if Marie's dead? What if Malcolm comes back?

Adrenaline surged through him, numbing his limbs. Inside the cage in his mind, the beast stirred. John bit back the terror, grasped the door handle, and stepped inside. Marie was tied up in the far corner of the room. She was naked, and her limbs were bound with blood-crusted white cables. Marie's extremities had turned purple. She looked up and opened her mouth, but John put a finger to his lips to silence her and rushed down the stairs to where she lay.

John untied the cables around her wrists and ankles and was relieved when the colour in her hands started to fade. Keeping his voice low, he asked, "Are you alright? Can you move?"

Marie's brow flushed with sweat, and she looked like she might throw up. "Give me a minute. Got the world's worst case of pins and needles, and it's going to take a little while for my body to handle the poison."

John looked shocked. "Poison? What did he do to you?"

She shook her head. "It's fine. Just the build-up of crap in my blood from the cables. Give me a second and don't hold it against me if I puke on your shoes, OK?"

Marie's complexion turned ashen, and she curled up into a foetal position. Sweat ran from her pores, forming a pool on the concrete floor. John put his arm around her and waited for the sickness to pass.

High Moor

The sound of exploding glass came from above. Marie looked at John. "What the fuck was that?"

"That was Steven keeping Malcolm off our backs. Come on, we need to get moving."

Marie got to her feet and shook her arms. John checked his pistol to make sure that a round was chambered and the safety catch was off, then started to move toward the staircase. Marie put her hand on his shoulder, and he turned around, "What, Marie? We need to go. Now."

Marie punched him in the face. He stumbled and fell to the floor. Marie followed up with a kick to his chin that lifted him off the ground and made the vertebrae in his neck crack. She picked up his pistol, removed the clip, and ejected the round in the chamber. Then she tossed the empty weapon into the corner of the room and walked to the staircase. Light brown hair was already flowing from her skin.

John tried to get to his feet, but his body was still healing the damage to his neck and wouldn't obey him. He tried to speak, but could only manage a hoarse whisper. "Marie? What the fuck? What are you doing?"

Marie stopped at the top of the stairs and looked back. Her eyes were shining green disks. Tears dampened the fur around her cheeks. "I'm sorry, John. I really am, but I have to do this."

John winced as the vertebrae in his neck realigned with a sickening crunch. "Do what?"

"Kill two bastards with one stone."

***

Steven stood with his back against the pebble-dashed concrete wall of the school building and checked the two possible entrances to the courtyard for any sign of the werewolf. Almost a minute had passed, and Steven was certain that an attack was imminent, yet nothing happened. Had their plan had failed?

If the creature realised that he was nothing but a distraction, then John could be in very serious trouble. The temptation to run to John's side was strong, but he fought against it. *Stick to the plan. John can handle himself.*

Then the window beside him exploded as the werewolf leaped through it.

Steven raised the Ingram and opened fire. The werewolf ran parallel to the wall, moving at impossible speed. Steven poured death after it. The machine pistol spat fire that destroyed the remaining windows on the ground floor and blew chunks from the concrete render, but failed to hit his target. The creature was too fast.

The Ingram clicked as the magazine emptied. Steven hit the release and brought up a fresh magazine with his left hand. He'd practiced the move over and over until he could be ready to fire again in less than two seconds. Two seconds turned out to be a second too long.

The werewolf changed direction as soon as the firing stopped and leaped. It collided with Steven just as the second clip clicked into place. Steven was thrown into the concrete wall, and his head hit the render with a wet crack.

The Ingram flew from his grip and skittered across the paving stones. Flashbulbs burst behind his eyes, and he was aware of a warm, wetness trickling down the back of his neck. That was the least of his problems. The werewolf was right beside him.

He fell onto his front and tried to crawl toward the discarded machine pistol. He almost made it when a shadow fell over him. He could smell the foul, animal reek of the thing. He slumped to the floor, resigned to his fate.

The werewolf's fangs punched through his lower back, tearing his kidneys into bloody fragments. The jaws closed around his spine and he felt a white-hot bolt of agony tear up his back, filling his entire being with unbearable blinding pain. He screamed as the bones crumbled under the force of the bite.

Then, the weight above him disappeared. The beast backed up and turned to face one of the courtyard entrances. In the shadows, Steven saw two green eyes, glowing with barely contained fury. Then Marie attacked.

The light brown werewolf was a blur, covering the distance before Steven had registered the movement. She slammed into the side of the huge grey beast and snapped at its throat. The fight would have been over there and then, but it ducked away from the attack, and her fangs tore away a chunk of its shoulder instead. The grey werewolf yelped in pain and slashed at Marie with its razor sharp talons, which sliced through the flesh against her ribs and carved grooves into the bones.

The two combatants circled each other, protecting their injuries from direct attack. Malcolm snapped at the air, and Marie responded by peeling back her lips and snarling at the other werewolf. Then she leaped and crashed into the other creature. They both rolled across the ground, biting and clawing one another.

Steven felt darkness closing in. Blood seeped from his ruined kidneys, and his lower back was a blaze of searing pain. He couldn't feel his legs. He pulled himself along the ground, digging his fingertips into the edges of the cold concrete slabs, not caring when his hand slipped and he peeled back two fingernails.

He brushed against the discarded Ingram with his fingertips. His hand closed around the grip. He rolled over, screaming as the shattered bones of his spine ground together. With the last fragments of his strength, he pointed the weapon at the two battling werewolves, and pulled the trigger.

The grey werewolf seemed to sense the danger at the last second. It threw its weight against Marie, and swung her into the line of fire. The Ingram's barrel spat flame. A round slammed into Marie's chest and another into her stomach, almost simultaneously. The back of the light brown werewolf exploded in a cloud of hair, bone, and blood. Hair retreated into pores. Talons retracted into fingers. Fangs slid into gums. The Ingram clicked empty. Marie's ruined, naked body lay on the ground in a spreading pool of blood. The last thing Steven saw before the black closed in and oblivion claimed him was the grey werewolf, unharmed and advancing across the courtyard.

High Moor

***

John burst from the basement door into the cold night air. His neck was still sore from the kick that Marie had administered, and he held his empty pistol in his right hand. He scanned the area outside of the door, hoping that Marie had left the ammunition close by, but there was no sign of it.

His fight-or-flight impulse screamed at him to flee. Unarmed, he wouldn't stand a chance against Malcolm. Then he heard the sounds of breaking glass, a scream of agony, the subdued staccato whisper of Steven's Ingram, and a brief yelp of pain. He couldn't leave them. Even if it meant his death. He swallowed his fear and sprinted towards the courtyard.

He emerged from between two buildings and almost dropped the empty pistol in shock. Marie lay naked and unmoving in a dark pool, with two fist-sized holes in her back. Steven was face down on the floor. His lower back was shredded, and blood oozed from the terrible wound. Malcolm stood over Steven, teeth bared, ready to tear the unconscious man's head off.

John pointed the pistol at the werewolf. "Don't you fucking move, Malcolm. You so much as twitch, and I'll blow your bloody head off."

John and Malcolm glared at each other. John's heart pounded in his chest. *Nice move, John. Now what the fuck do you do?*

The massive grey werewolf bunched its muscles. John got ready to die. Then Malcolm bolted for the gap between the buildings and disappeared from sight.

John stood still, too shocked to process what had just happened. He regained his senses and ran to Steven. He picked up the Ingram and checked the magazine. When he realised that it was empty, he dropped the weapon and checked the old man for any sign of life. Steven was still breathing, but only just. He was bleeding badly from the ragged wound on his back. He'd be dead before very much longer, and there was nothing that John could do about it.

He went over to Marie. He bit back the tears and forced himself to look at the wounds. The damage caused had been catastrophic, and the silver filings prevented the wounds from healing. Marie had been dead before she hit the floor.

A voice echoed around the courtyard. "Why won't you change, John? I don't want to fight you with your little popgun. I want to tear your throat out when you're at your strongest. When you're like me."

John dropped to his knees and let the pistol slide from his grasp. He picked up Marie's head and placed it on his lap.

"Don't ignore me, John. Change. Face me. It's no fun if you're not going to fight back."

"It doesn't work like that. Not for me. If you're going to kill me, then get it over with."

Malcolm stepped out from the shadows at the end of the courtyard. He was naked and bled from a dozen bites and scratches.

"You'll change. I know you will, because I'm going to count to three, then I'm going to change myself. If you're still human when I finish, then I'm going to come over there, I'm going to tear a fuck-hole in your stomach, and screw you like I screwed your little dead bitch."

John felt his grief transform in a second into a cold ball of anger. He got to his feet and turned to face the other man.

"One. Two."

John smiled at Malcolm, tore down the barriers in his mind, and let the wolf out.

The change began in an instant. The familiar agony tore through him, but instead of trying to hold back the flood, John let it take him. He welcomed the wave of pain and power that pulsated through every cell, knowing that it was his only chance of survival. The muscles in his arms thickened and expanded. His jaw dislocated and stretched to accommodate the fangs that burst through his gums. His vision shifted from full colour to shades of grey, tinged with blue and green. He heard rodents scurrying within the walls of the school building, and a flood of scents assailed his nostrils. The information combined into a three-dimensional awareness of every living thing within half a mile. The sensation was like trying to surf a tsunami, and he struggled to process the myriad smells and sounds.

Then Malcolm attacked.

The grey werewolf bounded across the courtyard on all fours and launched itself into the air. John tried to react, but by the time his mind registered the threat, Malcolm was already on him.

The impact hurled John backwards, and they both crashed through a pair of wood and glass doors into the main school building. Malcolm's fangs darted forward and sank into the flesh of John's chest. John howled in pain and swiped at his assailant with his right arm. Malcolm had expected the response, however, and darted back, out of range, before surging forward again. Claws tore at John's arm, tearing fur, flesh, and muscle. Sharp teeth ripped chunks of meat from his body.

He was losing. Already disoriented as a result of his enhanced senses, the pain and blood loss only made things worse. He couldn't think. An electric bolt of fear surged up his spine. He realised that he was going to die.

Then his beast spoke to him in a cascade of images and emotions. There were no words, but the meaning was clear.

GET OUT OF MY WAY.

John relinquished control, and the beast's consciousness hit him. Thought, indecision, and doubt washed away in a wave of instinct and fury, submerging him in the bottomless red waters of his beast's rage.

John dug his claws into the back of Malcolm's neck and hurled the two-hundred-pound werewolf away as if it weighed nothing. Malcolm crashed through a glass display cabinet into the unyielding concrete wall behind.

He regained his feet in a flash, lowered his head, and snarled a challenge to the seven-foot-tall, dark-haired monster that filled the corridor. Then the two creatures sprang forward, meeting in a flurry of claws, teeth, and blood.

High Moor

John's jaws clamped around Malcolm's right foreleg and crushed it to bloody pulp. Malcolm swiped with his left foreleg and tore four ragged, parallel wounds across John's muzzle. John brought his left arm up in a savage counter-attack and raked the right side of Malcolm's face, puncturing his eyeball with one of his claws. Malcolm's fangs bit down on John's leg and tore away a grapefruit-sized piece of muscle. The leg gave way, and John fell to the ground.

Malcolm thrust his jaws forward at impossible speed, towards John's exposed throat. John's claws flashed out and grabbed the underside of Malcolm's jaw. Malcolm thrashed and snarled, but John held him steady. Claws sank through fur and flesh. John curled back his black lips into a bloodstained snarl and drove his head forward, jaws agape. His teeth fastened around Malcolm's throat. Fangs crunched through cartilage. Hot, sweet blood filled his mouth. He closed his jaws and ripped his head back in a single movement. Blood sprayed from the open wound. Malcolm's thrashing weakened, then stopped. Hair retreated into flesh. Bones cracked and reformed. Within seconds the werewolf had transformed back into the ruined corpse of Malcolm Harrison.

Darkness closed in on John. Blood flowed from his terrible wounds, and with that blood flowed the last of his strength. The beast whined and collapsed beside the dead body of its enemy. The last thing that it was aware of was the sounds of sirens in the distance.

Epilogue

14th November 2008. King's Close School. 18.57.

The armed response unit was the first to arrive at the school. After the killings the previous day, the chief constable had ordered an ARV to be on constant patrol in the town so that any further reported incidents would have an immediate response. Despite this, the early evening traffic, combined with the road closures around the crime scenes, meant that it was over twenty-five minutes from the first report before the first responders arrived at the scene.

Constable Mark Briggs, the armed response vehicle's operator, got out of the passenger door of the BMW and opened the boot. Sergeant Rick Grey, the team's observer, got out of the back door, walked to the rear of the car, and unlocked the reinforced metal box within, then removed one of the MP5 carbines. Mark did the same.

Rick walked around to the driver's door and tapped on the window. Constable Paul Patterson, the driver and the last member of their three-man team, lowered the electric window.

"OK, Paul, Mark, and I are going in to take a look. Keep us updated on the ETA of the ambulance and the Specialist Firearms Officers. We'll stay in constant contact, so keep the channel open. Got it?"

Paul nodded. "OK, boss. Good hunting."

Rick moved away without saying another word, and Mark fell into step behind until they reached the locked gates. Mark cut the chain with a set of bolt cutters he'd retrieved from the boot along with his firearm, then set it down on the floor and pushed the gate open.

The two police officers moved along the driveway toward the dark outline of the school. Rick touched his throat mike. "Fifty meters inside. No sign of life. Over."

They made it to the side of the building without incident and flattened their backs against the concrete wall. Rick signalled for Mark to cover him, then moved to the corner and peered around.

"We have two, I repeat, two casualties in the courtyard at the northeast end of the building. One male, one female. Status unknown. Moving in."

Rick moved out into the yard while Mark covered him. He made his way to the first body: a naked female with two gaping holes in her back. "First casualty, female, mid-thirties, naked." He checked for a pulse and wasn't surprised when he didn't find one. "Cause of death appears to be multiple gunshot wounds. Proceeding to next casualty. Mark, make sure no one gets the drop on me."

He heard Mark's whispered affirmative in his earpiece as he moved to the next victim: an old man with terrible injuries to his lower back. "Next casualty, male, late sixties." He reached down and pressed two fingers against the man's neck. "This one's still alive, but he won't be for much longer. What's the ETA on the ambulance?"

Paul's voice crackled in his ear. "Two, maybe three minutes."

"Alright. Keep them away until we can secure the scene, then send them down with one of the SFO's. Hopefully the poor old sod will make it till then."

Rick signalled Mark, and the two men moved to the far side of the yard where the entrance to the school had once been. Rick moved into the building, conscious of the crunch of broken glass beneath his boots.

"Two more casualties inside the building. Two males, again, both naked."

The earpiece crackled. "What do you think, Sarge? Some swingers' party get out of hand?"

Rick ignored the younger officer and moved through the bloodstained hallway until he got to the bodies. Both men were covered in blood. Ragged wounds were apparent across their bodies. "First male, late thirties or early forties. Multiple wounds, but the cause of death appears to be a major trauma to the throat."

He moved around the bodies and checked the other man. "Second male, early to mid-thirties. He...it...it looks like he tore the other bloke's throat out with his teeth. He's still got most of it in his mouth."

The man groaned, and his eyes flickered open. Rick pushed the barrel of the MP5 into his face. "Sir, you are under arrest on suspicion of murder."

***

High Moor

14th November 2008. Nauchnnyy proyezd, Moscow. 22.57.

Michael sat by a desk in the dingy room and removed a silver knife from one of the drawers. He turned it over in his hand and let the glare from the table lamp reflect on the blade, then he pushed it against his left forearm and sliced through the flesh. Blood welled up in the wound and ran down his arm. Red raindrops spattered the green leather surface of the writing desk, then stopped as the wound healed. He grunted and pressed the silver into his arm, repeating the process over and over until there was a knock on the door. A small, grey-haired man entered the room without waiting for a response.

"Mikhail. We've had an update from England. I'm sorry, but it's been confirmed. Marie is among the reported casualties, and John Simpson is in police custody."

Michael pressed the silver into his arm again. "Did I ever tell you, Steffan, that John was turned because he tried to save me? For years, I felt responsible. When The Pack broke apart, I tried to find him and bring him into the fold. I even allowed my sister to execute her ridiculous plan because I thought it had a chance of working."

"You had no way of knowing he was moonstruck, Mikhail. Marie was experienced, and she knew the risks. You cannot blame yourself, and you can't let the others see you like this. I have no aspirations to be Alpha, but there are some that do not feel that way."

Michael looked up at the other man. "You are right, my old friend. We have a situation to handle, and I have no time for grief or regrets. I will mourn my sister later."

Steffan lowered his head. "What would you have me do?"

"Send two teams. Retrieve Marie before they can examine her body."

"And the moonstruck?"

Michael's lip curled into a snarl. "Bring me his fucking head."

***

15th November 2008. Durham Hospital. 13.26

Marie floated in darkness. She had no idea how long she'd been like this. Time ceased to have meaning when there was no frame of reference.

Is this what death is? Nothing? Then why can I think? Why do I still hurt like a bastard?

The inky blackness of her world exploded into red light.

What the fuck?

She heard voices. Quiet, muffled, as if she were underwater, becoming clearer as the pressure in her ears equalised.

"So, we have a female. Mid-thirties. Hmm, the chart says the cause of death appeared to be multiple gunshot wounds, but I can't see any evidence of that, just several contusions that seem to be from an animal attack," said a deep, male voice.

A woman's voice replied. "It'll be that idiot, Jenkins. He's fucked the paperwork up again. I'm going to put my foot up his arse when we get done here."

"Well, never mind that now. Let's see if we can establish exactly how Miss Williams, if that is her name, really did die. Susan, can you pass me the scalpel."

High Moor

Marie felt the cold steel of the blade press against her stomach.

Oh fuck!

Graeme Reynolds

ABOUT THE AUTHOR

Graeme Reynolds has been called many things over the years, most of which are unprintable.

By day, he breaks computers for a living, but when the sun goes down he hunches over a laptop and thinks of new and interesting ways to offend people with delicate sensibilities.

He lives somewhere in the UK with two cats, a flock of delinquent killer chickens and a girlfriend that is beginning to suspect that there is something deeply wrong with him.

He has over thirty short story publications to his name, and is a member of the Horror Writers Association and the British Fantasy Society.

http://www.graemereynolds.com
http://www.facebook.com/HighMoorNovel
@graemereynolds